Murder Can Be Murder

Murder Can Be Murder

The boundless

Chronicles of Brother Hermitage

by

Howard of Warwick

From the Scriptorium of
The Funny Book Company

The Funny Book Company

Published by The Funny Book Company
Crown House 27 Old Gloucester Street
London WC1N 3AX
www.funnybookcompany.com

Cover design by Double Dagger.
Cover image: Creative Commons, The British Library

ISBN 978-1-913383-52-7
Scriptorial appreciation is due to:
Mary
Susan Fanning
Karen Nevard-Downs
Lydia Reed
Claire Ward

Murder Can Be Murder

Caput I: Preliminary Enquiries

'Brother Hermitage?' The young man with bright, enthusiastic eyes was very well-presented and exuded confidence like a fresh spring on its way to becoming a major river.

'Erm, yes,' Hermitage replied carefully. He was young and enthusiastic but his habit had not been well-presented for many a year, and he had never got the hang of confidence.

Simply being approached was enough of a worry. As King William's duly appointed investigator, most of the approaches he experienced were connected with murder, which was truly awful. Being investigator at all was terrible but he had no choice. William and the Normans seldom offered choices about anything; unless it was life or death.

He had been walking down the main street of Derby on a bright summer morning, minding his own business on his way to the church when the young fellow bounded up. There was no question that this would be someone who wanted to join him. No one in Derby joined him on his daily visits to the church for prayer.

The face was not one he recognised, which was unusual for a small town. Strangers approaching Hermitage seldom brought anything but trouble.

'The King's Investigator?' the young man asked with more from a deep and bubbling reserve of enthusiasm.

'That's right.' Hermitage's spirits sank. No one ever called for the King's Investigator to ask about the weather. Or the post-Exodus prophets. They had a murder which would demand his attention.

Mind you, this youngster appeared to be Saxon, so perhaps he had not been sent by the king or any of the other ghastly Normans. And he seemed bright and cheerful, which was a bit of a contradiction if murder was involved.

'Marvellous.' The young man gave a bow. 'I am Fridolf. Fridolf of Gotham.'

'Gotham, you say?' This concerned Hermitage, as his previous dealings with that town had had a touch of madness about them.[1]

'But it is many a year since I was there,' Fridolf explained. 'Now, I am apprentice goldsmith to Master Scrydan of London.'

'A goldsmith, eh?' Hermitage was suitably impressed.

'Aye. A good trade and I near the end of my apprenticeship.'

It certainly was a good trade, judging by the quality of Fridolf's clothes and shoes. Naturally, goldsmiths were only ever employed by people who could afford the material in the first place. He could imagine that goldsmiths were very well rewarded for their skill.

'Trade continues, then?' Hermitage asked. 'The Normans and all?' He left the question hanging. It wouldn't do to disparage the Normans too much if this young man was a friend to the invaders.

'It does,' Fridolf confirmed. 'King William and his court want to show their magnificence as much as any rulers. Things were a bit difficult after Hastings, but Master Scrydan is a name of high regard. And goldsmiths are rare beasts.'

Hermitage nodded at this. If there was one thing a king needed to do it was show everyone that he was king. This

---

[1] *The 1066 To Hastings:* madness all round.

was especially true of a new king, who would be anxious to dispel any notion that the old king might come back. Not that this was a problem for William, King Harold having been very effectively dealt with, if the tales he spread were true.

And what better way to show what a successful and well-established king you were than by ostentatious displays of wealth? Preferably wealth taken from the people you just conquered.

This was all very interesting, but Hermitage had to ask the key question.

'What brings you away from your work, then? And from London, which is a good step away?'

'Let me stand you a mug of ale.' Fridolf suggested, beckoning towards the rough tavern close by. 'Then I can tell all in comfort.'

Hermitage nodded his acceptance. He was growing in confidence that this would not be murder after all. A comfortable discussion over a mug of ale was hardly the setting for such a subject.

Fridolf led the way, and in a few moments Ern, the tavern-keeper, supplied them with leather mugs, which they took at the large table outside.

Ern followed them and stood waiting to hear what this stranger had to say. There could be a week's gossip in this.

'Thank you, Ern,' Hermitage said, trying to indicate very clearly that Ern could return to his labour.

'Ern, get back in here,' Mistress Angel's voice pierced the air in a most un-angel-like manner. 'Is this floor supposed to be clean?'

Where Hermitage failed, Mistress Angel succeeded.

Fridolf supped and then began. 'I heard all about the

King's Investigator from the Normans. It seems a remarkable role.'

'That it is,' Hermitage confirmed. 'From the Latin, you know, vestigo, vestigare, to track.'

'A track,' Fridolf repeated with interest. 'Yes, that would make sense.'

'I just happened to be of assistance to King Harold in resolving a murder,' Hermitage explained. 'And then King William continued the role.' He didn't want Fridolf to think that he actually wanted to investigate murder. Nothing could be further from the truth.

'But I hear that you stay with Wat the Weaver?' Fridolf was clearly a bit concerned about this, which was not surprising. The reputation of Wat the Weaver was not one that most decent people would want to get anywhere near; some of it might rub off.

'An old and complex set of circumstances,' Hermitage explained. 'And anyway, Wat produces only pious tapestry now. His works of old are long gone.'

'Once seen, never forgotten.' Fridolf gave a conspiratorial wink.

'Best never seen or quickly forgotten,' Hermitage replied firmly. He had seen some of Wat's old tapestries. The human form was a work of God, and only He should be able to see quite so much of it.

'But what makes a young goldsmith's apprentice seek me out?' Hermitage asked. He didn't really want to open the door to discussion of murder, but he certainly wanted to move on from the subject of Wat the Weaver.

'You are the only King's Investigator,' Fridolf said.

'As far as I am aware.' Hermitage had long hoped that someone would take the job away from him. The appointment of another investigator would be just as good. He had his apprentice, Bart, or rather, his self-appointed apprentice, but, as far as he knew, he remained the only investigator.

'So, it is to you I must come.'

Hermitage couldn't tarry any longer. If it was coming, it was best to get it over with. 'A murder?' he asked with resignation.

'Just so.'

Hermitage sighed. 'You were sent by the Normans?'

'Oh no,' Fridolf replied brightly. 'This is my own doing. I thought it best to get things right.'

Hermitage didn't like to think what "getting things right" about a murder involved. 'I suppose it is. And there was no one in London who could deal with the matter?'

Even though there was no other investigator, murder was not that uncommon. Shire Reeves and county authorities had dealt with it in the past and presumably continued to do so. Only very specific matters came Hermitage's way. At least, he assumed that was the case. Usually when the Normans wanted it so.

'Once I had heard of the King's Investigator, I knew this was where I had to come.'

'A four-day walk,' Hermitage noted.

'I am travelling for business anyway, but seeing you is essential if matters are to be properly dealt with.'

Hermitage nodded reluctantly. 'To the heart of it then,' he said. 'Whose murder are we talking about?'

'My master, Scrydan.'

'Oh dear, you have my sympathy.' Hermitage thought the boy might have mentioned that Scrydan was dead when he first brought the name up.

Fridolf frowned deeply at this.

Hermitage knew that relations between apprentices and their masters could be difficult. Wat had reported his own experience of a harsh and cruel master, so perhaps this death had little effect on Fridolf. That would explain his cheery attitude. He hated to consider it, but perhaps this murder had come as a bit of a relief. However, if Fridolf was still an apprentice, he would now have no master, which could cause him problems.

'A master goldsmith and a great craftsman, but an awful fellow,' Fridolf explained. 'Sad to say, but I don't think he will be missed.'

Hermitage acknowledged this without further comment.

'So,' Fridolf said brightly. 'How do we proceed?'

'Well,' Hermitage began. Worryingly, he found it quite comfortable to talk about murder when there wasn't a body lying in front of him. Nor were there any Norman nobles demanding to know this instant, who did it.

'I have developed an approach that has proved to be quite informative.'

Fridolf looked at him like an attentive acolyte.

'I have identified three key factors in any murder; the method, the motive and the opportunity.'

'Fascinating.'

'First of all, the method. How was Scrydan killed?'

'How was he killed?' Fridolf didn't seem to understand the question.

'Yes,' Hermitage explained.' By what method did Scrydan meet his end? A knife, sword, poison?'

'Hm,' Fridolf seemed to think about this, which was odd. 'They're all possibilities, I suppose,' he said.

'They're all, what?' As usual, Hermitage didn't understand

what was going on but assumed it must be him.

'How Scrydan will be killed,' Fridolf explained happily. 'It could be any of them.'

Hermitage must have misheard. 'How will he be killed? What do you mean, how will he be killed?'

'Just that, I suppose.' Fridolf shrugged. 'How's he going to die?'

Hermitage gaped. 'You mean he is not dead yet?'

'Well, no.'

'Oh, Lord,' Hermitage breathed. 'If there is some threat to your master, why have you taken four days to come and tell me? You should go to the Shire Reeve and have some protection put in place.'

'I came because you're the investigator.'

'Yes, but..,'

'You keep track of all the murders. For the king.'

'I keep track of them?'

'A record of some sort, I suppose. A strange thing, if you ask me, but then there's no telling with Normans. They are terribly well organised about most things. Murder as well, it seems.'

'I, er,' Hermitage was lost. This was quite normal for most of his investigations, but he wasn't sure that this even was one.

'You keep a track of all the murders in the kingdom,' Fridolf explained, seemingly puzzled about why he was having to explain this to the man who kept the track. 'So I've come to let you know about this one. So you can put it on your list, I imagine.'

'My list?'

'The Normans said you investigate all the murders. Tracking. You said so yourself.'

'That doesn't mean keeping a track of them.' Surely the young man would understand that.

'Oh.' Fridolf sounded very disappointed.

There was one question that was burning a hole in Hermitage's head. 'If your master is in danger of murder, why on earth are you thinking about adding his name to some list, instead of how to stop it from happening?'

Hermitage started to wonder if this Fridolf really was an apprentice goldsmith and not simply some loon who went around the country making up stories to disturb ordinary working folk. And monks.

'Stop it happening?' Now Fridolf looked as confused as Hermitage felt. 'Why would I want to stop it?'

'Good Lord, how can you ask such a question?'

Fridolf scowled deeply, obviously worried that he was having to explain the blindingly obvious. 'Because I'm going to do it.'

'You're going to what?' Hermitage had heard the words and in the right order. As a sentence, it made perfect sense. But that was as far as it went.

Fridolf now cheered up and smiled broadly at the prospect. 'Going into the method and the opportunity bits could be quite helpful. I was thinking about a knife in the dark, but you may know better.'

The silence in Hermitage's head spread out around him like a very thick blanket. Fridolf was clearly as mad as a mad thing, but hopefully, he was harmless. Unless you were a master goldsmith, apparently.

'But, but,' Hermitage stuttered. 'My investigations of murder are to find out who did it.' It felt like a very weak argument in the face of all this.

'You won't need to this time,' Fridolf assured him. 'You'll

know.'

The most obvious thing to say was that Fridolf could not be serious. This must be the raving of a disturbed mind.

He considered the young man and didn't think he looked disturbed, but you could never tell. He was also very well-dressed. Not that well-dressed people didn't commit murder.

But no one in their right mind would just go and murder his master like that. Let alone would he come to the King's Investigator and let him know in advance. It was a sure sign of Fridolf's madness. But how to say it?

'This is madness,' he managed to croak out. 'You cannot seriously come here to tell me that you are going to commit a murder.'

Fridolf nodded seriously. 'I see.'

Hermitage felt a slight relief, but only a slight one.

'You mean I need to ask permission? I didn't know that.'

'No, you don't need to ask permission,' Hermitage found himself snapping.

'That's good then.'

'What you don't do is murder your master. You don't murder anyone. Whether you have permission or not.' Hermitage was glad to get that out in such plain language.

'Really?' Fridolf was still showing intense interest, which Hermitage assumed meant he wasn't getting through. 'Is there a queue? Do I have to wait my turn or something?'

'Have to wait?' All Hermitage could do was repeat the words as he had nothing else in his head.

'Oh, I say.' Fridolf snapped his fingers as he reached a conclusion. 'Have I got the wrong end of the stick altogether? I do apologise.'

Hermitage didn't want to risk breathing a sigh of relief too soon.

'King's Investigator and all that,' Fridolf said. 'Tracking of murder. You follow the track and come and do it for me? Is that the arrangement? That is good. He'd never suspect a monk.'

Hermitage was glad he hadn't released that sigh. He then took a much longer draught of ale than he was used to.

'Fridolf,' he said as calmly as he could manage. He looked into the young man's eyes. 'You cannot murder your master under any circumstances. You cannot murder anyone. It is the most awful sin. I don't know if this is some jest you are playing, or if the thoughts in your head are simply disordered.'

'The Normans do it,' Fridolf protested glumly.

'That's as may be, but they are sinning when they do it as well.'

Fridolf shook his head. 'This is all much more complicated than I thought.'

'How complicated did you think murder would be?' Hermitage asked with well-risen irritation. 'You don't seriously plan to kill your master, surely?'

'Of course, I do. And I thought you were supposed to help.'

'I do help with murder. I help by finding out who did the murder and I bring them to justice.' He hoped the threat in this was clear.

Fridolf did now look quite crestfallen, which Hermitage took as progress. 'I've got a perfectly good murder to do, I come and tell the King's Investigator of murder, just to do things right, and now this. If I'd known it was going to be this difficult, I wouldn't have come in the first place,' he grumbled.

10

'Which might have been for the best,' Hermitage agreed. 'Why do you even think about murdering your master at all?' he asked as gently as he could manage.

'Oh, he's awful. Terrible man. As I said, I'm sure he wouldn't be missed.'

'That's not the point.'

Fridolf appeared to find a new argument. 'If I don't do it, someone will.'

'You don't know that.'

'I'm pretty sure. Nobody likes him.'

'Just because you don't like someone doesn't mean that you kill them. Anyway,' Hermitage came up with a practical problem; applying reason, sanity and morality having had no effect. 'You're an apprentice. If you have no master, who will see you progress to master yourself?' It sounded awful to rationalise the avoidance of murder like this, but perhaps Fridolf would respond to such an approach.

'That's exactly the problem.' Fridolf was all enthusiasm once more. 'He's in the way. He sits there as master and won't progress anyone.'

'Are there other apprentices?'

'There are two others, but they aren't as far advanced as me. It's my time to be made up. I've even done my masterpiece for the test. It's a beautiful wristband. Intertwining strands, jewel encrustation, the lot.'

'It sounds wonderful.'

'But old Scrydan would rather see it melted down than admit it's the work of a master.'

'That is still no reason for murder. You can't kill a man simply because he's in your way.'

'Sounds like a very good reason to me,' Fridolf muttered. 'King William did it.'

'Why don't you set up your own workshop?'

'Without being a master? Who would come?'

'That's what Wat did,' Hermitage explained. 'He never was made a master yet has had great success.'

'I don't know how you'd make rude jewellery.'

Hermitage had to accept that Wat was probably not the best example.

'It could be a tradition,' Fridolf tried.

'A tradition?'

'Yes, you know. Apprentice kills master. For all we know, Scrydan killed his master before him. Now it's his turn.'

'I am confident that murder of a master is not the route to apprentice advancement.'

'Don't monks kill abbots?'

'No, they do not.' Hermitage could not contain his outrage at this suggestion. And he was starting to feel as if he were following this young man down the path of madness.

Fridolf sagged and looked defeated. Perhaps Hermitage could send him home with some wise words. He assumed that he had eliminated the suggestion of murder from the boy's mind.

'Just have a discussion with Scrydan. Ask him how you are to progress to master. What his plans are.'

'He'll probably kill me. Then how will you feel?'

'I am sure it will not come to that.'

Fridolf huffed. 'So, I can't kill him at all?'

'Not at all.'

There was a long and uncomfortable pause, but Fridolf did eventually speak, even if it was in the manner of a child who has been told to feed the pigs or there'll be no mead. 'All right.'

Hermitage relaxed.

Fridolf now spoke lightly, as if chatting about the weather in these parts. 'But, if I were to kill him, which I'm not, obviously. What would be the best method and opportunity? In your experience.'

'Fridolf,' Hermitage cautioned. 'We are not discussing the matter.'

'No, no, of course not. It's just out of interest, really.'

'You should not be interested in murder. You should be interested in goldsmithing.'

'Yes.' Fridolf said this very slowly and with a very scheming look on his face.

'What are you thinking?' Hermitage asked suspiciously.

'Oh, nothing really,' Fridolf said. "Just considering my craft, you know. The smelting with the fire, hot metal all over the place. Could be dangerous in the wrong hands. And then the gold itself. Very heavy is gold. You only see little bits of it as it's so valuable, but when you get a big lump of the stuff, it'd be enough to weigh a man down in say, a river. Or a pond. As long as it was deep enough.'

'Fridolf,' Hermitage cautioned. 'If I were to hear word that a goldsmith called Scrydan had been murdered, I would have a very strong suspicion about who did it. The Normans may go around killing people, but the rest of us do not. We are discovered and we are punished for it.'

'Right, right,' Fridolf said absent-mindedly. 'Just out of interest?'

'More interest?' Hermitage asked pointedly.

'As you mentioned it. What would the punishment be, do you think, for murdering, oh, I don't know, a goldsmith, say?'

'The punishment for murder is eternal damnation. God is the ultimate judge.'

'Of course, of course. But before Him?'

Hermitage sighed. 'Obviously, there would be the wergild.'

'Ah, the wergild, yes. A fine.'

'A substantial fine,' Hermitage insisted. 'For someone as valuable to his family as a goldsmith.'

'Shame that Scrydan doesn't have any family then, isn't it? His wife died. Which is a bit suspicious, come to think of it.'

'She died?'

'In childbirth.'

'Not that suspicious, then.'

'What are we talking about? Fifty shillings, maybe. Forty?'

'I do not know.' Hermitage took a sup of ale and then folded his arms in what he hoped was a very critical manner.

Fridolf also supped his ale and then leant forward on his stool.

'This wergild,' he said nodding at Hermitage and reaching to bring something up from his waistband. 'Do you think I could pay in advance?'

Caput II: Problems At Home

'Things have got completely out of hand.' Cwen made her conclusion perfectly plain. And it was a conclusion. This was not the opening statement of a debate, nor a proposal that demanded detailed analysis and consideration. Things were not getting out of hand, they had already arrived. Now that her audience had been informed of this fact, they needed to respond.

'Really?' Hermitage asked timidly, which he always preferred.

'Of course.' Cwen wasn't going to give him the opportunity to travel his usual path. Prevarication, a long discussion to confirm that everyone understood and agreed on the definition of "out of hand", or doing nothing and hoping everything turned out all right in the end was not going to work this time.

'Only yesterday, a total stranger approached you in the street and asked if you'd mind taking a note of the fact that he was going to murder his master.'

When it was put like that, it did sound rather extreme.

'It was unusual,' Hermitage admitted.

'Unusual? Is that what it was? Just unusual? Not completely mad and ridiculous?'

'Well,' Hermitage hummed a bit. 'I suppose it was better than him coming and telling me that he'd already done it.'

'Not much. Now he's on his way to do it, having had a nice conversation with you.'

'I'm sure I made it very clear that he should do no such thing.'

'He offered to pay you the wergild in advance, Hermitage.

What do you think his plans are?'

Hermitage grimaced at this as it woke memories of rather similar situations. Not involving murder, obviously, but times when he'd had a serious discussion with another brother about the nature of sin and the consequences for the immortal soul.

He had left those encounters confident that the correct course of action had been identified, only to find that the brother in question had gone off the map completely.

'Surely, he wouldn't,' Hermitage said more in hope than anticipation. If Fridolf did go and murder his master, Hermitage would be partly responsible. But he'd told him not to do it, surely that counted in his favour. And what more could he have done?

'From what you've said, he didn't sound dissuaded.'

'You should have brought him back here, Hermitage,' Wat put in.

'Back here?' Cwen's outrage at this suggestion reached great heights. 'Are you serious? Is that what we need? The place is already half full of people doing nothing useful but waiting for the next murder. Now we bring the potential killers in as well? I suppose it would keep things neat. You know, all in one place. If we put the body by the fire, we could have the whole thing sewn up by bedtime.' The folding of her arms indicated that this remark was not to be taken as a serious proposal.

'If you cast your mind back,' she went on, 'you might recall that this is supposed to be a weaving workshop. Where we make tapestry? Which people pay for. Unless we can start charging for the murders, we're all going to starve.'

'Hardly,' Wat said quietly. 'The apprentices are still working.'

16

'For now. How long before they get dragged into dealing with murders?'

'The point I was trying to make was that this Fridolf is a goldsmith's apprentice,' Wat explained. 'And nearing elevation to master, if what he said was true. They're rich people, goldsmiths.'

'He did indicate that was the case,' Hermitage confirmed, although he couldn't really see what Fridolf's actual or potential wealth had to do with anything.

'He might have wanted a tapestry.'

They both looked at Wat with mouths slightly open.

'I'm only saying,' he defended himself. 'Never let a customer pass you by. How many goldsmiths do you think come through Derby? And this one had forty or fifty shillings in his purse. Forty or fifty shillings that could have been in mine.' Wat sounded positively sorrowful that the money had left town without him.

'So, while he's asking Hermitage the best way to kill his master, we enquire whether he might like a tapestry to commemorate the event?'

'Now you're being silly. But he obviously had money to spend. I don't like seeing people with money to spend. I like to see them after they've spent it. On a tapestry.'

'Even potential killers?'

Wat shrugged. 'Everyone's a potential killer when you think about it.'

Hermitage didn't think anyone would think about that.

'There aren't many who tell you that they're going to do it,' Cwen pressed. 'The real problem is that this place is turning into some sort of home for investigation of murder instead of a weaving workshop. What would you call it, Hermitage?'

'Me?' in the face of Cwen's insistence, Hermitage found

that he could only agree with her assessment. Since his arrival, they had been consistently bothered by all manner of people turning up at the door with a murder. If it wasn't a force of Normans it could be the locals. It was an extraordinary situation for a weaving workshop to find itself in.

Wat had been kind enough to take him in and the two of them had helped with the hideous tasks thrown at him by the Normans. They hadn't complained about being taken away from the weaving. Until now.

Bart coming along hadn't helped. But at least the lad had been keen to help around the place. Well, not keen perhaps, but he'd done it.

Now, after visiting De'Ath's Dingle, they'd brought Siward back with them.[2] Three extra mouths to feed who were not contributing to the trade of the place really was a burden.

And was it possible that with the three of them here now, more murders would turn up?

It was a tricky situation, but he didn't like being asked to find the solution. Analysis of problems was his speciality. Someone else would do answers.

'The word,' Cwen specified.

'The word?'

'Yes, from your Latin. There must be a word for a place where investigators live while they're waiting for the next murder.'

Well, that was a relief. An etymological puzzle was much more comfortable than sorting out life's real dilemmas.

'Erm, well domus would be home, of course.'

'Let's assume it's not their home,' Cwen said very plainly. 'Just the place they wait for bodies.'

'Oh, in that case, perhaps statio, stationis. Standing still, a

---

[2] ***Return to the Dingle:*** The source of most of Hermitage's problems.

post? That sort of thing.'

'Station, eh?' Cwen concluded rather inaccurately. 'We need this to be a weaving workshop and not a station for people to report their murders. The place is going to end up with more investigators than weavers before long.'

'I don't think Siward has actually said he's going to be an investigator,' Hermitage pointed out.

'He spends all his time with Bart.'

'Well, yes, but they are of a similar age. It's natural.'

'There's nothing natural about him living in a weavers' workshop and not doing any weaving. Or any work at all, come to that.'

'He had nowhere else to go,' Hermitage pleaded the young man's case.

'Everyone's got somewhere else to go,' Cwen insisted. 'He could go home. How about that?'

'He told us of his awful life clearing filth, you know that.'

'Then he could at least clear our filth.'

'We've got a privy,' Hermitage pointed out.

'Are you going to say nothing useful?' Cwen asked Wat.

Wat supped at his ale and continued to warm his toes before the fire.

'I thought I might,' Wat replied. 'Now that I don't have fifty shillings to occupy me.'

'These boys are eating your food and taking up your space,' Cwen reminded him. 'Bart claims he's Hermitage's apprentice, but we're not actually investigating anything at the moment. And Siward doesn't claim anything at all.'

'What do you suggest then?' Wat asked. He clasped his tankard of ale before him and raised his eyebrows in polite enquiry.

'Suggest?'

'Yes. You've kindly raised the problem, so I assume you have a solution in mind.'

'Well..,'

'Ah. No solution, then? Just a list of problems.'

'Somebody's got to bring them up.'

'I'm sure the young men would be willing to work for their keep,' Hermitage said. 'And of course, if there's anything I can do, you know I'd be only too pleased.'

'You're not the problem, Hermitage,' Cwen said gently. 'It's just that we can't keep bringing new people back here after every investigation. Even Wat can understand that.'

Wat gave a tip of the head that indicated he acknowledged that something might need to be done.

'Perhaps there won't be any more investigations,' Hermitage suggested.

Wat and Cwen considered him in silence for a moment, a moment that they used to prepare for the burst of laughter they let out together.

'Oh, Hermitage,' Cwen smiled. 'You do say the silliest things.'

Hermitage didn't think it was silly at all. It was a laudable ambition. If there were no murders, there would be no investigation. Surely, that was a good thing in every sense of the word.

'Well.' Hermitage was thinking carefully about this.

The idea that people came to the weavers to get their murder solved was simply not right. Surely, there should be somewhere more appropriate for them to hold this station of theirs. 'What if we moved in with the Shire Reeve?'

'The sheriff?' Cwen asked, pronouncing the title incorrectly, as young people tended to do.

'He's miles away,' Wat said.

'Well, yes. But he's where people should go when there's been a murder. Or any other crime, come to that.'

'You have met our Shire Reeve?' Cwen questioned, pronouncing it carefully.

'Master Crandon, yes.'

'And would you want to live with him?'

Hermitage recalled what Master Crandon was like. 'I suppose we wouldn't have to live with him. We could just go there during the day when people might want their murders reported, and then come home in the evening.'

'You'd need a horse and cart,' Wat pointed out.

'And our dear Shire Reeve would probably sell your horse and cart from under you. I wouldn't trust that man to investigate a small hole in the ground and be able to get to the bottom of it. As for accommodating the three of you, well, you heard what he did when his old father was on his deathbed?'

'Erm, no.'

'Left him at the door of the church. Said it would save time.'

'How do you know that?' Hermitage thought that this sounded like a bit of malicious village gossip.

'I don't know how else an old man who can't get out of his bed ends up lying in it outside the church door.'

'At least being with the Shire Reeve would take the murders from the workshop,' Hermitage said.

'I'm not sure it would,' Cwen mused. 'William and his men know where you are. They'd still send for you here.'

'Then, what's to be done?' Hermitage's solution seemed to have been quickly dismissed.

'Don't ask Cwen,' Wat said. 'She only does problems.'

'It's not the murders that are the problem, really.' Cwen

was now thoughtful.

'Oh, isn't it?' Hermitage couldn't think what else would count.

'It's the people that go with them. Siward and Bart. If William says we all have to go and find some killer, we have to do it, don't we? Got no choice.'

Hermitage could only agree that King William was not strong on giving people choices.

'But now we've got those two loitering about not doing anything useful.' She put her hand to her chin and looked up at the ceiling.

'When we do get another murder, we'll be busy again,' she said mainly to herself.

'If,' Hermitage corrected.

'When,' Cwen corrected right back at him. 'But even then, we don't know what use Siward will be. Bart comes up with some good ideas now and again, but even then he comes back and eats our food.'

'How selfish of him,' Wat commented.

'It's what we do with them until we've got to go off again,' Cwen was mumbling now.

'There's a good chance we'll have Master Scrydan to do if Fridolf has his way,' Wat gave a little laugh.

Hermitage tried to ignore that idea. 'We've said many times that the Normans are settling down now. That battle near Hastings is long gone and they're firmly in charge. They can't possibly go on needing me to investigate all these murders for them. Perhaps I'll only have to do the special ones.'

'Special murders?' Wat enquired. 'I think there will still be plenty of them. There'll be all the ones they do themselves. But then, I suppose they never want you to investigate them.

That wouldn't be at all helpful.'

'Scrydan,' Cwen said for no immediately obvious reason.

'I'm sure he will be fine,' Hermitage said mainly for his own benefit. 'Fridolf may still wish his master ill, but I warned him that if anything did happen, I would know who did it.'

'Well, exactly,' Cwen agreed.

'Exactly, what?'

'How will you know who did it?'

'Erm, because Fridolf is the obvious suspect.'

'But you won't know if this Scrydan is even dead or not, what with him being in London and you in Derby.'

'Erm, yes.' Hermitage had no idea what Cwen was talking about, but it seemed rude to say so.

'What are you talking about?' Wat asked.

'There's a possible murder in the offing, yes?' Cwen sounded quite enthusiastic at the prospect.

'I don't really think..,' Hermitage began.

'Could be,' Wat said rather too nonchalantly.

'And we could put a stop to it,' Cwen went on. 'Which has got to be better than investigating after the event, when you think about it.'

'And just how do we do that?' Wat asked.

'Send Bart and Siward.' Cwen looked inordinately proud of her marvellous idea.

'Send Bart and Siward?' Hermitage enquired. 'Send them where?'

'To London, of course. To find Scrydan and stop Fridolf murdering him.'

Hermitage liked to think that he had already prevented the murder by giving Fridolf a stern talking-to.

'And it would get them out of here,' Cwen added another excellent feature. 'Give them something useful to do.'

'You can't simply send them to London like that.' Even as he said it, Hermitage couldn't see why Cwen couldn't send them anywhere.

'Why not? I'm sure they'd love to go to London.'

Wat sighed heavily. 'And what? We give them a pack full of our food and some coin for the journey? How does that save us the problem of looking after them?'

'They're on the King's Investigator's business,' Cwen announced. 'They can get people on the way to give them lodging.'

'Prising favours out of people because of your office,' Wat mused. 'Master Crandon really would be the best teacher in that regard.'

'But they won't be on my business,' Hermitage pointed out the fundamental dishonesty at the root of this suggestion.

'Yes, they will. Fridolf came to you as King's Investigator. He told you about a possible murder and now you're, what can we say, acting on information received?'

'Hardly at the instruction of the king, who doesn't know anything about it.'

'You have to act on your own, Hermitage,' Cwen said. 'Grasp the reins, that sort of thing.'

Hermitage didn't like the sound of that at all. He had grasped reins once but the subsequent damage to the cart meant that he was never trusted with them again. He'd explained that no matter how hard you grasped the reins, it wouldn't make the wheel fall off, but no one believed him.

'If William found out that you knew about a murder and had taken action, he'd probably be quite pleased.' Cwen sounded quite enthusiastic.

Hermitage wasn't concerned about pleasing William. Simply staying away from him was best.

'And you don't have to do anything yourself. You just send Siward and Bart. They can leave first thing tomorrow.'

It was very much sounding to Hermitage's ears that if he didn't send Siward and Bart, he would wake tomorrow to find they'd been sent anyway.

'But what if there's nothing to find?' Hermitage pleaded. 'Fridolf may have taken my talk to heart and Scrydan is alive and well, the master-apprentice relationship put back on a sound footing.'

Wat snorted at that idea.

'Then they get a trip to London out of it. Young men like going to London.'

'Do they?'

'Bound to.' Cwen nodded to herself in a very determined manner. 'I'll go and tell them.' She stood from her stool and headed to the stairs.

Hermitage looked at Wat, who looked back. From not knowing there was a problem at all, Hermitage was now complicit in a solution that he had made no contribution towards and wasn't even convinced was right.

Wat nodded gently as he took another sup of ale. 'Take my advice, Hermitage.'

Hermitage's eyebrows rose in hope.

'Do nothing and hope it all turns out all right in the end.'

Caput III: Problems Away

Master Scrydan, goldsmith of repute in the Saxon realm of England. was now very satisfied to be a goldsmith of repute in the Norman realm of England. Things had been very worrying for a little while, but his natural skills and talents had seen him through.

Those natural skills and talents covered more than simple goldsmithing; not that goldsmithing was in the least bit simple. No, Scrydan's personal craft was accompanied by that raft of abilities that elevates the humble, if talented, worker to the heights of success; he was avaricious, ruthless, scheming and, if need be, dishonest.

Skill with gold was the route by which he achieved his goal of wealth and power. If it hadn't been gold, it would have been something else.

In what would be a shock to any who knew him, he considered himself to be an honest and straightforward man. He knew exactly what he was like and made no efforts to hide it; unless the scheming or dishonesty were called for, obviously.

"People take me as they see me and I treat everyone alike, master or slave", was his common refrain. It was also common amongst all the other people who followed their own interests regardless of the needs of others.

He also managed to convince himself that he was not a greedy man, despite the simple fact that he had the girth of several of them. His needs were simple, he didn't seek the wealth of kings and desired no more power than what was required to make him beholden to no man. If all men and most women were beholden to him, that was fine. And the nearly fifty years of his life seemed to have been spent collecting people who were beholden to him.

This foundation of raw self-interest had ensured that he said the right things to the right people when the Normans arrived, even if they were the opposite of the things he had said the week before.

Others had not fared so well.

Unfortunately, it was also in Master Scrydan's nature to take equal measures of satisfaction from his own success as from the failure of others.

As a result of all of this, Fridolf was right; nobody liked him.

On this day, he hummed and pottered about his workshop with more than usual smug contentment. He criticised the work of an apprentice here, tutted at the state of the furnace there, moaned at the cost of the provisions the delivery boy deposited and generally expressed his disappointment with everyone and everything except himself.

For his own aggrandisement, which really didn't need any more aggrandising, he stopped every now and again and went over to the velvet-lined box of exquisitely fine walnut that occupied the prime spot on his own workbench.

The amount of money the carpenter wanted for this box had been truly shocking. Scrydan didn't know where some people got their ideas. The promise of the box being part of the presentation to the king had knocked the price down a bit, but the man was now nagging to come along and stand before William alongside Scrydan. Ridiculous.

Lifting the lid, he gazed at the marvel within.

Fit for a king was an expression bandied about by the less

talented as if such items were commonplace. Only from the hand of Scrydan himself could something come that truly was fit for a king.

The clasp that sat in this box had a weight about it that simply demanded attention. There was more gold in this single piece than Scrydan had handled in a very long time, and he felt he should take as much credit for its procurement as he did for its craft.

There was gold to be found, of course there was, but the Romans had so loved the metal that they had used most of it up. Welsh gold was good but in very short supply, hard to get hold of and ridiculously expensive. Rumour was that the druids kept most of it for their hideous ceremonies, and that which did become available was cursed.

Scrydan thought that any ceremony that kept gold out of his hands was hideous. As for curses, well, he was happy to pass them on to the new owner of his fine products. Mentioning a curse when making a profitable trade would be a dangerous thing to do; and incredibly stupid.

With the problems of Welsh gold and rare fresh supplies from the merchants who travelled from the east, alternative sources had to be exploited.

Those Romans may have taken their gold to the grave with them, but if an imaginative goldsmith knew where the graves were, he could easily replenish his stock. Well, late-night digging was never easy, but it was productive.

And the king didn't have to know. Not that William the Norman would be sensitive about anything like that if the tales were true.

Anyway, concern about the previous owner of the gold would dissipate in the face of the wonder that lay heavily before Scrydan's eyes.

This was a clasp to sit in the middle of the chest of a king, holding only robes of the very highest quality on the most special occasions. And the mighty who looked upon it would despair and come to Scrydan to ask for one of their own.

As long as he didn't run out of Romans, he'd be all right.

The piece was a ring of solid metal, engraved and hammered with utmost precision. The whole thing was at least a hand's-span wide and the thickness of a thumb. By any standard, it was a monstrous display of wealth.

This was not a work for some beggarly pauper to even dream of. The sight of it alone would be too much for the average working peasant. It sat beyond the ambition of a wealthy merchant and Scrydan would not waste his time even discussing it with the upstart rulers of small countries.

This was gold for popes and kings.

Embedded jewels glinted and the tiny shapes of lions scribed into the gold could be discerned upon close inspection.

Scrydan had heard that William liked lions. Obviously, he'd never seen a lion or had any idea of his own what they were supposed to look like, so he'd copied some from a book. At least, he assumed they were lions.

The pin of the clasp that crossed the middle of the circle needed to be stronger than gold, which would have bent too easily, and so Scrydan had cunningly enveloped a shard of steel with more gold.

He took the piece from the box for about the tenth time and felt the solidity of it in his hand. He truly marvelled at his own skill in producing such treasure. The direction he had given the apprentices, mainly Fridolf, had been of such high quality that a result of this excellence was inevitable.

And the boy had thought that he could become a master!

That trinket of a wristband of his would melt down to make a gift for one of William's nobles; Scrydan just had to work out which would be the most useful noble.

But the lad was getting above himself. It was best to have sent him off on the pretext of searching for commissions. Scrydan didn't want an apprentice making ridiculous claims when he made his presentation to the king.

Reluctantly, Scrydan closed the box once more and patted its lid in a horribly intimate manner.

'I'm going to court,' he announced to the apprentices who had their noses bent to their work.

No reply or acknowledgement was given or expected, and Scrydan threw his fine cloak about his shoulders. He took the box from the bench and tucked it under his arm, secreting it beneath the folds of the cloak.

He had told much about this work to some of the important Normans and now was the time to show it. A fellow called Ranulph de Sauveloy seemed to have the ear of the king and struck Scrydan as a like-minded individual.

That was not a man to be fooled into paying more than the work was worth, though. Such a route, Scrydan's normal practice, would be rash. The true value of the clasp would be enough and should give him an influential, and profitable position with the Normans. A position in advance of the other goldsmiths, many of whom were ridiculously precious about their work and the fact that their erstwhile Saxon customers had been slaughtered by the Normans. Idiots.

To give with one hand while taking with the other was only reasonable. Once Scrydan had fully established himself, he would settle into a more comfortable position; not giving at all and taking with both hands.

As he closed the door behind him, both apprentices turned

as one and made extremely rude gestures, accompanied by a cacophony of farmyard noises. One had even managed to contain a putrid accumulation of digestive gases, which he now released to what sounded like thunderous applause.

Laughing heartily, they both left their work, drew their stools up to the furnace fire and resumed their favourite conversation; all the things they'd do to Scrydan if they had the chance.

Oblivious to the disrespect being shown in his own workshop, the goldsmith turned on the street outside and headed for the new castle from where the Normans' power issued.

It was most inconsiderate of William to have set himself up so far to the east. Scrydan, along with several of the other goldsmiths of the town, was settled around Ceapan Street, hard by Saint Paul's Cathedral.

The Normans had put up a castle at Ludgate, which was only just around the corner. Why couldn't William be happy with that?

Scrydan would have to travel the full length of Ceapan Street and go beyond until the eastern wall of the old Roman town was reached. At least the Normans were fully in control of London and their patrols guaranteed some safety. Still, Scrydan was cautious about keeping his precious load away from prying eyes.

He could have taken one of the apprentices with him, but he wasn't about to let either of those wastrels anywhere near the Normans. He could also have hired some protection for the journey but there were two problems with that. One, it would have meant spending some money and two, you couldn't trust anyone these days. The protection from attack could well turn into the attack itself if the profit was high enough.

No, he was well enough known among these streets for his passage to be unhindered. No one even stopped to make conversation with Master Scrydan if they could avoid it.

Nonetheless, on this day, interested eyes closely observed the departure from the workshop.

The street was busy this early evening with people coming and going about their business. Churchmen scurried to and fro on the tasks of their day, traders moved their goods and stallholders hawked their wares.

It was all carried out in an atmosphere of nervous caution, though. There was still no way of reliably telling what the Normans would object to. The coming and going was completed as quickly as possible, the scurrying had an added urgency, and the hawking took the form of some polite requests instead of the usual aggressive demands.

Movement of goods was very careful indeed. It was now well known that if the Normans took a fancy to the goods in question they could vanish in an instant. Along with the trader, if they weren't too careful.

In the midst of all this activity, one pair of eyes followed the goldsmith with practised and comfortable efficiency.

These were eyes that knew how to follow their target as well as how not to be seen following anything at all. From under a dark hood, they peered out, not missing a detail, including the bulge in the cloak at Scrydan's side.

The hood nodded very slightly to itself, apparently satisfied with its observations, and the figure stirred from its place in the doorway of a storehouse where the hood merged into the shadows.

The movement hesitated, and inside the hood, an interested eyebrow rose.

Another specific movement in the crowd had been noticed and the eyes narrowed slightly while a crease of curiosity crossed the brow.

A slightly familiar face, this one blatantly open, followed Scrydan's back as he made his way along the street to the east.

The eyes under the hood observed this with wry amusement. If the young man thought that that was supposed to be discreet following, he had a lot to learn. One wrong turn at a corner and he would be spotted.

After only a few steps, this new presence turned and looked back to the west. Another act of ineptitude.

The hooded eyes followed the gaze and saw yet more movement that did not fit with the hustle and bustle. This time it was a woman who appeared to be loitering with unjustified interest at the door of a blacksmith. She gave the barest nod to the young man, lost her interest in metalwork, and sauntered along behind.

A hand reached up into the hood and scratched the chin. This was clearly an unexpected development and one that required thought.

Obviously, the woman would have to be allowed to pass by, but the situation was becoming overly complex. More complex than he had been told would be the case.

The woman wandered along the street as if only out for an idle stroll, or what she thought idle strolls were like. In fact, she couldn't have looked more obvious if she'd tried.

Only a truly idle stroller could really look like one, and they all stayed indoors now that the Normans were on the streets.

As she passed by at the closest point to the hooded one, he could see that she was old enough to be the boy's mother.

Either that or some woman who had a hold over him and was directing from behind.

Whatever their motivation, their interest was plainly in Scrydan.

With the train now past, the one in the hood made an habitual check of his surroundings before moving off.

He now spotted yet another pair of eyes, these following the followers. This was getting ridiculous.

At least these eyes appeared incapable of even seeing the road in front of them with any clarity. The man to whom they belonged swayed and wobbled as he stood on the opposite side of the street. He also had the look of one who would quite like to be sick very soon indeed.

He was an old fellow, dressed in a workman's smock. It was impossible to discern his trade as the cloth was dirty and creased as if it had been out all night with the workman still inside.

Containing internal disturbances that were obviously causing great distress, the bleary and bloodshot eyes forced themselves to move off.

To the one in the hood, it seemed that this latest participant was directly interested in Scrydan, having failed to notice either the young man or his companion.

The hooded one now took a deep breath and ran his fingertips over his thumbs, as if testing the quality of whatever scheme it was he had in mind.

He gave it a moment, just to make sure that the whole gaggle on the street was not going to turn and now follow the goldsmith before he left his spot and headed east. He was much better at idle strolling than the woman and looked quite convincing.

But, as if mirroring the very layers of heaven, a far superior being observed the departure of the hood with a level of patronising condescension that would have put a cardinal in his place.

This fellow didn't seem at all perturbed about the throng now following Scrydan on his way along the street. In fact, he appeared to consider this sort of thing quite normal.

Quite oblivious of the interest in his progress, Scrydan continued eastward until he came to the crossing of the River Walbrook. This was a substantial wooden bridge, capable of carrying significant loads. In olden days, which weren't actually that olden, it had separated the Saxon stalls of Ludgate and Corn hills. Now, it was simply a bridge over a river in Norman London.

From here, the old Roman road continued towards the east gate of the city, where Scrydan's route turned him south, along the line of the wall towards King William's new stronghold.

It was incredible to think that from this spot, over a thousand years previously, Roman soldiers had stood and probably gazed out to the east, wondering what savages lay out there waiting to attack.

Scrydan didn't find this incredible at all as he didn't even think about it. The sight of the old stones did make him consider those generous Romans and their propensity for taking their wealth with them wherever they went. And to keep it with them when they stopped going anywhere anymore.

The eastern cemetery was just beyond this wall, and the goldsmith did his best to out-haunt the Romans themselves where that place was concerned.

All of which idle speculation meant that Scrydan didn't even see his attack coming.

At first, he felt the heart-stopping shock of someone barging into him from behind and knocking him almost from his feet. An excess of the blood humour rushed through his body, preparing him for either flight or fight. Scrydan didn't really do either and so quickly assumed that this was a simple accident.

When the box was snatched from under his arm, his blood humour didn't know what to do with itself.

The agony of his treasure being taken from him was more than he could bear and he turned to face his assailant with a mountain of righteous indignation.

'Give that back this moment,' he instructed when he saw that the clasp had been taken from the box. He didn't even bother looking at who this outrageous individual was, only having eyes for his gold.

He did chance a quick look over his shoulder to see if any Normans might be available to come to his aid. There weren't.

'Of course,' the thief replied. 'You can have it straight away.'

Scrydan watched with some disgust as this pair of hands fiddled with his magnificent work and opened the steel clasp away from the body of the gold.

They even clasped the ring as if it were some sort of weapon, for heaven's sake.

They then used the weapon to stab Scrydan to death.

Caput IV: This Way To The Murder

'You really want us to go to London?' Bart checked as if unable to believe his luck.

He and Siward stood before Cwen, Hermitage and Wat in the upper chamber, soon after dawn. The previous evening having seen the firm conclusion that the boys would go to London. Well, it had seen Cwen's firm conclusion and the shrugged agreement of Wat and Hermitage.

'For about the tenth time, yes,' Cwen replied. It was actually only the third time, it just felt like the tenth.

'Because this Fridolf might be about to murder his master?' Siward did not sound quite so enthusiastic about the mission.

'It's a possibility,' Cwen said with a heavy sigh. She was obviously wondering why it was necessary to repeat herself several times before she was understood. The words were quite straightforward. She wasn't speaking Latin. In fact, she used precisely the same words over and over again. Weren't they listening or something?

'And what do we do about it if he is?' Siward enquired carefully.

'Hopefully, it hasn't happened,' Cwen said. 'In which case, you simply find Fridolf and tell him that you've been sent by Brother Hermitage to make sure that he doesn't go through with it.'

Hermitage wondered about that. As this was Cwen's idea and she was issuing the instructions, could the boys really say that they had been sent by him?

'But if it has happened?' Siward checked.

'What is the matter with you?' Cwen asked, getting a rather offended look back from Siward. 'You're the one who says you sailed the known world with Vikings.[3] Now you don't even want to go to London?'

'I just like to know what I'm facing,' Siward explained. 'On a boat, you can see for miles, nothing surprises you.

'And everything is natural. You're fighting against the wind and the water; it doesn't care who you are. It's not actually trying to kill you. You might get killed but that will probably be your own fault. And the wind and the water will simply carry on as if nothing has happened.

'Me and Bart alone in London looking for someone who sets out to kill is not the same at all. People are horrible, you never know what they're up to. They lie and cheat and might want to do you harm simply because they like doing harm. Give me a mountain of waves any day.'

The others all looked at him after this strange speech.

'I'm just saying,' Siward added meekly.

'I don't think Fridolf is a killer, really,' Hermitage assured him. 'He is simply a young man with some very wrong ideas.'

'You said he was planning to stick a knife in this Scrydan's back,' Siward reminded him.

'Well, yes, but I don't think he meant it.'

'Oh, that's all right, then.'

'I mean he hadn't really thought it through. It's all well and good to talk about putting a knife in someone's back, but when it comes to the real deed, it's a different matter.' Hermitage didn't really believe it was all well and good to talk about putting a knife in someone else's back, but he couldn't think how else to explain the situation.

'And if we find that Scrydan is lying there with a knife in

---

[3] *The Domesday Book (Still Not That One):* Siward getting about a bit.

his back?'

'Then you report to the authorities,' Cwen snapped. 'Go and tell the sheriff.'

'Will there be one?'

'For heaven's sake.' Cwen slapped her arms at her side. 'Do you want me to come with you and hold your hand? You're a big boy now. One who's played with Vikings. Go to London and work it out for yourself.'

'We can do that,' Bart nodded. 'We'll be on official business. King's Investigator's business.'

'Ah, now.' Hermitage saw quite quickly how that could go wrong.

'You are not the King's Investigator,' Cwen made it quite clear, for which Hermitage was grateful. 'You are just running an errand for him. You can say that to get lodging and food and so forth, but you're not to go strutting about the place telling people you are the King's Investigator.'

Bart had that look on his face that said he had heard the instruction and had absolutely no intention of following it.

'Remember who is in London,' Cwen said coldly. 'In his tower by the river? The king. William. The Norman. Yes? Word gets to him that his investigator is shouting about in his streets and you'll have a very uncomfortable experience.'

Bart grimaced at this and could obviously see the problem.

'Shall I say it all over again?' Cwen asked sarcastically. 'Go to London. Find Fridolf and tell him not to kill his master. If the master is already dead, go and tell the sheriff. Otherwise, keep your heads down and out of trouble.'

Bart nodded sharply and took Siward's arm to lead him away.

As they went down the steps from the upstairs room, Siward continued to express his concerns.

'I'm not sure telling the sheriff about a killer is sensible. Killers probably don't like you doing things like that.'

Cwen shook her head as the two young men left. 'With any luck,' she said to Wat and Hermitage, 'they won't come back.'

'What?' Hermitage was horrified at that idea.

'I mean that they'll find London so exciting, they'll want to stay.'

'Doesn't sound like Siward likes excitement,' Wat observed.

'Yes, what's wrong with him?' Cwen scowled. 'He keeps going on about his adventures on the sea and he doesn't want to go to London?'

'I think it's the murder.' Hermitage had every sympathy. 'Fighting the raging sea on a longship is one thing. Dealing with someone who stabs people in the back is very different.' He knew this because he hated both in very different ways.

'Well, perhaps they'll make a good pair,' Wat speculated over his ale. 'Bart's all for finding murder wherever he can and Siward wants to avoid it.'

'I trust that they will find no murder at all,' Hermitage said as if insisting on the fact would make it so.

...

Bart and Siward's departure from the workshop the following dawn was as organised as it had to be and as quick as Cwen wanted it. There was no point in loitering, she said. Scrydan's life was at stake.

Fridolf's immortal soul was also at stake, as Hermitage pointed out, but that got treated as less of a priority.

Despite Cwen's arguments that they should be able to take care of themselves on the road as they were on the king's business, of a sort, they still managed to leave with packs weighed down with a lot of the workshop's food.

Wat's raised eyebrows at the supplies that were being given away to the boys who were apparently a waste of supplies, were met with stony silence.

More worrying to Hermitage's mind was the question Bart asked a moment later.

'It's south, yes?'

'London?' Cwen checked with some alarm. 'Yes, of course, it's south.'

'Just checking. I've never been there before.'

'Me neither,' Siward admitted. He scanned the southerly horizon from east to west as if he'd be able to spot the place.

'Just head south down the old tracks, cross the river and carry on until you come to the Roman road,' Wat advised. 'Follow that all the way and you'll be in London. It's a big place, you can't miss it. If you see the sea, you've gone too far. Be about three days, if you get a step on.'

'Three days?' Siward sounded quite horrified.

'Of course. Where did you think it was?'

'Not three days away.'

'Oh, just get on with it,' Cwen instructed. 'And when you get there, find Fridolf.'

'Hm,' Bart hummed.

'What is it now?'

'If it's a big place, will they know who Fridolf is?'

'Just ask for the goldsmiths. There won't be many of them,' Wat said.

'And if Scrydan has been murdered, everyone will be talking about it,' Cwen assured them, which seemed not to be a very welcome assurance.

With a final wave, accompanied by a hearty push in the

back, the boys made their way down the path from the workshop and onto the Derby road.

Bart turned right, while Siward turned left.

'And Derby is that way,' Cwen shouted pointing in the right direction.

Siward gave a wave of acknowledgement and turned around to follow Bart.

'Good God,' Cwen swore despite Hermitage's scowl. 'At least they're out of here now, but the chances of them actually finding London between them are a bit slim.'

'Perhaps I should go with them?' Hermitage half-offered, not wanting to go with them at all.

'Absolutely not,' Cwen said firmly. 'They've got to look after themselves. They'll manage.'

'Of course,' Wat said nonchalantly as he turned back towards the workshop, 'if we get word that they've both been murdered in London, we can all go.'

Hermitage skipped after Wat, anxious to hear that this was extremely unlikely and that Wat was only joking.

...

Siward and Bart, once out of the workshop and the organisation that went with it, found that they were quite capable of looking after themselves. They even started moaning about Cwen and how she bustled and ordered everyone about so much, that no one did anything for fear that it would be wrong.

There was no need to do anything other than walk along the road at this point. They had made sure they had more than enough supplies for the journey, Cwen not knowing about the extras they had prepared earlier and left by the road.

They exchanged nods of acknowledgement with a few people on the main street of Derby and, as they walked down the road in their sturdy boots with packs on their backs, slowly grew exasperated at such questions and comments as; "going on a journey, then?", "you'll be off somewhere, I reckon?" and "you've got your sturdy boots on, I see."

The two of them walking along was probably the most exciting thing that had happened in days, but surely there were limits as to what constituted a topic of conversation.

Bart even tried engaging for entertainment's sake.

'Heading south then, boys?' Ern called from outside the tavern.

'That we are,' Bart replied. 'Still running the tavern, eh, Ern?'

'That I am,' Ern said with horrible interest, looking ready to embark on a whole morning of idle chatter.

They moved quickly on.

Once beyond the confines of the town, they took the southern road straight towards the ford across the River Trent. Or it might be a bridge. There was no telling these days as bridges seemed to be put up, only for them to fall down again soon afterwards.

People with money fancied the idea of taking in the tolls from a bridge, but they weren't so keen on giving the money out to build a decent bridge in the first place.

At this time, the crossing seemed to be half and half. There were some bits of bridge sticking out of the water here and there, but you had to wade out to get to them. With feet already wet, it was sensible to simply walk all the way across.

On the far bank, the track continued its path southward.

A few people were on the road either coming from or going

to Derby, and Siward and Bart joined the steady procession. Ahead of them, a tradesman of some sort walked, a truly massive pack upon his back dwarfing the man himself.

His burden was so great that the two of them soon caught him up.

'This is the road to the south, is it?' Bart asked brightly.

The man with the pack did not stop but glanced up from under his load.

'No,' he said. 'It's the Appian Way, and just over that hill is the Forum of Rome.'

'Erm,' Bart was confused.

'Of course, it's the road to the south, you idiot,' the tradesman explained. 'Look at the sun.'

Bart and Siward did so and saw that they were heading south.

'Have you been to Rome, then?' Siward asked with some awe.

'I have,' the man answered with what sounded like pride. 'In my time, for my trade.'

'I say, you're not a goldsmith, are you?' Bart enquired.

'A goldsmith?' the man asked incredulously. 'Would I be carrying a pack the size of Nottingham castle if I was a goldsmith? Would I be trudging this wretched road if I was a goldsmith? Would I be having to put up with stupid questions like this if I was a goldsmith?'

Bart assumed the answer to each of these questions was no.

'What do you want a goldsmith for, anyway?' the man asked with a little more interest.

'He might be dead,' Bart explained.

'A dead goldsmith's going to be no good. You want a live one. Are you looking for some gold?'

'No, no, nothing like that. We're going to London because

44

a goldsmith might have been murdered.'

'Oh, ar?'

'Or he's going to be murdered,' Siward added. 'We don't know yet.'

'Is that right?'

'No, really. We've been sent by the King's Investigator, Brother Hermitage.'

'Been sent by something,' the man muttered, seemingly now quite grateful that he had a large pack between himself and these two.

'Well, we'll leave you to your journey,' Siward promised. 'Is it far to the Roman road?'

'About fifteen mile or so.'

'Fifteen miles?' Bart exclaimed with disappointment at the great distance. 'And then it's London, is it?'

'London is a hundred miles away,' the tradesman informed them. 'And I'm not sure that you two are going to make it.'

'Wat was right,' Siward moaned. 'It is going to take days.'

'Did you say Wat?' the pack-bearer asked.

'That's right.'

'Wat the Weaver?'

'That's him. We live at his workshop.'

'You live with Wat the Weaver?'

'Yes.' Siward was wondering where this was leading.

The tradesman spat on the ground. 'Then I hope you get murdered as well.'

Siward and Bart simply looked at one another and let the man wander on under his pack. With shrugs that they didn't know what that was about, they resumed their journey, quickly stepping past the tradesman without further comment.

Learning from their first encounter, they kept to

themselves as they trudged on down the road. Occasionally, they exchanged a glance and a nod with someone, but never stopped for conversation.

Naturally, they were bothered by beggars quite regularly, but robbers and ne'er-do-wells were probably dissuaded by the number of travellers on the road, which made for a straightforward passage.

Their stomachs were telling them that the noonday meal was in order when they finally arrived at the Roman road.

This was a busier thoroughfare, bringing people from the northwest, and they stopped in what was almost a camp of people all taking their food together.

On the far side of the road, the scraps of a fort remained, peeping out of the fields.

'I wonder what the Romans were like,' Siward speculated as they partook of Wat's finest provisions.

'Same as us, I should think,' Bart replied as he supped from a skin of Wat's ale.

'They must have liked walking a lot, to have built all these roads.'

'It is a lot of trouble to go to,' Bart agreed. 'But at least it'll be downhill to London from here.'

Caput V: London

Disappointment at the number of hills they had to go up simply in order to go down them again bothered the boys for the rest of the journey.

At least the travel itself was uneventful, and the number of people using the roads increased the closer they got to London.

Nights were spent in quite large camps of travellers as they settled once darkness made walking too dangerous. The first light of dawn saw everyone up and off once more, and there was something in the air on the third day that said this would see their arrival in London.

Unfortunately, the number of Normans increased the closer they got. Bright chatter between the Saxons on the first two days, died to a worried mutter as more and more uniformed men appeared, many of them on horses.

These Normans all looked anxious to find a recalcitrant Saxon or two to deal with and so all the Saxons avoided the gazes and stares and found the stones of the road absolutely fascinating.

Cresting yet one more hill, Siward and Bart stopped and looked out at the view spread before them. On either side, the ever-present woodland opened to reveal a striking vista.

In the distance, a huge river snaked across the landscape, breaking its bounds here and there to form pools and lakes. Various small settlements could be seen dotted about the countryside and way off to their left, a more substantial town sat, still too distant to be seen in any detail.

'London,' Siward breathed.

'I think it must be,' Bart agreed.

'Get a move on,' a woman's voice called from behind, and they realised they were obstructing the street. 'We haven't got all day to stand here and gawp.'

'London,' Bart told the woman.

'Of course, it's London. Have you never seen it before?'

'Well, no.'

'Well, now you have. Get a move on.'

Bart and Siward moved with jolting steps, trying to take in the view even as they descended the hill.

'How long until we get there?' Siward asked the woman.

'With you two dawdling about? A week, probably. For the rest of us an hour or so.'

The excitement of finally arriving in London drove them on, and their steps were livelier than they had been for some time.

Once off the hill, the walking was largely flat and level and before long, the great walls of London came into view.

Siward and Bart exchanged glances at this incredible structure, which, even from a distance, towered over them. They marvelled at what beings had been able to create such an edifice. It didn't look like wattle and daub and there was no thatch on top, so it was a complete shock to their sensibilities.

'It's amazing,' Siward breathed.

Bart could only nod his agreement.

One of the travellers nearby coughed a snort of contempt, but Bart supposed that if you saw this sort of thing every day, it wouldn't inspire such awe.

As they drew closer, the awe began to wear off a bit.

The tops of the walls were still high but weren't quite complete. It was true that the wall appeared to stretch all around the city, but it wasn't in one single span anymore. There were bits of the wall that were high, but in between those bits, there were gaps where it had fallen, or been pushed.

Piles of rubble lay here and there, overgrown with moss, bushes and even small trees. It was still a lot of stone, but you could see a lot of stone in all sorts of places.

If this was meant to be the defensive bulwark of London, it wasn't going to work against anyone who was capable of walking around a pile of stone.

Drawing nearer still, they saw that the gaps and failures in the wall outnumbered the solid sections. Goodness knew when all of this had started to fail, but it was clear no one had bothered even making the attempt to put it back together again.

Perhaps the Normans had plans, but there was no sign of any work going on at all.

The great entrance into the city, Alders Gate, was even more of a disappointment. True, it was a gate, a real wooden gate, or rather a pair of gates that hung from two stone pillars on either side of the road.

The fact that anyone who felt like it could simply walk around either side of the pillars to get into the town detracted somewhat from the impact of the gate itself. That and the fact the left-hand gate was hanging from its hinges and looked ready to collapse on anyone who got too close.

The modest stream of people coming and going by Alders Gate ignored the gate itself and created new paths heading off into the east and west of the city according to their destinations.

There was no sign of the great Roman walls here at all. Presumably, the bits had been taken away to be more useful than lying in a field defending a town that obviously didn't want to be defended.

Stepping across the threshold into the great city of London continued the theme of a huge let down.

The tracks were rutted and more like streams of mud than solid paths. The smell was quite revolting, even to Siward who was used to filth. And the people pushed and barged their way around as if everyone else was there purposefully to get in their way.

Many Normans were amongst the crowd, some of them going about their own business, others watching the coming and going with suspicious eyes, as well as swords. They did not seem the sort of people to approach and ask where all the goldsmiths lived.

'This is London?' Bart asked with a sag in his voice.

'I suppose so,' Siward sighed.

'And they have goldsmiths here?'

'I imagine this is one of the busy bits,' Siward suggested. 'All the rich people will live somewhere else. Away from the muck. Like they always do.'

Bart nodded at this truth.

They scanned what there was to be scanned and concluded that walking straight on down towards the river that lay in front of them was not something they wanted to do. It was perfectly clear that this was the source of the smell that hung in the air, like dead things left to hang too long in a hunter's hut.

A miasma of mist loitered above the sluggish stream, clearly in league with the water below, if it was still water.

There were boats on the river, presumably plying their trade. Any boatmen hardy enough to ply on this stream deserved all the trade they could get.

To their left, a great bridge spanned the river; great in size, not in strength. One look at the crumbling wooden edifice confirmed that they would not be visiting the south bank.

The walls of the city continued their haphazard journey to the right but further up the riverbank, as if protecting them from any plans the river might have, a magnificent church arose.

This was obviously the best-maintained building in the city and towered over everything around it. Here was something in London to be impressed by. It even seemed to be built of stone, probably taken from the walls that fell all around it.

The boys gazed at this wonder and with no better idea, silently agreed that this was where they would go.

'If anyone wants a goldsmith, it'll be a churchman,' Bart reasoned.

'Or a king,' Siward said seriously as he nodded towards the east.

Over there, perhaps just over a mile away, and closer to the river than seemed comfortable, a large wooden construction could be seen. This was clearly new as ladders and wooden scaffolding crawled up its sides.

'How do you know he's there?' Bart asked.

'I don't. But that's got to be the Normans. And Cwen warned us that he lived in his tower.'

Bart took a slow breath. 'We won't go there, then.'

'Best not,' Siward agreed.

Ignored by and ignoring the bustle around them, Siward and Bart made their way through the disgusting streets until, as they approached the precincts of the church, they became considerably less disgusting.

Hard paving emerged from the mud, and rather desperate-looking individuals moved about with shovels and brushes, struggling against nature and man to keep the pathways clear.

The entrance into the demesne of the church was better built and better protected than the city itself.

'Clear off.' A large fellow wearing a fine black cloak over otherwise revolting clothes barred their way.

A solid palisade stretched off to left and right and in the middle of it a gateway stood open; open but for the large shape blocking the way.

'We have business here,' Siward said rather officiously.

Bart was impressed by this approach. Perhaps Siward really had sailed around with Vikings and knew how to deal with people who got in their way.

'I don't think so,' the big one replied, looking them up and down.

'We are on the king's business.' Siward said this not to protest their treatment, but as a warning to this obstruction that he better get out of their way.

'And I'm the king himself, so you can be off.'

Siward sighed. 'The King's Investigator,' he said.

'No, he isn't,' the man retorted with a snarl. 'And you don't go round saying things like that about the king.'

'We are on the business of the King's Investigator, Brother Hermitage.'

'Brother what?'

'Hermitage'

'Stupid name for a monk. And what's a monk got to do with anything?'

Siward explained patiently, as if to a child, which Bart thought might be a bit risky. 'We are here on behalf of the King's Investigator, Brother Hermitage. He has sent us on the matter of one Scrydan and so we have to get..,'

'Did you say Scrydan?' The large one asked with obvious interest.

'That's right.'

'Scrydan the goldsmith?'

'The same.'

The fellow scowled hard at them both as if hoping to discern their intent from their clothes.

'How do you know about him?'

'I just told you. We have been sent by the King's Investigator.'

'It's no good you simply repeating nonsense,' the man instructed them.

'I am his apprentice,' Bart added.

'What, his?' The man looked to Siward.

'No, not his. The King's Investigator's. Brother Hermitage. He's the investigator and I'm his apprentice.'

'Very nice for you, I'm sure. And what's this got to do with Scrydan?'

'The investigator tracks murderers,' Bart explained with some mischievous pleasure. 'That's what investigator means. To track.'

'Does it?' The big man did not sound convinced.

'And we've come to track Scrydan,' Siward added. 'He may be in danger.'

'I'll say,' the man agreed rather too readily. He seemed to reach his conclusion. 'You'd better come in, then.'

'Thank you.' Bart spoke as if this had taken far too long already. 'You know of Scrydan, then. Where will we find him?'

'Find him?' the man didn't seem to understand the question.

'Of course. Where is his workshop?'

'Oh, right. It's at the end of Ceapen Street. Over the east side of the church.'

'And how will we find Scrydan's workshop?'

'Oh, you can't miss it,' the man said with a snorting laugh that didn't seem to make sense.

Leaving the awkward fellow to his guarding, Bart and Siward made their way around the side of the church towards the east.

'It is pretty amazing, isn't it?' Siward said, looking up at the height of the building.

'Hermitage would love it,' Bart said. 'Perhaps we'd better go in before we head back. So that we can tell him all about it.'

'I wonder whose it is?' Siward asked.

'Whose it is?'

'Yes, you know, which saint. All churches belong to a saint, don't they?'

'Oh, right.' Bart considered the place. 'A pretty big saint, I'd have thought.'

'We'd better find out; it's the first thing Hermitage will ask.'

'If he doesn't know already.'

They exchanged weary expressions at this.

Rounding the rear of the church they came upon what must be Ceapen Street and a small crowd of people who were gathered there.

'Busy part of town,' Siward observed.

'I said churchmen would want goldsmiths, didn't I.' Bart said.

They approached the group, which didn't seem to be doing anything particular except standing about outside one specific building.

'London must be a rich place if you have to queue up for the goldsmiths,' Siward said.

Bart nudged him in the side and indicated one of the crowd who was standing off to the side.

This was a Norman soldier, armed and ready for action, by the look of him.

'Here to keep order, I suppose,' Siward hissed.

With no other idea than to join the assembly, they slowly sauntered over and exchanged silent nods with one or two of the number.

After a few moments, during which they started to wonder what the procedure was here, and whether they shouldn't go to the front and give their names in, or something, there was a disturbance at the door.

As if a river had suddenly burst its banks and thrown out the very big person who had been floating along, an imposing figure emerged from the building, accompanied by two very much less imposing men, who nearly bobbed in his wake.

Behind them, two timid-looking boys emerged, each of them in leather aprons as if they had just stepped away from their workbenches.

The leader, dressed in very fine cloth and standing a good head above everyone else, surveyed the scene. He was clearly a Saxon; his long hair being tied behind his head instead of sliced off in a circle around his ears in the Norman style.

He looked to be of good fighting age, which was a surprise these days, Saxons of good fighting age having fought to the death and lost quite recently.

The man threw his gaze around the crowd as if looking for something.

'Do you think that's Scrydan?' Bart whispered.

'Doesn't look like a goldsmith to me,' Siward replied.

'What do goldsmiths look like?'

Siward considered this reasonable question. 'Not like that,' he replied.

'Who are you?' the imposing one asked, picking them out of the crowd. 'I don't know your faces.' All the other faces in the crowd, the ones he did know, quite quickly moved aside to get out of the way of the gaze.

'Oh, erm,' Bart began.

'Who are we addressing?' Siward asked with a nice balance of polite enquiry and self-importance.

The man strode over to them, the crowd having parted before him. 'You are addressing Ansgar the Staller, Shire Reeve of Middelseaxe.' He informed them of this in a manner that made it quite clear that they had to answer his question.

Siward gave a very good obsequious bow. 'My Lord. My name is Siward, and this is my companion, Bart.'

Ansgar considered them both from his great height.

'And what brought Siward and Bart to London? To Ceapen Street? To the workshop of Scrydan the goldsmith, no less?'

Siward gave another humble nod of the head. 'We have been sent by Brother Hermitage.'

Ansgar the Staller had clearly never heard of Hermitage and his piercing look said he wanted more than this.

'The King's Investigator,' Bart explained to another silence. 'He, erm, investigates murder, you know, finds out who did it?' What had started as an assertive statement ended as a mild question, asking Ansgar if that would be all right.

But it didn't get through either.

'So, we're investigators and we've come to do Scrydan's murder,' Siward specified.

The silence at this did not sound like a good one.

56

'Say that again,' Ansgar instructed slowly.

Suddenly Siward didn't feel like saying it again. He had a horrible feeling that something had just gone terribly wrong.

'We, er, were sent. By Brother Hermitage, the King's Investigator, to do the murder of Scrydan.'

'Or not,' Bart added quickly. 'He may not have been murdered at all, of course.'

'Oh, he's been murdered all right,' Ansgar assured them. 'And you two just confessed.' He turned to the Norman. 'Take them away.'

Caput VI: Downhill Very Quickly

'No, no,' Bart bleated and hopped as he was dragged along by the Norman, who seemed quite content to follow Ansgar's orders. He held Bart in one hand and Siward in the other, apparently quite confident that neither of them would try to escape.

'You don't understand. We didn't kill Scrydan. We couldn't have. We've only just arrived.'

'And we didn't come to kill him,' Siward added. 'That's not what I meant.'

Ansgar, the Norman and the small crowd of people who were following along to see where this entertainment would end took no notice of either of them.

'Brother Hermitage is the King's Investigator,' Bart explained. 'King William.'

'And King Harold before that,' Siward added, perhaps hoping this would have some influence with the giant Saxon.

'That's right,' Bart agreed. 'And he investigates murder. He finds out who did it. For the king.'

'William,' Siward reminded everyone.

'He thought that Scrydan might be in danger and so he sent us to make sure.'

'Not make sure he was in danger,' Siward added quickly. 'Make sure he was all right.'

'Which he isn't, obviously,' Bart acknowledged. 'So, we can help, really. That's what we're here for. To help.' Bart didn't want to mention Fridolf at this point. Accusing someone else without any real evidence seemed unjust and rather cowardly.

True, Fridolf had said that he was planning to kill Scrydan and now here Scrydan was, killed, but that wasn't proof. Or

58

was it?

With the way this Ansgar was behaving, he thought that giving Fridolf's name might make the man do something rash.

If there was any sign of him doing something rash to them, Fridolf's name would be the first thing out of Bart's mouth.

Their pleadings had no effect whatsoever and Bart wondered why these people wouldn't listen. Well, why this Ansgar the Staller wouldn't listen.

Only now did he start to question what a Saxon called Ansgar was doing as sheriff at all. What was a Saxon doing anything for? Surely, they were in the heart of Norman rule, now. Shouldn't the sheriff be a Norman?

If this man was one of those Saxons who had supported William, he could have been rewarded with the position. In which case, he might be very dangerous indeed. What better way to show his loyalty to William than find a couple of Saxon killers and do something horrible to them?

Saxon strangers, at that. No one in London would care what happened to the two of them.

And now he had an even more horrible thought.

As no one was paying them any attention at all, he thought it safe to talk to Siward. Perhaps the Norman holding them couldn't understand English anyway.

'What did Hermitage say the punishment for killing Scrydan was going to be?' he whispered across to Siward.

Siward looked puzzled at the question, or perhaps at whether now was the best time to be asking things like that.

'Eternal damnation, I think,' Siward hissed impatiently.

'No, the wergild, the fine.'

'Oh, erm, forty or fifty shillings, wasn't it? I think he said that's what Fridolf offered.'

Bart was in enough despair at being hauled through the streets by this Norman. Now he took on an extra load.

'Where are we going to find forty shillings?'

'Or fifty,' Siward prompted.

'Forty, fifty, four or five. It makes no difference. We haven't got anything.'

They locked eyes as they saw the truly horrible situation this put them in.

'We'd have to ask Wat for it,' Siward breathed.

Bart nodded very slowly. 'And then he'll murder us.'

'I think he'd let Cwen do it,' Siward said hopelessly.

Bart wasn't sure whether the prospect of being dealt with by the sheriff over a murder or dealing with Wat over forty shillings was worse. Either prospect was awful and so something had to be done.

'Where are you taking us?' he asked Ansgar. 'At least tell us that.'

'To be dealt with,' Ansgar replied simply and with horrible significance.

'Dealt with?' Surely, as Ansgar was the sheriff, he would do any dealing with people. Why did they have to go somewhere else at all? Perhaps there was a moot hall somewhere where this sort of thing was done. There would be a scribe to take notes and an official to take their money.

He wasn't sure what would happen when it was found that they had no money. Locked up somewhere, probably. Which made it even more important that this Ansgar understood that they had nothing to do with Scrydan's death.

'Dealt with by the Normans,' Ansgar specified.

There was a note in his voice that said he wasn't entirely happy about this, but that the situation was beyond his control.

Bart was comprehensively unhappy about this, and the look on Siward's face said that he shared the concern.

Normans were funny people. There was no telling what they'd do most of the time, and they might have strange ideas about murder and the like.

On the other hand, coming before the Normans could be a good thing. They might know Hermitage, or at least be aware of the existence of the King's Investigator. Once that was clear, Bart and Siward's presence here, and their mission would finally be understood.

Ansgar would probably be quite embarrassed when some Norman told him to let them go.

It was a comforting thought that delivered very little comfort. They were still being dragged through the street accused of murder. It was hard to think of any way that was a good thing.

'The Normans will know all about Brother Hermitage,' Bart protested. 'They'll know he's the King's Investigator and that we have come from him. They'll see that we couldn't have done anything to Scrydan.'

'We'll see,' Ansgar said with worrying confidence.

They now moved out of the cathedral precincts once more, passing through another gate, after which the roadway returned to its rutted and muddy state.

At this point, quite a few of the followers lost interest and decided to stay where they could keep their feet dry. The two attendants to Ansgar still followed at his heels and the lads from the workshop tagged along at the back, although they looked like they'd prefer to simply slip away and do something else; anything else.

Bart looked around and saw that this was the eastern gate from the cathedral, and so would be leading them towards the Norman part of town.

While he tried to tell himself that this was good, he couldn't help but think it was bad.

A more useful thought occurred to him. 'When was Scrydan murdered?' he asked.

'Shut up,' Ansgar replied.

'It's important. We only arrived in London today. We came straight to the church area because that was where we thought the goldsmiths might be.

'If Scrydan was murdered before then, we can't have done it, can we?'

Ansgar beckoned the Norman to stop and came around to stand before them.

'Here's a thought,' he said with a little snarl. 'You're lying. You didn't arrive today. You came here to kill Scrydan, which you did. You then came back to his workshop to see what you could steal. You even told me you'd come to do the murder.'

'Why would we do that?' Bart pleaded. 'We'd have to be stupid.'

'And you're also stupid,' Ansgar concluded. 'Now be silent. I can just as well deliver some dead murderers to the Normans. In fact, that might be easier. Save listening to any more of your whining nonsense.'

The Norman holding them obviously understood this and smiled at them as if he would be taking an active part in making them dead.

'But..,' Bart protested.

'Silence,' Ansgar reminded him angrily.

Bart swallowed. He gave Siward a hopeless look that said they would just have to take this to the Normans and sort it out then.

It was disappointing that Ansgar, a fellow Saxon, was not being at all helpful.

They were led on through the town, a few people stopping to look at what was going on, but soon losing interest when they saw that the sheriff and a Norman were involved.

It wasn't at all long before they rounded one corner and emerged in front of the Norman fortress.

Reluctantly, Bart and Siward thought it quite impressive.

A large wooden structure had been built on the bank of the river, much more than the usual Norman stockade on top of a pile of mud.

This place had an air of permanence about it. There were several separate buildings making up the whole site, including guard houses, stables and the main keep in the middle.

This was clearly where King William resided, and it looked as drear and foreboding as it should. Even men as completely innocent as Bart and Siward would tremble before that edifice.

The whole was surrounded by a great wooden wall at least ten feet high, and the only way in seemed to be through a main gate, that was itself at the end of a bridge.

This bridge spanned a moat that had been dug for protection, although what this place needed protection from was a bit of a mystery.

The walls, the bridge and the surrounding land were swarming with Normans, all of them armed and dangerous. Serious Saxon resistance had been left on the hillside near Hastings, and London seemed to be going about its business as if the Normans had always been in charge.

There were even loads of stone being moved about by cart, all of it heading into the fortress.

Neither Bart nor Siward could imagine building a castle

out of stone, but if it was done, there would be no moving it.

In the grip of the Norman, Bart and Siward were led straight towards the bridge, Ansgar striding along behind.

The sheriff's two attendants followed, but the two lads from the workshop showed commendable reluctance.

'You don't really need us now, do you?' one of them asked.

'Of course, we do,' Ansgar said simply. 'It was your master who was murdered.'

'Yes, but we don't know anything about it.'

'And you know where we are if you want us,' the second put in. 'We could go back to work.'

'You're coming with us.'

Bart could understand the two young boys not wanting to go into this Norman stronghold. He didn't want to go in himself, but he also wondered if there might be more to their reluctance.

Fridolf had been Scrydan's apprentice and he had wanted to kill his master. What if all the apprentices did?

Hermitage's report had been that the others weren't as advanced in their craft as Fridolf, but could they all have been in it together? Had Fridolf persuaded them to join his scheme of murder, with the promise of advancement?

He was quite proud of this line of thinking and wanted to question the two boys as soon as possible. Doing so in the middle of a Norman fortress was probably not sensible, or even possible.

'Get in there,' Ansgar made their lack of choice in the matter clear.

The boys looked more sheepish than a flock on a hillside but did as they were told.

None of the Norman guards on the bridge or the gate did anything to impede their progress, Ansgar obviously being recognised by all

'Where are we going?' Siward asked. 'What are you going to do with us?'

'You're going somewhere safe until the Normans can deal with you.'

'Deal with us? What do you mean, deal with us?'

'What do you think I mean?' Ansgar now led the way towards the keep.

'We didn't do this,' Siward insisted. 'You've got to listen to us.'

'Tell the Normans we've come from Brother Hermitage,' Bart added. 'We didn't even know Scrydan. Never met him.'

'Yet you knew his name, you knew that he'd been murdered, and you said you'd come to do it.' Ansgar said confidently. 'That'll be enough for anyone.'

'Enough? Enough for what?' Bart didn't like to say that they had no money to pay the fine. People who couldn't pay their fines ended up with a more physical punishment. Usually something public and humiliating.

'The Normans will decide. The king himself, probably.'

'The king?' Siward sounded very concerned about that. 'What does the king have to do with it?'

'He's the king,' Ansgar explained carefully.

'The king will be good,' Bart said. 'Brother Hermitage is his investigator, after all. Everything will be clear.'

Siward looked even more worried.

'What's the problem?' Bart hissed at him as Ansgar pushed them on.

'I may have met the king before,' Siward's voice was weak.

'You may have met him before?'

'all right, I have met him before. And he wasn't very happy

65

with me then[4]. He might remember.'

'I think he's probably met a lot of Saxons and killed quite a few of them. He can't remember them all.'

Siward was not comforted.

'Surely the king doesn't deal with minor matters like this,' Bart suggested to Ansgar. 'You're the sheriff, I mean Shire Reeve, after all.'

'The king wants his order imposed,' Ansgar explained. 'Everyone must know that he commands now.'

It was slightly gratifying to detect that Ansgar was as unhappy about this as he should be. Bart was itching to know how the Saxon came to be this involved with the Normans.

'So, he dispenses justice in person?' Bart asked. Neither Harold nor Edward before him had done much of that. They left it to the local lords. Not that Harold had had much time as king to do anything, really.

'He will have London in order, and if he needs to take action himself, he will do so.'

Bart shrugged that this seemed to be taking things to extremes and that surely the king must have better things to do with his time.

'So, we lock you up until the king can deal with you.'

'Oh, wonderful,' Bart complained. 'And how long is that going to take?'

'As long as the king sees fit,' Ansgar snapped.

'Look,' Bart said. 'If we could see him straight away, we can get on with trying to find out who really killed Scrydan. King William will know all about Brother Hermitage. He'll explain. Then we won't have to waste a lot of time being locked up, see?'

It was slightly worrying to see that Ansgar was now

---

[4] The Domesday Book (Still Not That One), remember?

clenching and unclenching his fists.

'You will be locked up until the king decides to see you.' Ansgar pointed a large finger at them. 'And if I can arrange it, it will be somewhere very dark and uncomfortable. Somewhere no one can hear you two prattling on. If you happen to die down there, it will save us all a lot of bother.'

'Die?' Siward squeaked.

'We need to explain to the king,' Bart pressed urgently. 'He doesn't even need to go to the bother of imposing the fine.'

'What fine?' Ansgar asked. 'Where did you get that idea?'

'The fine for murder. The wergild,' Bart explained. 'Not that we had anything to do with it, as we keep telling you.'

'No, no,' Ansgar explained with horrible intensity. 'We're under Norman rule now and King William wants to set an example to ensure this sort of thing doesn't get out of hand.'

'What sort of thing?'

'Murder. We can't have people going around murdering one another. It's got to stop.'

'Erm?' Siward couldn't get the question out.

'There's a whole new punishment for murder,' Ansgar said. He left a horrible pause before announcing it. 'Death.'

'Death?' Bart didn't quite understand.

'Yes. Your death. You killed Scrydan, so you will be executed. It'll be a, what did he call it? Discouragement? Deterrent, that's it.'

Bart's stomach turned completely over, and his legs felt as if they wanted to leave without him. 'We have got to see the king,' he insisted in a quivering voice.

'You will,' Ansgar said nonchalantly. 'Eventually. Unless, of course, he decides to simply have you executed anyway. He is a busy man, after all.'

Caput VII: A Night In The Cells

They're going to kill us,' Siward complained bitterly as the door to the cell thumped shut behind them. 'I said this would happen. Didn't I say this would happen? Give me the wind and the waves, I said. Didn't I?'

'Yes, you said,' Bart agreed wearily. 'But that doesn't help much, does it?'

'And who puts cells in their new castle? What sort of person, upon building a thing like this to establish their rule, thinks, where shall we put the cells?'

'A king.'

'It's not right. The first idea shouldn't be, where can I lock people up.'

'We've got to get word out,' Bart ignored the complaints.

Siward pointedly looked around the small space they occupied.

'I don't think anyone's going to hear us.'

'Someone will come by.'

'Really? You think passers-by will be wandering along just waiting for the latest captive to ask nicely if they can be let out?'

'For heaven's sake, Siward, we are where we are. Now we have to work out what to do next.'

'We are where we are? What on earth does that mean? We're always where we are.'

'I mean,' Bart said pointedly, 'that we are locked in a cell in King William's new castle under threat of death. Now, that's where we are, so what are we going to do about it? You've tried just standing there and complaining and I haven't

68

noticed it achieve anything. Shall we try something else? Do you think?'

Siward sulked a bit but didn't have any more complaints to offer.

'Someone is going to come by,' Bart repeated. 'They have to give us food and water.'

Siward said nothing, by which he meant that no, they didn't have to give anyone food and water.

'Or we can talk when they come to get us. You know, later.'

'Later when they come to get us for the execution,' Siward checked. 'If they bother.' He held up his hands to fend off further complaints from Bart that he wasn't being helpful.

'That Ansgar is obviously in with the Normans,' Siward went on. 'I don't know why the king is making such a fuss over one dead goldsmith, but he is. It could be right that William wants to make an example of us. And Ansgar has to be seen to cooperate.

'So, if he can tell the king that he's found the killers and we're already dead, so much the better. And the easy way to do that is simply leave us down here until we oblige by dying ourselves.'

Bart looked at him with some shock. 'Have you done this sort of thing before?'

'No, but I've been around kings and nobles before and I've seen what they're like. That's why I prefer a ship that only kills you if you get something wrong.'

Bart thought about this and tried to pace up and down their enclosure. He only managed two paces before he had to turn around.

It might be a worrying sign that William had built cells into his castle, but at least he hadn't spent much effort making them a reasonable size.

Like the rest of the place, the cell was all wood, but the walls comprised logs so close-fitting that they wouldn't even pass a butterfly wing. The door was as tight fitting as a new door on a cell should be. The only sliver of light came from an opening high on one wall; a butterfly probably could get through if it lay flat and crawled.

'He does want to set an example, though,' Bart reasoned.

'Of us.'

'Yes, of us. And we're not much of an example if we simply stay here and then die, are we? He'll want us on display. Gather all the locals, you know. Show off our horrible death to all the Saxons so they can see that murdering goldsmiths is now frowned upon.'

'So, when we're on the way to being hanged, we say what?' Siward asked. 'Would you mind taking word to Brother Hermitage in Derby? It'll be a bit late for that.'

Bart nodded that he had to accept that. 'Even if we could get a message to the Normans that we're with Hermitage, it would take days to get word to Derby and then more days for him to come down.'

'Come down for what?' Siward asked. 'All we need to do is let the Normans know that we're with the King's Investigator. Then they'll know we didn't kill Scrydan.'

'Well, Hermitage can come and work out who did do it,' Bart offered.

'Who did do it?' Siward didn't seem to understand the question. 'We know who did it.'

'Do we?'

Siward stared at Bart as if unable to believe how he could have missed this point. 'Fridolf.'

'Oh, right, yes.'

'Oh, right, yes?'

'I thought about mentioning Fridolf to Ausgar.'

'You thought about mentioning Fridolf.' Siward's voice was cold. 'While we were being taken away for execution for murdering Scrydan, you thought about mentioning Fridolf? And that he probably murdered Scrydan.'

'We didn't know we were going to be executed,' Bart protested.

'Oh, that's all right, then.'

'But we haven't got any real evidence that Fridolf did it.'

'Apart from his coming all the way to Derby to let Hermitage know he was going to kill Scrydan. I think that's enough to be going on with.'

Bart opened his mouth to speak.

'And don't say that the Normans might execute the wrong man, because they're already planning to execute the wrong men. I don't know about you, but I would rather they executed a wrong man who wasn't me.'

Bart didn't have anything to offer to that.

'So, we have to get word out.'

'Have we started again?' Siward asked.

Bart ignored him and stepped over to the door.

This might as well have been part of the wall, and they only knew where it was because they had come in that way. It was clearly barred from the outside and no amount of pushing or kicking would get it to move.

'Hello?' Bart called out. He waited for a reply, which didn't come.

'Hello,' Siward repeated sarcastically. He went to the door. 'Help,' he screamed at the top of his voice. He then screamed it a few more times. Nothing.

'There's no one there,' Bart accepted reluctantly.

'We could be the only ones in cells,' Siward said. 'After all, the Normans haven't had that long to fill them up.'

'And if no one comes to give us water,' Bart didn't finish the sentence.

Siward considered this. 'We wait until it's dark and then call out.'

'Calling works better in the dark, does it?' Bart sneered a bit.

'No,' Siward sneered back. 'But everything will be quiet. People will be in their beds. They're more likely to hear us.'

'Normans probably like hearing people cry out in the dark. They'd likely find it restful.'

'Someone will find it annoying and might come to shut us up.'

'And what is it we are going to tell them?' Bart asked. 'We've already told Ansgar that we're with the King's Investigator and he didn't seem that interested. If we get some horrible guard, he's not likely to pop off and wake the king at our request.'

Siward sighed. 'We tell them that we know who killed Scrydan. Fridolf.'

Bart said nothing this time, reasoning that Fridolf had brought this on himself, really. And for all they knew, he actually had killed Scrydan. He was the most likely, after all.

'So, whoever comes, we tell them that we're prepared to say who killed Scrydan.'

Bart gave a short nod and they settled to wait for dark.

...

Darkness arrived very quickly in the cell. The small opening that passed what little light they had, passed the darkness much more effectively. It was as if the daylight had been cut off like the snuffing of a candle.

Siward cupped a hand and lifted Bart up to peer out of the opening, after which he confirmed that the day had simply drifted into the evening. They would have to wait a lot longer before the castle settled into its night time routine.

They both took spots on the rough floor and kicked them clear of stones to get as comfortable as they could. Sleep was obviously out of the question in this place.

Siward woke to complete blackness and had no idea how he had managed to sleep, or for how long. It could have been a moment or two, or it might have been hours.

His sleep had been restless, the kind that felt as if you hadn't really slept at all but instead drifted on the edge of wakefulness, not getting the satisfaction of real rest.

'Bart, wake up.'

'Eh, what?' Bart started from what sounded like a very deep sleep and seemed quite surprised.

'We've slept,' Siward told him.

There was no point trying to find one another as they were now in the most profound darkness, and still in the tiny space that meant locating one another would not be a problem.

'What hour is it?' Bart asked.

'How the devil should I know? A dark one.'

'all right, all right.' Bart could be heard stretching the sleep from his bones and untying the knots that the hard floor had caused in his flesh. 'Everyone must be at rest by now.'

'We don't know what Normans get up to in the dark.'

'Whatever it is, it'll be quiet.'

They both listened hard and couldn't hear anything at all. The silence itself felt oppressive and the close walls of the cell seemed even closer.

'Right,' Bart instructed. 'Help,' he cried out loud.

'Help, help,' Siward repeated.

'Help,' they called together.

They continued this for some time without any discernible result.

They paused for a moment, just to give the Normans a chance to come running.

'What do we do now?' Siward asked when the Normans didn't come running.

Bart didn't have an answer.

'Murder,' Siward said after a moment.

'Yes, I know. Don't keep going on about it.'

'No, murder. It's what the Normans hate just at the moment, or so Ansgar told us.'

'So?'

'Murder!' Siward cried at the top of his voice.

Bart got the message and joined in.

'Murder, murder, help, murder,' they called enthusiastically.

After a brief pause to evaluate the silence, they resumed their cries.

Bart even found the door once more and took to kicking it as hard as he dare without breaking his foot.

After three rounds of this, they thought they detected some movement off in the corridors of the castle. It could just be someone going to the privy in the night, or it could be a response.

They started up again.

During the next rest, they listened and there was definitely someone out there in the dark.

'Murder, murder,' they tried to call a bit more quietly so that they could listen at the same time.

At their next silence, they were surprised to hear a distinct shuffle outside the door.

'What's going on in there?' A gruff voice asked. It was a Saxon voice, which could be good news or bad. 'Disturbing the castle at this time of night. You got me out of my bed.'

'Murder,' Siward blurted out.

'Murder? What murder?'

'We know who did the murder,' Bart got in quickly. 'We're prepared to tell Ansgar.'

'I heard you were the murderers.' The voice was not convinced.

'No. No. It wasn't us at all, but we know who it was.'

'What are you doing in there if you didn't do it?'

'Exactly,' Siward agreed. 'It's all a mistake. We tried to tell Ansgar but he, erm..,'

'Was in a bit of a hurry,' Bart continued. 'We didn't get the chance to explain.'

'We don't want no explanations this time of night,' the voice complained.

'We have to let Ansgar know,' Bart pressed. 'Otherwise, you could execute the wrong people.'

The voice grumbled but didn't seem too concerned about that prospect.

'Which is murder,' Siward pointed out. 'Executing people who shouldn't be executed. That's murder, that is.'

'Ansgar's not here,' the other side of the door said. 'He's gone back to his home. The castle's locked up for the night. Everyone's asleep. Except for me, of course. I have to go wandering the corridors shutting people up.'

'Will he be back in the morning?' Bart asked.

'How should I know? He's the Shire Reeve. Be about Shire Reeve business, I should think.'

'What about us?'

'He's caught you and put you in a cell. Don't know what he'd want to come back for.'

'Then we need to speak to a Norman,' Siward said.

'Oh, you don't want to do that,' the voice cautioned. 'They're best not disturbed.'

'But the king wants to kill us,' Siward protested.

'He wants to kill a lot of people. Does it a lot of time, as well.'

'You must tell someone that we know who killed Scrydan and we can give them the name.'

The voice seemed to think about this for a moment. 'Why don't you tell me?' it asked in a blatantly scheming sort of way.

'Because we want to do it ourselves and avoid being executed,' Bart pointed out.

'Fair enough. Don't know who I'd tell, though.'

'It would have to be someone in charge. The king, ideally.'

'You think the likes of me gets to talk to the likes of him?' the voice scoffed at this idea.

'Well, who else is there?' Bart asked. 'Us not being familiar with the place.'

'I suppose I could let the captain of the guard know.'

'Who's that?'

'Fellow called John. He's one of the more reasonable Normans.'

'There are reasonable Normans?' Bart asked.

'Not many. And I can't promise he'll do anything about it,' the voice cautioned.

'It's got to be better than sitting in here waiting to be executed.'

'Yes, I suppose it would be. I'm not going to go waking him, though. Even reasonable Normans don't like being woken in the middle of the night.'

'The morning will be fine,' Bart assured their messenger.

'What time is it?' Siward asked. 'We can't tell from in here.'

'Oh,' the voice explained in a friendly manner. 'It's nearly dawn anyway. I was just getting up to do the fires when I heard you howling like a pair of cats.'

Quite apart from the fact that cats didn't howl, Bart struggled to take this in.

'You mean we didn't wake you at all?'

'Ah, well, I was about to get up, I said. I didn't say I was up.'

Bart breathed deeply. 'Just tell this John that we have information about the murder of Scrydan that he needs to hear.'

'I'll do me best.'

'What's your name?' Bart asked.

The voice guffawed. 'Oh no, I'm not falling for that.'

'Falling for what?'

'Giving you my name.'

'We only want it so the captain of the guard will know that it's us who sent you.'

'Exactly,' the voice agreed. 'I'm not getting caught out like that.'

Bart gave Siward a look of hopelessness, but this was the only help they had.

'Well, tell him quickly,' Bart urged. 'We don't want anyone deciding this is a nice morning for an execution or two.'

Caput VIII: Help At Hand?

The dawn crept into the cell, and its pace was not helped by Siward and Bart staring at the opening urging it to get a move on.

'Normans must get up with the dawn,' Siward reasoned.

'Especially a captain of the guard. He'd want to be about before everyone.'

'You'd think so. Perhaps Norman captains are lazy and get everyone else to do the work.'

They both took to hopping from foot to foot, wringing their hands, turning round in small circles and blowing their breath out with increasing exasperation.

'I want the privy,' Siward announced at one point.

'Me too,' Bart said. 'Perhaps someone comes to let us out in the morning.'

The light of the day was dribbling into the cell now and Bart paused in his pacing when he thought he heard a noise.

'Is there someone there?' He called at the door. 'Is that the captain? John?'

The noise of someone moving about was clear, but there was no reply.

'We need the privy,' Siward called.

'Perhaps he doesn't speak English?'

'What's Norman for privy?' Siward asked.

'How should I know? You're the one who's travelled.'

'Only with Vikings. I know it in Danish.'

'Well, try that.'

Siward looked at the door. 'Borð före', he said. Or something like that.

'Of course,' Bart mused. 'It's unlikely a Viking is out there, come to think of it.'

Siward stepped up and hammered on the door. 'Hello,' he shouted. 'That's got to be the same in Norman.'

'Quiet,' a new voice replied in heavily accented English.

'How can we be quiet? We need the privy,' Siward called back.

This got no response.

'Privy,' he said plainly and a lot louder, which was bound to work.

'Privy, privy,' the voice muttered as if this was a complete nuisance and was ruining his day.

There was some scuffling about on the other side of the door and hope was kindled at the sound of the bar being lifted.

Barely able to believe their luck, they took a step back as the door was opened, even if it was just a crack.

An arm appeared through the gap and a small handful of straw was thrown in. The door closed once more and the bar was dropped back in place.

'Privy,' the voice announced with a cackle.

'Oh, very nice,' Bart called back.

They both considered the straw on the floor, which wouldn't serve a small family of mice.

Exchanging shrugs that there was nothing for it, Bart kicked the straw over into the back corner of their small space.

Before they could make use of the facility, there was further noise outside the door.

Some loud words of Norman French were barked out, and the barker did not sound happy.

In response, a now timid voice replied something that sounded apologetic, and scrabbling at the door indicated that it was about to be opened once more.

Leaving the straw, hopefully no longer required, Bart and Siward stood waiting.

It was now swung fully open and a well-dressed man stood there, clearly someone of importance, and hopefully John, the captain of the guard.

'Now, what's going on here?' the man asked in reasonable English.

'Are you John?' Bart asked.

'I am. What do you want?' John did not sound very sympathetic.

'Well, we'd like to use the privy,' Siward said. 'To begin with.'

John huffed. 'Grond has been told not to come down here teasing the prisoners.' He said this with a pointed stare at a much more humble, and actually quite revolting figure, who stood at his side.

Grond touched his forelock and scurried away.

'This way,' John instructed.

He led them out of the cell and back the way they had arrived. After a few paces, he came to a widening of the enclosed corridor where a good pile of straw was piled up against the wall.

'Ah,' Bart breathed. 'A decent privy.'

Both boys sagged with relief as they made use of the straw, while John stood back, obviously making sure that they weren't going to use the opportunity to escape.

'Thank you very much,' Siward said when they'd finished.

'You're the prisoners,' John said with a shrug. 'You'll be cleaning it up later. Now, back to the cell.'

'We need to talk to you,' Bart said as they slowly did as they were told. 'About the murder of Scrydan.'

80

'So I hear.'

'We didn't do it,' Siward told him.

'I gather that's what you've been saying since Ansgar took you.'

'Yes, because we didn't.'

'But we think we know who did,' Bart added.

'And who would that be?' John was not sounding convinced of their argument.

'Fridolf.'

'Who is Fridolf.'

'Scrydan's apprentice.'

'I understand Ansgar's already spoken to the apprentices.'

Siward gave Bart a worried look at this.

Bart was thinking hard. 'The two lads who came out of the workshop?'

'I wasn't there,' John pointed out. 'I don't know.'

'There's another one. By the name of Fridolf.'

'I see.' John clearly thought they were making this up.

'No, really. There is.'

John sighed heavily. 'Very interesting. There's another apprentice no one knows about except you two, and he's the one who did the murder.'

'That's right.'

'Despite the fact that you two confessed. Then, when you find that it's going to be execution instead of a fine, you come up with this mystery apprentice.'

'We didn't confess,' Bart complained.

'You told Ansgar that you'd come to London to do Scrydan's murder.'

'Well yes. We came to investigate it, not do it.'

'You came to what?' John asked urgently.

'Investigate,' Bart explained. 'It means..,'

'I know what it means.'

'Oh,' Bart was surprised at that. 'Well, that's good, then.'

'Why were you coming to London to investigate the murder?' John asked very seriously.

'It's a bit of a long story,' Bart replied.

'I don't think you've got anywhere else to be.'

'Right,' Bart agreed. He looked to Siward and got a silent agreement that they had better tell this John the truth. 'Well, we live with Wat the Weaver in Derby.'

'And with Cwen and Brother Hermitage?' John asked.

'Erm, yes.' Now Bart was confused.

'You know them?' Siward asked hopefully.

'I do. They were here some time ago, dealing with the death of Malf.[5]'

'Who's Malf?' Siward asked.

'A dead Norman,' John explained simply. 'But if there's an investigation needed into Scrydan, why didn't Hermitage come himself?'

'I was getting to that,' Bart said. 'Hermitage was visited by this Fridolf, who said that he wanted to kill his master. Hermitage thought he'd dissuaded him, but then Cwen said we could come to London just to check.'

'Why you?' John considered them both.

'I'm Hermitage's apprentice,' Bart said proudly.

'As I recall,' John said. 'Hermitage didn't want to be investigator at all. Why would he have an apprentice?'

'Just for things like this. I can save him the bother.'

John didn't look content with this explanation.

'But then, when we got here, we found that Scrydan really had been murdered,' Siward said. 'And Ansgar misunderstood what we were saying.'

---

[5] *The King's Investigator;* the reference work for the period.

John looked hard at them both and scratched his head. 'You could simply be making this up to avoid your execution.'

'It's a bit of a complicated tale to make up,' Bart pointed out. 'And you obviously know Brother Hermitage.'

'And Wat and Cwen,' Siward added.

'Hm.' John was very thoughtful.

'It's true,' Siward pleaded.

'What's Brother Hermitage's title?' John asked. 'Quickly now.'

'His title?' Bart thought it was Brother.

'The job he has.'

'Oh right. He's the King's Investigator. From what he's told us. He was first appointed by Harold and then William carried it on.'

'And when did he take on an apprentice.'

'Oh, well, I sort of offered myself, I suppose. Hermitage investigated my old mistress, a Saxon noble.[6] And, after all that business near Hastings, jobs with Saxon nobles were hard to come by.'

John was starting to look as if they might be convincing him.

'And just before this,' Siward went on, 'we went to De'Ath's Dingle with Hermitage. His old monastery, you know.'

'Anyone could know that.'

'And there were a lot of other people there,' Siward hurried on. 'Erm, his old prior, Athan.'

'Athan, eh?' That was a name John recognised.

'And a ferryman they seemed to know. Name of More.'

John started at this and looked around in a bit of a panic. 'God. You haven't got him here with you?'

---

[6] *The 1066 To Hastings*. Ignoble is more like it.

'No, no. We dropped him off in Lincoln.'

John breathed deeply. 'Remind me never to go to Lincoln.'

'Do you believe us, then?' Bart asked.

John considered his answer. 'I believe you know Hermitage. That doesn't mean that you didn't kill a goldsmith. Hermitage knows a lot of people who kill other people.'

'We'd have to be pretty stupid to tell Ansgar that we'd done it, wouldn't we?' Bart suggested.

'Hm, I suppose so.'

'And we do know about Fridolf.'

'Who you could have made up.'

'We'd just need to ask the other apprentices. The two lads. They'd know if Fridolf was real.'

'And if he is,' John mused. 'Why would he kill his master?'

'Because Scrydan wouldn't make him up to master. He told Hermitage that he had all the skills but that Scrydan was in the way.'

'Why was he telling Hermitage any of this in the first place?'

'Fridolf didn't understand what an investigator was,' Siward explained. 'He thought that he had to tell Hermitage he was going to do a murder so that a track of them all could be kept.'

'Ha.' John barked a laugh at that. 'Sounds like an idiot, not a goldsmith's apprentice.'

'Whoever he is,' Bart pressed. 'He said he was going to kill Scrydan and now Scrydan is dead. Brother Hermitage sent us here to make sure it didn't happen and we were too late. We can't be executed for that.'

John's face said he wasn't sure about that at all.

'We just have to go to the workshop and ask the apprentices,' Bart said.

'I think you're locked up in King William's new Tower of London,' John pointed out. 'You're not going anywhere.'

'You go, then,' Siward said. 'It wouldn't take a moment. And if you find that there is a Fridolf, you'll know we're telling the truth.'

'The captain of the guard running errands for Saxon prisoners?' It was clear that this wasn't going to happen.

'Send someone else then. Anyone.' Bart was getting frustrated. 'Ask Ansgar to find out, he's the sheriff, I mean Shire Reeve.'

'And he's a Saxon,' Siward added. 'He probably has to do what you tell him.'

'Or send that Grond creature,' Bart suggested.

'I'm not letting him out of the castle again.' John folded his arms. He reached his conclusion. 'Very well.'

Bart and Siward sighed their relief.

'I'll send someone to find out if there was an apprentice called Fridolf.'

'And you'll do it soon?' Bart asked.

'Before we're executed would be good,' Siward added.

'I shall do it straight away,' John agreed.

'And come back quickly to let us out,' Bart said.

'If there is an apprentice called Fridolf.'

'Which there will be.'

'We'll still need to settle the matter with Ansgar,' John seemed to be speaking mainly to himself. 'He's reported that he's found the killers. He won't like hearing that he could be wrong.'

'Bloody Saxons,' Bart complained.

'Yes, quite.' John regarded them both. 'Well, back in the cell with you. I shall see what can be discovered.'

'One thing before you go?' Siward asked.

'Yes?'
'Can I use the privy again?'

Left to their own devices once more, the worry of not knowing what was going on was almost worse than the worry of being executed. Almost, but not quite.

What if John didn't send anyone? Or what if he did and they misunderstood what they were supposed to do? They could come back and say there was no Fridolf because they hadn't asked the right question.

Or if Ansgar got involved, he might not want to find Fridolf. He might prefer it if the people he'd already accused were simply executed. After all, he wouldn't want to look bad in front of the Normans.

Could Fridolf still be about and simply deny everything? He might be back in the workshop, saying that he'd never been near Derby, had never heard of Brother Hermitage and that anyone who said otherwise was only trying to get out of execution. After all, Scrydan was dead and the two of them stood accused.

What if someone came to execute them before John got back?

That did seem unlikely. It was clear the king would want to make an example of them, and he couldn't do that without some sort of display. All of London would need to know about it and that would take a while.

They had no idea how much time was passing. The hole in the wall didn't even create a shadow that they could follow.

Thus, Bart's suggestion that John, "must have sent someone by now", made little real sense.

And there was no sign of anyone attending to their needs who they could ask. That idea of food and water was proving to be hopelessly optimistic. Still, with the privy on the other side of the locked door, they didn't want to drink too much anyway.

They had both sat on the floor and drifted off into a stupor of terrified anticipation when more movement outside the door almost caused them to use the privy there and then.

Leaping to their feet they stood by the entrance, anxious for good news.

The bar was lifted and the figure of Grond was revealed once more.

'Has John had word?' Siward asked immediately.

'Come, come,' Grond beckoned.

'Ah, the truth has been found,' Bart said with relief.

'Come, come,' Grond repeated as he set off down the corridor, past the privy.

The boys followed, nodding to one another that this ordeal was coming to an end.

Grond led them on through the winding ways of the castle until they came to a flight of steps, which he indicated that they should climb.

'Up here?' Bart asked.

'Grond not allowed,' Grond explained.

'This is more like it,' Bart said. 'Getting some decent treatment now they know we're innocent.'

They climbed the steps and emerged into the daylight, blinking the shock from their eyes. Looking around, they saw that they had emerged at the front of the keep, the stairs they had climbed leading back down into its depths.

In front of the keep, there was quite a large crowd, which seemed odd.

'Ah, there you are,' a very sophisticated voice spoke up.

They both turned and saw a Norman lord. He had to be a

lord because he was very well-dressed, had a number of people gathered around him, and was standing in front of a set of gallows as if he owned them.

Caput IX: Time To Die

'What, what?' Bart blurted out in horrible recognition of what was going on.

'Come along,' the Norman said encouragingly. 'Let's get on, shall we?'

'Get on, get on?' Siward bleated. He took a look at the gallows and was not going to ask what they needed to get on with.

'You can't do this,' Bart protested, looking all around for a way out. 'We didn't do anything.'

'Yes, yes,' the Norman said as if he wasn't listening.

Bart did now look at the man and his eyes widened.

'I know you,' he said.

The Norman cast a lazy eye.

'Yes, yes.' Bart even pointed quite rudely. 'Lord Ranulph. Ranulph de something or other.'

'De Sauveloy,' Lord Ranulph provided the information with practised condescension.

'That's it.'

De Sauveloy seemed to think that was the end of the conversation.

'It's me, Bart.'

Lord Ranulph gave him slightly more attention and looked him up and down.

'What about your bart?'

'No, that's my name, Bart. We've met.'

Ranulph de Sauveloy gave what was clearly a sneer.

'You'll have to remind me. I have a terrible memory for Saxons.'

'I was with Brother Hermitage. In that business at Blore.'

'Blore?'

'That's right. We met. You and your scribe.[7]'

Ranulph frowned and peered at Bart as if trying to see someone different. 'Possibly,' he admitted.

For some reason, Siward had worked his way around behind Bart and seemed to be doing his best to keep out of the way.

'Absolutely,' Bart enthused.

'If you say so,' de Sauveloy reluctantly agreed. 'We've met before and now you're going to be executed. It happens.'

'But I was with Brother Hermitage, the King's Investigator.'

'I wouldn't offer that in your defence if I were you.'

'Don't you see? I'm with Brother Hermitage, the investigator.'

'And saying the same thing over and over again isn't helping.'

Bart breathed deeply and tried to make as much sense as he could, as quickly as possible. 'Hermitage sent me here, well, us here, to look into the possible murder of Scrydan. We're investigating. We didn't come here to do it.

'When we said to Ansgar that we'd come here to do the murder, we meant to investigate it. Didn't we?' He turned to Siward who seemed to be shading his face with his hand.

'That's right,' Siward confirmed in a rather odd voice.

De Sauveloy cast a glance at Siward but it was only a cursory one. 'Fascinating.' He sounded more bored than fascinated.

'So you can't execute us.' As the words left his mouth, Bart knew that de Sauveloy could do what he liked.

'We know who did do it,' He quickly added. 'John's gone

---

[7] *The Investigator's Kingdom;* he was, you know.

to find him.'

'John?' De Sauveloy seemed to register this name.

'The captain of the guard.'

'What has the captain of the guard gone to find anyone for? He's supposed to be in charge of the guard.'

'Well, he hasn't gone in person. He's sent someone.'

Ranulph de Sauveloy released a heavy sigh that said he was finding this all terribly tedious.

'He sent someone to fetch the killer?' the Norman checked.

'Erm, that's right.'

De Sauveloy looked up at the sky. 'And how long is he going to be?'

'Oh, erm, I don't know, really. Won't be long, I'm sure. Just got to get to the goldsmith's workshop and back.'

'We can't loiter all day, you know. These people have gathered for an execution.' De Sauveloy indicated the crowd. 'They won't want to be disappointed.'

Bart felt as if he were being asked to apologise for inconveniencing everyone by holding up his own death.

De Sauveloy appeared to consider the situation for a moment. 'I think we'll get on,' he concluded as if deciding that they would start the meal before the final guests had arrived.

'No, no,' Bart blurted, looking desperately around. 'Look, there's John. You can check with him.'

Bart's relief at seeing John walking across the castle yard with some purpose was so powerful it made him sag.

At least Ranulph de Sauveloy seemed willing to wait until John had joined them.

'What's this about another murderer?' he asked when John arrived.

'That's what I'm checking,' John replied with a short bow

of the head.

'So, we do these two and then another one?' de Sauveloy asked. 'Or do we wait and do them all together?'

'These two say they didn't do it,' John pointed out.

'Yes, they told me that as well. It's the sort of thing they would say, I imagine. And does it really matter?'

'Does it matter?' Bart managed to mouth the horrified words instead of shouting them out loud into the ear of a Norman noble; the Norman noble in charge of the gallows.

'We might execute the wrong people,' John suggested far too lightly.

'I repeat, does that matter?'

John gave this very serious question some thought. 'Might cause more trouble with the Saxons if we execute the wrong people and the right one turns up. You know, they could get restless.'

'I'm not sure we really need to worry about that.'

'It shouldn't take long,' John said casually. 'I've sent to the goldsmith's workshop.'

'Is the killer still going to be there, then? I thought Ansgar had sorted the place out.'

'It's an apprentice called Fridolf we're looking for,' John explained. 'Apparently, he actually went to Brother Hermitage and announced his intention to kill his master.'

'Nothing about Saxons surprises me,' Ranulph said wearily. 'If it's so simple, why did Ansgar bring these two?'

'I don't think Fridolf is there,' John explained. 'He could be off hiding somewhere.'

'Oh, for heaven's sake,' de Sauveloy said with irritation. 'What's the point of us chasing about, then?' He looked at Bart and Siward with clear intent. 'You know what they say. A man on the gallows is worth two hiding in the woods. Let's just get this over with. I've got a lot to do today.'

'We didn't do anything,' Bart insisted, feeling that he really had to speak up.

De Sauveloy looked at him thoughtfully. 'You came from Brother Hermitage, you say.'

'That's right.' Bart nodded enthusiastically.

'The monk?' de Sauveloy checked.

'Erm, yes.' Bart couldn't think why else he'd be called Brother Hermitage.

'From Derby yes?'

'Derby, that's it.'

'So you're not known in London?'

'Absolutely not.' Bart was gratified that this man was finally seeing that they could not have killed Scrydan.

De Sauveloy reached his conclusion. 'No one here will care if we kill you, then. Good.' He clapped his hands as if everything had turned out for the best.

'My lord,' John said in a hesitantly, doubtful sort of way.

'Oh, what is it? You've got to stop worrying about Saxons, John, we've told you this before.'

'But if there's a chance of catching the right killer, shouldn't we take it?'

'Now?' Ranulph asked with a gesture towards the crowd, who were starting to fidget and chat amongst themselves.

Bart felt that he had to take a risk with what he said next. Currently, their chances of surviving the next few moments did not seem good.

'Why do you want to kill us anyway?' he asked. 'I don't mean to sound disrespectful, but some goldsmith has been killed. It's very bad, I admit. Not the sort of thing anyone should do. But under King, erm, I mean, in olden days, it would have just been a fine. That's what Saxons did, before, you, erm, you know, arrived.'

'We're setting an example,' de Sauveloy explained. 'Quite a good one, as it happens.' He gave an appreciative nod towards the crowd gathered to see the example.

'We can't have murder under our noses. You Saxons need to behave. And this Scrydan was bringing a gift to the king. If people bringing gifts to the king get murdered, where will it end, I ask you?'

Bart didn't really know where it would end. Not with them, he hoped. 'That's very suspicious, isn't it?' he asked seriously, a glimmer of hope troubling the back of his head.

'Suspicious? Of course, it's suspicious. It's murder, it's always suspicious.'

'Well, quite. And a gift bearer to the king getting murdered is awful. Do you know what the gift was, by the way?'

'Do I know what it was?' de Sauveloy seemed confused by the question.

'Yes. Just out of interest. I assume it was gold, coming from a goldsmith.'

'I would have thought you'd have other things to be interested in, just at the moment.' De Sauveloy tipped his head towards the gallows.

'Just trying to help.'

'Really?'

'What harm can it do?'

De Sauveloy sighed. 'It was a large gold clasp.'

'Hm,' Bart considered this carefully. Or rather he tried to give the very best impression of considering it carefully, hoping that his glimmer of hope might make itself a bit more explicit.

'Well, if that's all you've got to say..,'

'How do you know it was a clasp?' Bart asked quickly. 'Did

the killer not take it?'

'No, it was left in the body.'

'In the body?' Bart didn't like the sound of that at all.

'Scrydan was stabbed with it,' John explained.

'Oh, my.'

'Yes, well this is all very interesting,' Ranulph de Sauveloy was getting impatient.

Bart's next sentence had better work.

'So, let's assume for a moment that we're telling the truth and we didn't do it. That means the killer is still out there,' he said. 'The killer of gift-bearers to the king. A killer who, for some reason, wasn't interested in stealing a large gold clasp.'

De Sauveloy's eyes narrowed at this, which was a great relief.

'A killer who may now have other people in mind.'

'Fridolf?' John asked.

Bart nodded as sombrely as he could in the circumstances. 'Probably quite important that he's caught, I'd have thought.'

'Unless, of course..,' de Sauveloy mused.

'Yes?'

'It was you and this is a tapestry of lies to get out of being executed.' He considered his own suggestion. 'Yes, I think that's probably it.' He instantly lost interest in anything else. 'On with the execution, then.'

Bart gaped and looked to Siward, wishing that he'd do something. Anything at all would be useful.

'Is that your messenger?' Siward asked John, pointing over towards the castle entrance.

A small figure in a servant's smock came running through the gate and looked about the courtyard. This was noticeable as they were the only person running anywhere.

'Yes, that's her,' John confirmed.

'Now we'll hear about Fridolf,' Bart said confidently, praying that they'd hear about Fridolf.

The servant spotted John and hurried over.

'Well, Margaret, what have you found?' John asked.

Margaret bent over, gasping her breath and Bart saw that she was only a young woman, probably taken from her own duties and despatched on this peculiar mission. And she was a Saxon. He wondered if she had any choice in being a servant to the Normans.

She had had a scarf tied around her head, but this had fallen in the hurry, and dark brown hair dropped around a mostly dirty face.

'Fridolf,' Margaret nodded. 'The other apprentices said that there was a Fridolf but he left.'

'When did he leave? Did they say?'

'Some days ago. Scrydan sent him away to seek commissions for the workshop.'

'Any mention of him wanting to kill Scrydan?'

Margaret swallowed as she recovered her composure. 'They all did. It was a common topic of conversation, apparently.'

'Really?'

'Yes. Although they said that they would never do anything about it, they used to talk quite often about how good it would be if Scrydan was dead.'

'There you are.' Bart couldn't resist crowing at de Sauveloy.

'You could be in it together,' the Norman grumbled.

'Oh, really! We told you about Fridolf, and now you've had it confirmed. We said he came to Brother Hermitage, who sent us. We didn't do it. Did we, Siward?'

'Erm, no,' Siward mumbled.

'What is the matter with you?' Bart hissed at him. 'I'm

arguing for our lives here.'

'Tell you later,' Siward whispered back.

'If we have a later.'

'It does sound as if this Fridolf is real,' John said to de Sauveloy as if the rest of them weren't there. 'If he did kill his master, we ought to deal with him.'

De Sauveloy did not look happy at having his carefully planned execution taken away from him like this.

'And if he has other motivation for killing someone bearing a gift to the king, rebellion, for example, that could be dangerous.'

Ranulph blew out a long slow breath.

'Further,' John went on. 'If these two know what this Fridolf looks like, they can be of use finding him.'

The Norman noble now gave the two of them more of a detailed examination. He looked hard at Siward. 'Don't I know you?' he said.

Siward shook his head but kept his face down. 'Oh no, shouldn't think so.'

'I never forget a face,' de Sauveloy said suspiciously.

Bart thought this was not the moment to point out that only a few moments ago, the Norman had said he never remembered a Saxon

'It'll come to me,' de Sauveloy warned. He seemed to reach a conclusion and turned to the crowd, now largely uninterested in what was going on at the gallows.

'Clear off,' he instructed as if it was their fault that they'd gathered here for no good reason. 'Guards. Clear these people away.'

De Sauveloy's attendants moved to do their master's bidding.

'And you,' he pointed at them all, Bart, Siward, John and

even Margaret. 'Find this Fridolf and bring him to me.' He thought about this for a moment. 'Or rather, bring him to the gallows, then come and get me.'

'My lord,' John acknowledged the instruction.

With Ranulph de Sauveloy gone, Bart felt as if he were breathing again for the first time in hours.

The crowd wandered off under the instruction of the guards, showing little interest in anything, really. Perhaps being called for executions that then got cancelled was quite common.

'Why didn't you speak up?' Bart demanded of Siward.

'He knows me,' Siward said urgently. 'We've met. And not in happy circumstances. When he remembers, he might want to execute me anyway.'

'What did you do?' Bart asked with interest.

'The fewer people who know, the better,' Siward said with a look to John and Margaret.

'Right, then,' John smiled at them. 'I'm glad we got that sorted out. For now, anyway. We can't afford to linger if we're going to find this Fridolf.' He looked to Bart. 'What does he look like?'

'Ah, well.'

Caput X: Hunting Who?

ou never met him?' John checked. He did not sound at all happy about this piece of information.

'Hermitage reported what Fridolf said,' Siward explained. 'He never actually came to the workshop.'

John had taken them down to the guardhouse by the castle entrance, explaining that it was out of Ranulph de Sauveloy's range, and so he would be less likely to decide to execute them after all.

To Siward and Bart's way of thinking, it was a lot more comfortable to be close to the way out, even if that way out was barred by the Norman army.

Margaret had accompanied them, and the boys assumed she must be one of John's own servants as she didn't seem to have anything else to do.

'How are we supposed to find him, then?' John pressed.

'If he's in London at all,' Siward added.

'What?'

'Well, we don't know that he is.'

'Just a moment.' John took a breath. 'This Fridolf, the one you said murdered Scrydan, might not even be here?'

'Well, would you be?' Bart asked. 'If you'd just murdered your master and you had the Normans after you, you wouldn't wait around.'

John spelt out the problem very plainly. 'We have just told Lord Ranulph de Sauveloy, one of the king's most trusted companions, that Fridolf is our killer and that we're going to find him.'

'We didn't say how long it would take,' Siward tried to be helpful.

'Lord Ranulph didn't ask, because he expects it to be done immediately.' John was obviously struggling not to raise his voice.

'We could ask the other apprentices if they've seen him,' Siward suggested.

'I did,' Margaret said. 'And they haven't.'

'Oh, wonderful.' John threw his hands in the air and walked around in a small circle.

'Didn't they tell all this to Ansgar?' Siward asked. He sounded quite aggrieved that they may have been threatened with execution when the Shire Reeve knew they couldn't have done it.

'Of course not,' Margaret replied as if that should be obvious. 'Ansgar's an idiot. He thinks that shouting at people and threatening them makes them cooperate. He's always been the same.'

'Never mind Ansgar,' John persisted. 'How are you going to find this Fridolf and deliver him to de Sauveloy?' He even folded his arms and looked expectant.

'Erm,' Siward offered.

'We investigate,' Bart said confidently.

John did not seem impressed. 'Investigate a man you never met who might not even be here.'

'We go and ask around. He must be reasonably well known in London, what with being a goldsmith's apprentice. We find out if anyone else has seen him.'

'We ask everyone in London if they've seen Fridolf?'

'Not everyone. People involved in the gold business.'

'And if he's not here?'

'He must have come back from Derby to kill Scrydan,' Bart said. 'When did that actually happen?'

'What, Fridolf getting here from Derby? How are we

supposed to know that?' Margaret asked.

'No, no. Scrydan's murder.'

'Oh, right. Days ago. He was found one morning,' Margaret said.

'Days ago, you see.' Siward was insistent. 'We only got here yesterday. We can't have had anything to do with it.'

'I don't think Lord Ranulph will let details like that get in his way,' John pointed out.

'If he was killed days ago, Fridolf could well have been seen around town,' Siward went on. 'He must have come straight back here after meeting Hermitage.'

'The other apprentices can give us a description,' Bart enthused. 'And Hermitage said he was young and well-dressed.'

'That narrows it down,' John said sarcastically.

Bart was looking very thoughtful. 'Method, motive and opportunity,' he said quietly.

'What and what?' Margaret asked.

'It's what Hermitage says.'

'Who's this Hermitage? You keep mentioning him. I assume it's a him.'

'Brother Hermitage. He's the King's investigator.'

'Is he?' Margaret asked. 'Funny name for a monk, if you ask me.'

'He investigates murder for the king.'

'That's good, then. He can do this one.'

'Unfortunately, he's in Derby.'

'Can't we fetch him?'

'Do you know where Derby is? It's miles away.'

'Near Westminster?'

'No, it's not near Westminster. It's five days' journey away. But I'm his apprentice.'

Margaret was not looking overawed at this.

'When you look for a killer you consider the method, who could have done it, the motive, who wanted to do it and the opportunity, who had the, erm, opportunity,' Bart explained.

'And that helps how? Scrydan was stabbed with his own gold clasp. Fridolf wanted to do it and he had the chance.'

'Who found him?' Bart asked. 'Where and exactly when?'

'One of the guards,' John explained. 'Patrolling the tower boundary around dawn. He was in the moat.

'In the moat?' Siward asked with some disgust.

'Well, not in the water. Down on the bank, off the road.'

'And he still had this gold clasp in him?'

'He did.'

'You'd think someone must have seen something,' Siward suggested. 'A goldsmith stabbed with his own gold right outside the castle. When he was bringing it as a gift to the king.'

'Which means it must have happened the previous evening,' Bart concluded.

'Why?' John asked.

'I don't imagine gifts are brought to the king at dawn. Scrydan would want to show off, wouldn't he? You wouldn't give a gold clasp to the king without some sort of ceremony, at least not without a lot of people around to see you do it.'

'I suppose so,' John admitted.

'Does the king have audiences?' Siward asked. 'Times when the Saxons appear before him?'

'Depends on the business,' John explained. 'Mostly during the day. Some evenings, if it's someone of use.'

'Why would Scrydan be left lying on the ground with a gold clasp sticking out of him?' Siward asked. 'If it was done the previous day, you'd think someone would have seen the body and helped themselves to the gold.'

Margaret nodded as if that was what she'd do.

'Is this getting us anywhere?' John asked. 'Scrydan was stabbed and left. What's the killer supposed to do, sit with the body?'

'We need to get out there and ask around.' Bart was decisive. 'Scrydan must have been seen coming here. He walked all the way from near Saint Paul's. Fridolf must have been following him. And the castle seems a busy place. Are we suggesting that no one spotted a body lying there with gold sticking out of it all night?'

The look on John's face said that he was reluctantly accepting this. 'Come on then,' he said. 'We need to deal with this quickly or Lord de Sauveloy will get back to dealing with you.'

He ushered them out of the guardhouse and right, towards the main castle entrance.

At the gate, two uniformed men stood upright as John passed them by. He turned to one. 'Tell Guillaume that he's in charge. I'm going out to find a killer.'

The guards seemed to take little interest in this, but Bart was concerned as John made it sound like a rather hopeless task.

They passed across the wooden bridge out of the castle, unavoidably staring down at the dank moat that lay beneath them looking as if it might rise up to take anyone who put a foot wrong.

The great Thames was a bad enough drain of stink and revulsion, but this moat made the river seem like a tinkling brook of sparkling light. The smell of the thing would be enough to put off most invaders, and there were things floating down there that looked like they were watching you.

The thought that Scrydan had been left on the bank of this evil drain, might explain why no one went near him.

Once out of the confines of the castle, Siward and Bart felt some sense of relief, as if a weight had been lifted from them. Unfortunately, Ranulf de Sauveloy was holding on to the weight and would probably use it on them if this didn't go well.

'Where do we begin, then?' John asked.

'Erm,' Bart tried to sound decisive. 'The scene of the crime.'

'The what?'

'Scene of the crime. You know, the place where Scrydan was found.'

'Why don't you just say the place where Scrydan was found, then?'

'All right,' Bart huffed. 'The place where Scrydan was found. Do you know where it is?'

'Not exactly,' John admitted. 'But the report was that it was by the western wall at the end of the road that comes from the town.'

'Let's go there then.'

John shrugged and turned right to walk along the edge of the moat; not too close to the edge of the moat, obviously.

After only a short walk he came to a halt where a road off to their left headed away towards Saint Paul's, clearly visible as it towered over the surrounding buildings.

'About here, I'd think,' John said. 'Or hereabouts.'

Margaret bent and considered the ground at their feet. 'What are we looking for?' she asked.

'Nothing down there,' Bart explained. 'It's people we want.'

He looked around the area at the few people who were coming and going along the rough streets. He supposed that if you didn't have any business with the Normans, you'd probably try to keep away.

The Saxon faces did their best to turn away from the Norman who was standing there looking at people.

'We'll ask there,' Bart said, nodding towards a simple hut that sat at the side of the road. Outside the door, a cart of sorts sat idle. It had two wheels and a wooden frame on top, but the wheels weren't as round as they might have been and the wood looked as if it had been rotten before it was made into a cart. It was clearly used for straw, as scraps and even small piles of the stuff were scattered about.

'Hello?' Bart called as he approached the door and peered in.

He then backed off quite quickly with a look of disgust on his face. The waving of his hand under his nose indicated what the problem with this place was.

'Ar?' A quite cheery voice emerged from this dark and stinking hovel, which was a bit of a worry in its own right.

'Can we have a word out here?' Bart called. There was no way he wanted a word inside.

A face appeared at the door and looked interested and expectant. It was an old face, lined and creased with the years, but one that looked quite content with its place in the world.

The clothes, the hair and the smell made it perfectly clear what that place in the world involved and explained what the cart was for.

'You must be the dung gatherer,' Bart said.

'How did you know that?' the old man asked in wonder.

'Oh, just something in the air, I suppose.'

'Har, har,' the old man cackled happily as if no one had ever said anything like that before. 'Edric,' he announced when he'd recovered from his fit of humour. 'Edric dung-gatherer.'

'You live here.' This wasn't a question as no one else in their right mind would live here.

'That I do. And have done long years now.'

'That's good.'

'Business has never been better,' Edric enthused. 'What with the castle. I'm as busy as a bee with lots to do.'

'Excellent.'

'Started off in animals,' Edric explained. 'But these days, everything's grist to my mill.'

Bart did not want to think about that mill at all.

Edric stepped over towards Bart, who tried not to step back. 'You're not thinking of setting up in the dung-gathering line of work?' he asked in a worried tone.

'Er, no. Definitely not.'

'That's good then,' Edric cheered. 'It's one of the excellent features of dung-gathering; no one else wants to do it.' He cackled to himself some more as if he really couldn't understand this.

'We want to ask about Scrydan,' Siward interjected, sounding worried about how much longer they might have to stand in this invisible fog of dung.

'Oh, the gold man,' Edric nodded. 'He's dead, you know.'

'Yes, we know. He died near here, we're told.'

'That he did. I was just coming out for the morning rounds when I saw the place was all soldiers.'

'All soldiers?'

'And they was looking at something on the ground down by the moat. Well, I wasn't having that, was I?'

'Weren't you?' Bart asked.

'Of course not. Anything on the ground is mine for the gathering. Everything between the moat and Saint Paul's. That's my patch.'

'You thought the soldiers were looking at some dung?' Siward asked, wondering why anyone would think the stuff was so fascinating.

Dung gatherers were everywhere, and it was a vital trade, but it was rather taken for granted and ignored completely when it could be. The removal and management of the material were obviously essential and it had many uses, from tanning to farming, and heating to medicine. That wasn't to say that people who weren't dung-gatherers took any interest in it, nor that they wouldn't find something else to do when the dung-gatherer called.

'I don't know what else would be on the ground that soldiers want to look at,' Edric explained. 'But then, when I got up close, I saw it was a dead man. I don't do dead men.'

'Scrydan,' Bart confirmed. 'Did you know him?'

'His workshop's in my patch,' Edric explained. 'I've handled his dung as long as there was dung to be handled.'

'So you'd met him before.' Bart nodded.

'No, of course not. Man like Scrydan wouldn't want to meet his dung gatherer, would he? Too good for the likes of me.'

Edric didn't seem at all put out that the likes of him weren't good enough for Scrydan.

'So, who did you deal with?' Siward asked carefully. 'Who paid you when the time was due?'

'Be the apprentices,' Edric explained. 'Most of the places I gather from, I deal with the servants or the slaves. In Scrydan's workshop, that was the apprentices.'

'Fridolf?' Bart asked as lightly as he could.

'Oh yes, back in the day. But young Fridolf's nearly a master now. It's the younger lads I talk to these days.'

'Have you erm, seen Fridolf about at all. Recently?'

'Have I seen Fridolf?' Edric didn't seem to understand why the question was being asked.

'Yes,' Bart pressed, without wanting to sound anxious about the answer.

'Recently?' Edric prolonged the agony.

'Yes, recently,' Bart growled the words out.

'Oh, my, yes,' Edric confirmed with a happy nod.

Bart sagged with relief.

'When, where?' Siward asked.

'Oh,' Edric scratched under his arms, which was not anywhere anyone else would go. 'Be the night before they found Scrydan.'

'So he was here,' Siward said triumphantly.

'And it was nearby?'

'Right here, it was. In fact, come to think of it, he was a bit rude.'

'A bit rude?'

'Yes. I called out, hello Fridolf, and he ignored me and ran off.'

'Did he now?' Bart asked with interest.

'I just said he did.'

'Erm, yes. And when was this? Exactly?'

'I don't generally keep track of time,' Edric explained, dung being pretty timeless.

'You said night?' Siward prompted. 'Late night? Early?'

Edric gave it his very best careful thought, which took a bit too long for everyone's comfort. 'Be the evening, I reckon. Just getting dark and I was about to stop. No point gathering dung in the dark, you never know what you might pick up.'

Bart thought that might be better than doing it during the day.

'The evening, eh? Siward said with some triumph. 'Right

about the time Scrydan was killed.'

'You think Fridolf did it?' Edric asked with obvious horror and some outrage at the suggestion.

'Do you think he couldn't have done it?' Bart asked.

Edric quickly lost his horror and outrage. 'Oh, not at all. Hated one another those two did. It was probably Fridolf.'

Caput XI: Secondary Enquiries

It is said that nothing travels as fast as bad news. This is true, but within the family of bad news, the speediest variety is bad news about other people. Such is the natural glee at hearing that an awful fate has befallen someone who isn't you, word flies upon the freshest wings.

The murder of Scrydan, while obviously being the worst possible news for him, was a marvel for everyone else. It flitted and skittered about the town with all the life of a newborn lamb. It bounced over the walls of the city and off into the surrounding countryside, gambolling in every field and village.

A few days later, when the execution was announced of not one, but two strangers for the murder, there wasn't a speed fast enough to accommodate the subsequent gossip. Even people who weren't there spread the word like fleas in a crowd. And being further away from the truth and any actual facts, made for a much more fascinating tale.

The subsequent release of the murderers was far less interesting and so barely made it out of the castle courtyard. Good news for other people moved as sluggishly as a sluggish slug.

Thus, when Bart, Siward, John and Margaret moved off into the town to search for Fridolf, the responses they got mainly comprised of sworn affirmations that Scrydan's murder had been the most spectacular event and that his murderers had been caught and dealt with in the most awful way imaginable. In fact, in many different awful ways imaginable, depending on the imagination of the one being questioned.

110

'This is ridiculous,' Siward complained. 'Half these people are convinced that we did it and that we've been executed.'

'And the other half don't believe that because they don't believe anything,' Bart added. 'Scrydan isn't dead at all. It's all part of a Norman plot to spirit all the goldsmiths out of the country. Why on earth anyone would want to do that isn't very clear.'

'Margaret,' John instructed. 'Go back to the castle and tell Guillaume to send me four men. We'll simply have to go from house to house looking for Fridolf, or anyone who's seen him.'

Margaret nodded at her instruction and headed back.

'And avoid Lord de Sauveloy, if you see him,' John called after.

Margaret raised an arm in acknowledgement.

'What if he ran all the way out of town?' Siward asked. 'He might not be here at all.'

John considered this for a moment. 'We send word to the gates to see if he's been seen. Every gate has Norman guards on it and they have orders to watch everyone coming and going.'

'We still don't know what he looks like,' Bart reminded them.

'Well-dressed and young, you said.'

'Well, yes.'

'John held his hands out to draw their attention to the people of London who were now going about their business. Not one of them was well-dressed and young.

'He could have left days ago,' Siward, said. 'As soon as Edric saw him.'

John put his hands on his hips. 'Shall we give up and get back to the execution, then? We can if you like.'

Siward didn't have an answer.

'Right. As soon as Margaret's here with the men, I'll send one off to each gate. Meanwhile, we start asking people if they've seen Fridolf. If Edric knew him on sight, there's a good chance others will too.' He strode off away from Edric's hovel towards the next one, which was similarly poor, if of slightly better odour.

'Ho, within,' John called into the interior.

This place was a simple dwelling, no bigger than a single body needed. Considering its condition, it might keep out some of the wind and a bit of the rain, but it was clearly not a place of any reputable tradesman or woman.

A youngish face appeared at the entrance and considered the visitors. Dressed in cloth that was on its way to being rags and had nearly arrived, the woman's face screwed up with suspicion as she appraised the Norman.

'Good day, mistress,' John said.

The woman looked back over her shoulder to see if he was talking to someone else.

'We're looking for Fridolf, the goldsmith's apprentice. Do you know him?'

The clear look on her face said that she didn't like answering questions from Normans.

'It's important that we find him,' Bart spoke up. 'Edric the dung-gatherer said that he was here the night Scrydan died.'

'Edric did?' the woman asked cautiously. She sounded quite impressed that someone of Edric's standing would have provided information.

'That's right,' Siward confirmed. 'Edric said hello to him but he ran away.'

'No, he didn't,' the woman said as if they'd said something quite silly. 'He's right there.' She nodded towards Edric's dwelling.

'No, not Edric.' Bart was impatient. 'Fridolf. Fridolf ran away.'

'That'd be right, then,' the woman agreed.

'You saw it?'

'If Edric said it, it must be right.'

'I see,' Bart sighed that this was going to be no help at all. 'Well, thank you, mistress, erm..?'

'Helg,' the woman introduced herself.

'Thank you, Mistress Helg.'

'Helg, dung-gatherer's apprentice,' she introduced her trade.

'Ah. Excellent.' Bart couldn't think what else to say.

'Did you see anything at all?' Siward asked. 'Any sign of Fridolf?'

'Not me. I keeps myself to myself.'

'Very wise.' Bart started to move away.

'You want Mistress Mildrith.'

'Really?' Bart had little interest.

'She's a one who doesn't keep herself to herself. If anyone's going to see anyone, it'd be Mistress Mildrith.'

'And where will we find Mistress Mildrith?' Siward asked.

'Just down a ways.' Helg nodded her head away from the river, further up the hill, which was obviously down a ways.

'That's very helpful, thank you.' Siward gave her a little bow.

Helg sneered and ducked back into her hovel.

'Is this getting us anywhere?' Bart asked. 'We can't go round the whole of London like this, it'll take weeks.'

'We'll just try this Mistress Mildrith,' John said. 'It sounds as if she could be the street gossip. After we've seen her, we'll split up. It'll be quicker. Then, when my men arrive we can cover even more ground.'

'Isn't de Sauveloy going to be getting impatient for his executions?' Siward asked.

'Lord de Sauveloy is always impatient about something. The problem is, he never forgets anything either. At least we have some firm evidence that this Fridolf may be involved. That should hold him off for a while.'

'Firm evidence from the dung-gatherer,' Bart pointed out.

'Important people, dung-gatherers,' John observed.

'This is very good of you,' Siward said. 'You didn't have to help us and you don't have to do all this.'

'If I find that you don't really know Brother Hermitage, I shall be quite annoyed.'

'Oh, we do, I assure you.'

'Right. Let's get on then.'

They all walked up the hill, not having a clue where Mistress Mildrith might be, but there weren't really many places to choose from.

The first enquiry into a dark hovel produced a very rude response. Apparently, the very idea that the occupier would have anything to do with the likes of Mistress Mildrith was the most appalling insult. And no, they didn't know anyone called Fridolf and wouldn't tell the Normans if they did.

With a shrug of resignation, John moved on.

The next place along was a more substantial dwelling. It was as if the greater the distance from the river, the more improved people became. This was quite understandable as the river was profoundly disgusting. As it was the method of removal for any material from the town that didn't meet the dung-gatherer's low standards, it was also no surprise.

'Mistress Mildrith?' John called at the door.

At least this place had a door, even if it was rough and

crooked. That condition meant that it sat quite comfortably in the rest of the place. There was a thatch roof and there were whitewashed walls, but they all looked as if they were slowly moving in different directions and would, at any moment now, part company completely.

The door was opened very slowly and carefully, and a woman's head peered around the corner while she held it ajar.

The head was tightly bound in a scarf, which made it hard to discern any specific or even general age. The features though, said that this was a woman of curiosity. The eyes were bright and lively, the head poked forward into the air as if trying to uncover some secret, and the nose was built for sniffing things out. This had to be Mistress Mildrith.

As this nose lived just up the road from the dung-gatherer, it must be of hardy construction.

'Well, well,' Mistress Mildrith said with the interest of town gossips up and down the land. 'What have we here?' She glanced at the others but her main interest was in John.

He gave her a short bow. 'We are looking for Fridolf, the goldsmith's apprentice. Do you know him?'

'Know him?' Mildrith asked. 'Well, I wouldn't say I know him.' She made no move to open the door further, or to come out from behind it. Perhaps that was wise as Bart was sure he had noticed the wall move slightly of its own accord.

'You know what he looks like?' John checked. 'Have you seen him recently?'

'Oh, yes, we all know what young Fridolf looks like. Why, what's he been up to?' Mistress Mildrith was plainly more interested in getting the details of what Fridolf had been up to than she was in answering the rest of the question.

'We want to talk to him, that's all.' John made it plain that he was the Norman in this conversation and that she wasn't going to get anything out of him.

'Is it to do with Scrydan?' Mildrith asked as if she hadn't heard a word. 'I expect it is, what with Scrydan dying like that. Fridolf was his apprentice you know. Nice boy.'

'Yes, we know he was Scrydan's apprentice,' John said slowly. 'Have you seen him recently?'

'Recently?' Mildrith seemed to have trouble with the concept.

'The night Scrydan died,' Bart specified. 'Did you see him then?'

'In the night?' Mildrith sounded quite offended. 'I most certainly did not. What sort of woman do you take me for?'

'I meant did you see him out in the street? Edric saw him. And he saw him run off. What did you see?'

'Nothing.' Mildrith said this a bit too quickly and was starting to sound annoyed at being questioned, which was a bit odd for a gossip.

'What do you know?' Siward asked her suspiciously. 'What are you hiding? Did you talk to him? Did he tell you where he was going?'

'Absolutely not,' Mildrith said stiffly.

'Absolutely not to what?' Siward asked. 'The talking or the telling?'

'If there's something you're not telling us, mistress,' John said. 'You'd better start, erm, telling us.' His sentence petered out.

'I know nothing,' Mildrith said quite haughtily.

'You won't mind if we come in, then,' Bart said.

'You are not coming in my house. The very thought.'

'We can wait until my men get here and then kick the door down,' John suggested. 'I don't think it would put up much of a fight.'

Mildrith retreated slightly behind her half-open door.

'She's hiding something,' Bart concluded.

Just then, a strange noise emerged from behind Mistress Mildrith. It was a sort of moving noise as if something of significant size had shifted when it wasn't supposed to; like the back wall of a hovel.

The three of them took a sharp step backwards, while Mildrith looked over her shoulder and let go a scream. She seemed torn between whether to go back into her house or get out of it, and her indecision left the door firmly stuck in her hand as she alternately tugged and pushed at it.

For a moment, Bart thought about stepping up to help her, but it was only for a moment. The moment after he had had the thought, he saw the roof fall down.

It hadn't been much of a roof to begin with, being a simple layer of thatch on top of a frame of some sort, but it had been higher than the walls it rested upon. Now it was lower.

Mildrith, standing under the frame of the door, neatly avoided her roof's collapse

Their sole means of support having been taken away, the walls had lost all motivation to stay upright. With nothing else to do, they started to make for their final resting place.

First, the wall on the left slowly wavered as if caught in some invisible wind. Everyone held their breath while they waited to see if it would fall in or out.

With a somewhat pathetic crash, it lumbered inward, down onto the top of the roof, which had now become the floor.

Following its brother's lead, the right-hand wall threw itself to its death and added to the general mess.

It now seemed that the only thing holding up the front of

Mistress Mildrith's house was Mistress Mildrith. She appeared to be acutely aware of her perilous situation and her eyes darted about with energy her body could not display. Everyone present knew that one wrong move would see the remaining structure collapse, quite possibly on top of her.

She couldn't go back into the house as there was no house to go into. Nor could she come out as that would require letting go of the door, a step which would almost certainly see her vanish under a pile of wattle and daub.

'Hold the wall,' John instructed the others as he took a step forward.

'Don't move,' Mildrith shouted. 'You'll bring the whole lot down.'

As if thinking this instruction was meant for it, the front of the house came down of its own accord.

Bart thought it a strange sensation, to see a house coming towards him, but it wasn't so strange that he didn't manage to step backwards out of the way.

Mistress Mildrith vanished from sight as the front wall collapsed onto the ground, creating a cloud of dust that rose up around them.

Waving the resultant fog away from their faces they looked to where the house of Mistress Mildrith used to stand.

The door was no longer ajar as there was no house left to hold it ajar to. Nonetheless, the mistress of the house still stood at her door, holding it while littered fragments of her home sank in the air around her.

She coughed once, let go of the door and seemed to watch with interest as it fell at her feet.

'Oh,' Siward said. It seemed that he wanted to add something along the lines of, "your house has fallen down", but realised that a description wasn't really necessary.

'Good Lord,' Bart said with some sympathy.

'Who's that?' John asked, pointing at Mildrith.

Bart and Siward looked over, wondering why John was asking, but they soon spotted a figure behind the mistress, standing looking at the back of the house as they were looking at the front.

As soon as each side of the erstwhile dwelling spotted the other, the figure turned and ran. Even from this distance and through the haze of what used to be a house, it was clear that this was a young and well-dressed man.

'Fridolf!' Bart cried.

'After him,' John shouted.

Scrambling over the recently deposited pile of sticks and mud, and past the still-stunned Mistress Mildrith, the three of them passed by the thatched floor and out the rear, following Fridolf who was now heading in towards the centre of the town.

'He must have been in there and tried to get out through the back,' Bart said.

'When there wasn't a door,' Siward added.

'Why's he still here?' John asked. 'If he killed Scrydan and ran from Edric, why go to Mistress Mildrith and stay here? He could have been long gone.'

'It was hardly a safe house,' Bart observed.

'And where's he going now?' Siward called.

'Let's just get him and find out.' John urged them on.

Not having a fallen house to negotiate, Fridolf had a head start on his pursuers and he made the most of it. He also knew these streets better than most, including where the dangerous holes were.

Skipping from side to side where necessary, he made excellent speed and was soon back on Ceapen Street. He cast a look over his shoulder and was pleased to see that his followers were some way off.

With one stride, the mud beneath his feet gave way to solid ground and he knew that he had crossed to within the bounds of Saint Paul's.

He stopped, bent double to gather his breath and waited for his pursuers.

Bart and Siward were first to arrive, but John was hard on their heels.

'Are you Fridolf?' Bart gasped.

Siward and John stood expectantly, waiting for the only possible reply. This had to be Fridolf. He was young, he was well-dressed and he had run from them.

Fridolf looked at them all quite boldly and gave a one-word reply.

'Sanctuary.'

Caput XII: Sanctuary

'Sanctuary?' Siward asked. 'What do you mean, sanctuary?'

'I mean sanctuary,' Fridolf explained. He sounded more relieved than anything at being able to say the word. 'I claim sanctuary.'

Bart and Siward exchanged glances. 'Can he do that?' Bart asked.

'I think he can,' John said with resignation.

'Really?' Bart sounded surprised. 'Doesn't King William simply do what he likes?'

'Not where the church is concerned,' John explained. 'The king is a very devout man. He worships and prays regularly, pays heed to the Pope and acts in the name of God.'

'Unless you're a Saxon,' Siward half muttered.

'He killed Scrydan,' Bart protested, gesturing at Fridolf. 'And we were about to be executed for it. Now he comes here, says, "sanctuary" and we have to do nothing?'

'If he claims the sanctuary of the church, there's nothing we can do.'

'So we could claim sanctuary as well. Everyone could do what they liked and then claim sanctuary. What's the point of that?'

'You have to stay in the church,' John said. 'You can never leave.'

That did cause some silent thought, even for Fridolf.

'You might be allowed to go into exile, but if your pursuers say not, then it's the church for the rest of your life. You couldn't even leave the bounds without being taken.'

Bart didn't seem so keen on sanctuary anymore.

'It's better than being executed,' Siward pointed out.

Bart looked hard at Fridolf and then back at John.

'At least we've got him, now. Lord de Sauveloy can't execute us when we know where the real killer is.'

Fridolf stepped up to the border of his sanctuary. 'I didn't kill anyone.'

'No,' Bart sneered. 'Of course, you didn't. You didn't come to Derby and ask Brother Hermitage to take a note of your murder plans, then? That wasn't you? Must have been another Fridolf, apprentice to Scrydan. The Scrydan who's been murdered.'

Fridolf was clearly taken aback by this accusation. 'Who told you that?'

'Brother Hermitage himself. The King's Investigator,' Bart crowed. 'I am his apprentice. He told me everything.'

'He told us everything,' Siward added.

Fridolf tried to recover himself. 'Then he told you that he said not to do it. That I couldn't. That it was a sin.'

'And that you offered to pay the wergild in advance,' Bart now added a sneer to his crow.

'I didn't do it,' Fridolf insisted.

'You didn't come back to London to do the deed. You weren't seen by Edric the dung-gatherer on the evening of Scrydan's murder and you didn't run away when you were challenged.

'Then, you didn't hide out in Mistress Mildrith's house until we found you, at which point you didn't run away again. And you haven't even claimed sanctuary, I suppose?'

'I knew people would think I'd done it, but I didn't,' Fridolf protested.

'What have you claimed sanctuary for, then? If you haven't done anything wrong, you haven't got anything to worry about, have you?'

'Like you?' Fridolf asked.

'Eh, what?'

'You've done nothing wrong yet you were about to be executed by the Normans. How was that going for you? Get a fair hearing, did you?'

'That's completely different.'

'No, it isn't. It's exactly the same.'

'We didn't murder Scrydan,' Bart insisted. 'We couldn't have done it as we weren't even here.'

'Neither was I.'

'Oh, yes?'

'Yes. I got back from Derby and went back to the workshop. The boys told me he'd gone off with his precious clasp and I knew where he was taking it.'

'Wait a moment,' Bart said very directly. 'They told Margaret they hadn't seen you.'

'Who?' Fridolf asked.

'Margaret. John sent her to find out about you so that we might avoid being executed. The apprentices said they hadn't seen you.'

'Ah, yes, well,' Fridolf hummed and hesitated. 'I may have told them not to mention that I was around. You know, in case Scrydan asked.'

'Oh, really? That would be helpful for when you wanted to follow him and kill him.'

'I did not,' Fridolf almost shouted. 'I followed him, yes, but only so that the king wouldn't think he'd made the clasp. I made it, and he was going to claim all the credit.'

'That obviously made you angry,' Bart reasoned. 'So, now we have the motive for murder. Another one. On top of all the reasons you gave Hermitage. And you asked the other apprentices to lie for you.'

'What actually happened?' John asked, interrupting what had become a simple series of accusations and denials. 'Tell us your version and we will listen.' He said these last words directly at Bart.

Fridolf took a breath. 'I left the workshop and headed for the castle. Scrydan had been boasting about how this clasp was going to make him the king's chosen goldsmith when he hadn't even made the thing. He hasn't got the skill anymore. It's another reason he can't have me made up to master.'

'Another reason to kill him,' Bart spoke up.

'We are listening,' John said firmly. He nodded to Fridolf to carry on.

'So, I went as fast as I could because I didn't know if Scrydan had already got to the king.'

'What were you planning to do?' Siward asked quite gently.

'I didn't know, really. I'd protested to Scrydan, but I'd been doing that for months. I'd insist on going with him. I'd tell the guards at the castle that I was with him. Anything, really. I didn't have time to think.'

'And you did find him?'

'I did.' Fridolf lowered his head. 'He was already dead.'

'Ha!' Bart dismissed that very quickly.

'He was,' Fridolf insisted. 'He was lying on the bank of the moat with the wretched clasp sticking out of him.'

'Why didn't you do something?' John asked. 'Call the guard, summon help?'

'Because I knew everyone would say I'd done it. I needed time to think. That's why I ran off when Edric called out.'

'To Mistress Mildrith?' John clearly couldn't see the reason for that decision.

Fridolf hesitated for a moment. 'She's my aunt.'

'Your aunt?' Siward asked.

'My father's sister. He died a long time back, along with mother. Mildrith's the only relation I've got. I knew she'd hide me. I couldn't go back to the workshop.'

'All the actions of a guilty man,' Bart concluded.

'Just like you,' Fridolf tried a sneer of his own. 'Heard all about Scrydan the goldsmith from Brother Hermitage. Came to London to do the murder yourself, knowing that I'd be accused.'

'We weren't even here,' Bart was outraged at this suggestion.

'So you say. Lord Ranulph de Sauveloy was ready to execute you. You must be guilty.'

'Be quiet, everyone,' John instructed. 'This is getting us nowhere. Fridolf has claimed sanctuary and there's nothing we can do about that.'

'We can tell de Sauveloy where the killer is,' Bart insisted. 'Who else would run away to the church?'

'Someone who was going to be executed for something they didn't do,' Fridolf said. 'Ring any bells? Give it half a day and you'll be in here with me.'

Siward was looking thoughtful. 'How did Scrydan manage to lie undisturbed all night?' he asked. 'And why was the clasp still in him when they found him? Surely someone must have come by?'

'I scared them off,' Fridolf said quietly.

'You what?'

'Scared them off. I thought it was best if the guards found Scrydan of their own accord. You know, just come upon him. That clasp is very valuable. If I took it, everyone would assume I'd killed Scrydan. If anyone else came along, all that gold could be lost.'

'We have assumed you killed Scrydan,' Bart said.

'Oh, shut up,' Fridolf snapped.

'How did you scare people off?' Siward asked.

'The body was just there, by the moat, not far from Aunt Mildrith's house. I just had to keep an eye on it and make noises if anyone came near.'

'Noises?'

'Yes, you know Like spirits. Woo woo, that sort of thing.'

'Woo woo?' John asked.

'Like a spirit,' Fridolf clearly thought that was obvious. 'A few people did come along and they went over to Scrydan. I went woo woo, and they ran off.'

John shook his head. 'Saxons! Why did you stay at all? Wouldn't it have been better to leave town?'

'I thought that, to begin with. But then I talked to Mildrith and we came to the conclusion that I'd be giving everything up. I'd never be a goldsmith or anything because I wouldn't be able to show my face again. We needed to know who really did it.'

'And you were going to achieve that by leaving the body out for the guards?' John asked.

'What else was there to do? I couldn't get involved, people would think I did it. I thought that if the Normans found him, they'd work it out.'

'How were we going to do that?'

'It's like Brother Hermitage said. He investigates and discovers who killed who.'

'But he's in Derby.'

'I thought you might send for him. Instead, that wretched Ansgar got involved.'

'He is the Shire Reeve,' John pointed out.

'Yes, but he's also a fool. He just stomped about the place shouting at people, like he always does, and was looking for me. Then you two turned up and confessed, apparently.' He made this remark in Bart's direction.

'We only said Hermitage had sent us to check that Scrydan hadn't been murdered,' Bart retorted. 'How were we to know that he had. By you!'

'Why would I stay if I'd done it?' Fridolf bit back. 'Answer me that. This Norman's right. I should have left town with the gold clasp. There was enough metal in that for a man to live a comfortable life. What idiot kills a goldsmith with pounds of gold and then leaves the gold behind? Eh?'

'I don't know, do I?' Bart replied. 'I don't go round killing goldsmiths.'

'If you didn't kill him, who did?' John asked.

'If I knew that, I wouldn't be claiming sanctuary, would I? I'd be telling everyone who did it and having them found.'

'Which is just what we were doing,' Bart replied.

'Except you were telling people a name without knowing whether they'd done it or not. If you're supposed to be Brother Hermitage's apprentice, you're not very good,' Fridolf observed nastily. 'He seemed quite a clever fellow. Thoughtful, not given to doing anything stupid.'

Bart took a deep breath. 'Is there anything to stop me going in there and dragging him out?' he asked John.

'Nothing to stop you going in there, no. But the laws of land and church allow no action to be taken against him while he is in sanctuary. If you dragged him out, you would be punished.'

'How's that fair?'

'It's not fair, it's the law. They're completely different things.'

The continuing argument, with Bart and Fridolf both raising their voices, had drawn the attention of those nearby. Unnoticed by the participants, a young cleric had considered the dispute and hurried into the church, a look of mild panic on his face.

He now emerged from the building with an older and wiser-looking cleric, who didn't seem ready to panic about anything.

'I am Father Thomas. What is the meaning of this?' the elder demanded in the way that only people who are very sure of themselves can demand.

Fridolf was the first to speak. 'I claim sanctuary, Father.'

The priest raised his eyebrows. 'Do you, indeed? We'll see about that.' He turned to John, who, being obviously Norman, must be in charge. 'Is this individual with you?'

'He is not with us,' John acknowledged the churchman with a short nod of the head. 'We pursued him from the castle and he came here.'

'Pursued him?' Father Thomas sounded as if pursuing people was one of the most disgusting things anyone could do.

'In the matter of the murder of Scrydan.'

'The goldsmith?'

'Just so.'

Thomas now peered at Fridolf, apparently seeing him for the first time. 'Don't I know you?'

'I am Fridolf. Scrydan's apprentice.'

'Yes, that's right. You're Scrydan's apprentice.'

No one seemed sure why the man had repeated this as if he had just worked it out for himself.

'And you killed Scrydan?'

'No, I didn't.'

'Then why are you seeking sanctuary?'

'That's what I said,' Bart piped up.

Father Thomas gave Bart a glance so withering, it could kill flowers.

'Because people of little thought have concluded that I did do it. But I didn't.'

'I see.' Father Thomas rubbed his chin and seemed to reach a conclusion. 'Well, we can't have people seeking sanctuary for every little problem. Be off with you now.' He waved Fridolf away.

'I'm not seeking it, I'm claiming it,' Fridolf insisted.

'I'm sure you are.' Thomas spoke as if to a child. 'But we don't want to inconvenience the king's men, do we now?'

John was looking serious. 'Are you denying his claim of sanctuary?' he asked.

'Denying? Oh, that's a strong word. No, no, but we need to be sensible about these matters, don't we?' Thomas looked John up and down and obviously didn't see any cause for concern.

'We wouldn't want our noble lords dragged into a lot of nonsense about sanctuary when the important matter of Scrydan's murder is being considered. In fact, I thought two miscreants had already been executed for the deed.'

'That was us,' Siward said.

Father Thomas looked at him with some surprise.

'But we didn't do it.'

'The town seems full of people who didn't do it,' Thomas observed.

'One of whom has claimed sanctuary,' John pointed out.

'Yes, yes.' Father Thomas was starting to sound a little irritated that this matter wasn't going away. 'But the church is anxious to cooperate with our new rulers in any way we can.

If you need this fellow to go with you, I'm sure that won't be a problem.'

'Really?' John sounded very interested in this. 'Despite me having heard him claim sanctuary.'

'Oh, don't worry about that.'

'Interesting,' John nodded lightly. 'I'm sure my father, Lord Le Pedvin will be interested to discover this change in ecclesiastical law. As will the king, who is very firm on that sort of thing, as I'm sure you know.'

Father Thomas was looking a bit pale now.

'Is this the Archbishop's word, or purely a local arrangement?' John inquired.

'Well, erm, of course, if you support his claim of sanctuary, that is a different matter.'

'Is it?'

'Oh, absolutely.' Thomas seemed to regain some of his composure. 'As I said, we are only seeking to cooperate in the finding of Scrydan's killer. A most heinous sin.'

'That will be most helpful.' A new voice piped up behind Thomas and made him spin in his gown.

'Who the devil are you?' he demanded of the interloper. He was more taken aback by the small female figure who was glaring at him with blatant impertinence.

'Me?' the speaker replied with a modest bow. 'I am Brother Hermitage. I am the King's Investigator.'

Caput XIII: To The Rescue

'Hermitage!' Bart shouted, half question, half exclamation. 'But you're in Derby, I mean were, that is. How did you..? Why..?, What's going on?' He looked from Hermitage to Wat to Cwen and back to Hermitage again. Wat gave him a smile and raised a hand. Cwen did not.

'Have you come about Scrydan?' Siward asked.

'All in good time,' Cwen said. 'So this is Fridolf, eh? We've heard a lot about you.' It was clear that none of it was good. 'It sounds as if you've claimed sanctuary, or not?' She stared at Father Thomas whose gaze flitted between her and John.

'It does seem that we have a most reliable witness to confirm that.' Thomas bowed an acknowledgement to John, his confidence seeping back into the moment. 'Me not having heard the claim myself. In which case, of course, sanctuary is in place.'

'Glad that's clear,' Cwen sniffed. 'All we need to do is answer Bart's question; what's going on?' She turned her attention to Fridolf, who wilted slightly under its force.

'Why have you claimed sanctuary, Fridolf?' Hermitage asked.

'They think I killed Scrydan,' Fridolf bleated.

'And you didn't?' Cwen was plainly sceptical.

'No, of course, I didn't.'

'Hm.'

'Is there somewhere we can go to talk?' Wat asked. 'Standing out here chatting about who killed who could take all day and we've had a long journey.'

John made a suggestion. 'Perhaps Father Thomas can find us somewhere within the bounds of sanctuary? As Lord Le

131

Pedvin's son and King William's own investigator want to discuss this matter?'

'Of course, of course. I was about to offer our hospitality to you all.' Father Thomas's words were full of enthusiasm, but none of it showed on his face.

'Of course, you were,' Cwen noted. 'Lead on, then.'

Father Thomas considered the small crowd he now had with obvious distaste, but was clearly a man who knew how to behave in front of power.

He beckoned them all to follow and headed off towards the church.

'It is good to see you again, Brother,' John said to Hermitage. 'Even if the circumstances are the same as usual.[8]

'You too, John,' Hermitage replied. 'I try to avoid all this, but it seems to follow me around.'

The young cleric, who had stood in attendance of Thomas all this time, looked positively horrified at the latest development but skipped off ahead of everyone in response to a gesture from the priest.

Leading the way through the main door of the church, Thomas made his obeisance to the altar and then moved off to the right.

In the wall of the church on this side, a small and humble-looking door squatted as if trying to hide from any passing interest.

Thomas delved into his robes and extracted a key from the end of an expensive-looking cord. He looked around as if checking that no one was watching him when in fact, he had a small gaggle watching every move.

He turned the key in the lock on the door, another expensive luxury, and pushed it open. Ducking his head, he

---

8 *The King's Investigator;* more of the usual.

stepped through and everyone else followed.

The other side of the door was not small or humble in any way whatsoever.

A most magnificent chamber opened up with more than enough room for everyone. In the far wall, a magnificent fire blazed and a high ceiling stretched away above their heads. The whole place was beautifully fragrant as the heat from the fire roused herbs scattered in the rush matting on the floor.

'Nice spot for a sanctuary,' Wat observed, walking straight over to the fire where he warmed himself. 'Is that wine?' He spotted a jug and leather cups on a table and, to the obvious horror of Thomas, went over and helped himself.

'Hm,' Wat supped with pleasure. 'Always trust the church to have the good stuff.'

'Wat, really,' Hermitage chastised. 'Perhaps we could all just take seats while we try to understand the situation.' While this room was beyond anything a humble churchman should need, he did feel that discussing a murder in a church was both more comfortable than it might be, and slightly more sinful.

There were more than enough seats for everyone, all of them well-padded with straw or even horse hair. This was plainly a room of some import in the church, doubtless somewhere all the clerics and officials gathered when not saying or taking part in Mass.

Thomas took himself to the largest chair by the fire and magnanimously indicated that the others should find somewhere.

'So,' Hermitage said when everyone was settled. 'It seems that Master Scrydan has been murdered.'

'How did you know?' Bart asked.

'Word travels,' Wat explained. 'Especially word about dead

goldsmiths. You hadn't been gone from Derby a few days before travellers came through gossiping about the big murder in London.'

'Which set Hermitage into a fit of fretting, of course,' Cwen added. 'He insisted we come all the way here immediately.' She sounded as if she thought this was a complete overreaction.

'Bart and Siward had come down to check on Scrydan,' Hermitage repeated this simple fact as he had had to do many times over the last days. 'What else were we supposed to do?'

'Leave them to it,' Cwen repeated herself as well. 'Bart says he's your apprentice anyway. It's probably good for him to do a murder on his own.'

'That's what she's been saying all the way,' Wat explained.

'But then,' Hermitage continued. 'We got to the outer reaches of London and all the talk was of two strangers who had been taken for the murder and executed.'

'We just assumed it was you two.' Wat nodded to Bart and Siward.

'Which put Hermitage in a complete daze,' Cwen noted.

'Quite understandably,' Hermitage said. 'Fortunately, even fresher gossip inside the gates was that there had been no execution and that the strangers had flown over the walls of William's castle into the river, where they were taken away by whales.'

'To Wales?' Siward asked incredulously.

'No, by whales. It's ridiculous the things some people make up.'

'It certainly is,' Bart agreed.

'And what do we find just as we arrive?' Cwen asked. 'Fridolf here, claiming sanctuary because he's being chased for the murder of Scrydan.'

'Which I didn't do,' Fridolf insisted.

'You came to Derby specifically to let Hermitage know that that's exactly what you were going to do. Murder Scrydan, your master. That was the plan.'

'Yes, I know it was,' Fridolf admitted. 'But that was then. I didn't really do it.'

'Tell us what you have done, Fridolf,' Hermitage asked gently. 'Explain how you came to this situation.'

Fridolf took a breath and looked around his audience, all of whom were listening intently.

'I did go to Derby to talk to Brother Hermitage about killing Scrydan, I admit that. I thought it would be routine. But he told me I couldn't.'

Cwen snorted. 'Brother Hermitage told you not to murder the man you'd been planning to murder, so you said, oh, all right, if you say so?'

'Not exactly, but the journey back here gave me time to think. I knew it was wrong to murder anyone, but that's why you pay the wergild. To right the wrong.'

'I think there was also a bit about eternal damnation,' Hermitage mentioned.

'Oh, yes, that too.' Fridolf didn't seem as concerned about eternity.

'They weren't going to make us pay wergild,' Siward protested. 'They were going to execute us.'

'And I'd hardly murder anyone if I had to die myself,' Fridolf said. 'Would I?'

'If you knew it would lead to execution at all,' Cwen responded.

Hermitage addressed Bart. 'Why did anyone think you had anything to do with it? Surely, you arrived well after

Scrydan was murdered.'

'We did,' Siward insisted. 'That's what we kept telling everyone, but Ranulph de Sauveloy wanted an execution.'

'Ranulph de Sauveloy?' Hermitage repeated the name with a tremble.

'I'm afraid so,' John confirmed.

'And surely, they can't just decide that execution is the punishment for murder instead of a fine,' Siward complained. 'That's hardly fair.'

'We bumped into the Shire Reeve,' Bart explained. 'Rough fellow called Ansgar. We just happened to mention that we'd come from you to do Scrydan's murder, and he assumed we meant that we'd done it.'

'Which is what you said,' Cwen pointed out.

'Not really,' Siward grumbled. 'Anyway, we managed to talk to John and told him about Fridolf. He got us out of being executed.'

'Thank you, John,' Hermitage said sincerely.

John waved the praise away.

'All roads lead to Fridolf,' Cwen observed.

'Who was not going to kill anyone,' Fridolf said. 'When I got back to London, I found that Scrydan was on his way to take the clasp to William.'

'Take the what?' Hermitage asked.

'Scrydan made a huge clasp of solid gold that he was going to present to the king. Except he didn't.'

'Because he was murdered,' Hermitage nodded.

'No, I mean he didn't make it. I did.'

'You made this clasp?'

'Yes. Scrydan doesn't have the skill any more, if he ever did. He told me what he wanted and I made it. Then, he was going to take all the credit from the king.'

'Sounds reasonable to me,' Wat muttered over his wine.

'What?' Fridolf was outraged.

'You're the apprentice, he's the master. What's he going to do? Does he say to the king, "here you are, Majesty, have a nice clasp my apprentice made"? That doesn't sound very good, does it. I wouldn't be impressed by that if I was the king. I'd want gold from the master.'

'He wasn't even going to give me any acknowledgement. I think he deliberately sent me out of town so that he could go to the king on his own.'

Wat didn't seem disturbed by that, either.

'So, you came back and killed him?' Father Thomas asked as if this were quite reasonable.

'No, I didn't,' Fridolf insisted. 'I'd listened to Brother Hermitage's words and decided that I would talk to him again. After all, it was my skill keeping the workshop going, he owed me something.'

'You were seen at the time Scrydan was killed,' Bart put in. 'Edric the dung-gatherer said so.'

'The dung-gatherer?' Cwen asked. 'What does he have to do with anything?'

'His hovel is near the scene of the crime.'

'The place where Scrydan was murdered,' John corrected.

'That is good work,' Hermitage commented.

Bart smiled.

'And how does Fridolf explain this?' Cwen enquired not very politely.

'I just found him,' Fridolf said. 'I was looking for him like I told you. The apprentices told me that he'd taken the clasp so I knew where he was going. I followed. When I found him, he was already dead. Stabbed with the clasp.'

'With gold?' Wat asked. 'How do you stab someone with

gold? It's very soft.'

'I built a steel pin for the clasp and covered it in gold. It was that that stabbed him.'

Wat looked impressed by this work.

'And then,' Bart added. 'Instead of reporting the matter, or summoning the guard, Fridolf hid and kept watch over the body with his aunt, Mistress Mildrith.'

'There are too many people involved in this already,' Cwen complained. 'What's Fridolf's aunt doing there?'

'Her home was nearby.'

'The dung-gatherer's wife?'

'Hardly. She had her own hovel. Or did. It fell down when Fridolf ran through the wall.'

Cwen ran her hands over her face. 'Are we seriously being asked to believe all this?'

'It's true,' Fridolf said.

'You came to Derby to let Hermitage know that you were going to kill Scrydan. You then come back to London and arrive just at the moment Scrydan happens to be murdered. Then you hide, after which you run away. And you still say you didn't do it?'

'I didn't,' Fridolf protested. 'I promise, I didn't do it.'

'Your arrival does seem coincidental,' Hermitage said thoughtfully. 'All the way from Derby and you arrive the very evening Scrydan is going to the king?'

'Yes, well..,' Fridolf was hesitant. 'I might have arrived a bit earlier than that.'

'Oh, might you?' Cwen asked. 'Time to plan the murder, eh?'

'No. Time to have a think.'

'You were doing a lot of thinking,' Wat observed.

'I had a new idea during the walk from Derby.'

'Go on,' Hermitage encouraged.

Fridolf considered the floor in front of him. 'It's not really, erm, decent.'

'Not decent?' Cwen asked with disbelief. 'We are talking about a murder here.'

'What was the idea, Fridolf?' Hermitage pressed.

Fridolf took a deep breath and plunged in. 'I thought I could change master.'

'What?' Wat was startled from his wine at that. 'You did what?'

'I know, I know. It was outrageous.'

'I'll say,' Wat agreed.

'But Scrydan wasn't going to make me up to master. Perhaps someone else would.'

Wat explained the problem with this very carefully. 'Apprentices do not decide who their masters are.'

'Not normally, no. But I was desperate.'

'So, you went and talked to some of the other goldsmiths?' Hermitage asked.

'I did.' Fridolf hung his head in shame.

'And what did they say?'

'Much the same as Master Wat.'

'Quite right too,' Wat agreed.

'Remind us how your master made you up, Wat,' Cwen said slyly.

'That was completely different.'

'Didn't he die as well?'

'Everyone dies,' Wat shrugged. 'What no one does is go looking for another master.'

'They all rejected you?' Hermitage asked.

'They did,' Fridolf's dejection was clear. 'I even told them about the clasp. And the masterpiece I'd made.'

'Did you now?' Wat asked this in a very thoughtful way. 'And what did they say to that?'

'They were very interested, but still said there was nothing they could do.'

'Yes, I imagine they did. How many goldsmiths are there in London?'

'About six.'

'About six? What do you mean, about six?'

'Some aren't really recognised by the others.'

'Why not?'

'Suspicions about the quality of the metal, that sort of thing.'

'They sound like an honourable bunch,' Wat observed. 'And Scrydan was one of them.'

'Oh, he thought he was better than them like he was better than me. Ha!'

'So,' Father Thomas said thoughtfully. 'That's why you killed him.'

'What?' Fridolf rose from his chair. 'I have told you that I didn't kill him. Why won't you believe me?'

Thomas didn't seem put off by the outburst. 'Scrydan would not make you up to master and the other masters turned you down. It seems you had many reasons to wish him dead.'

'We all wish a lot of people dead, but that doesn't mean we kill them,' Fridolf argued.

'But Scrydan is dead. Somebody did it, and you seem the most likely.'

'Hardly a sound conclusion, Father,' Hermitage observed. 'We must eliminate all those who might have done it to identify the one who must have.'

Father Thomas looked at Hermitage for some moments as

he considered this. 'What?' he said.

'It is true that Fridolf may well have committed the murder,' Hermitage went on.

'What?' Fridolf was still on his feet.

'But it is also possible that he did not.'

'It's more than possible,' Fridolf protested.

'Until we are certain, we cannot draw our conclusion. Much less can we send anyone to their execution.' Hermitage thought that must be clear.

'Who are you suggesting?' Thomas asked.

'No one at all, that's what we need to find out.'

'Ridiculous,' Thomas huffed. 'This young man is all we need.'

'Or six goldsmiths,' Wat offered. 'Six goldsmiths who didn't get on with Scrydan. Who would not want to see him gain favour with the king ahead of them.'

'Are you seriously suggesting that craftsmen kill one another to advance their own trade?' Thomas was incredulous.

'Suggesting?' Wat asked. 'No, I don't suppose I'm suggesting it.' He left a pause for effect. 'I'm stating a fact.'

Caput XIV: Division of Labour

It took some time to drag Wat from Father Thomas's fireside and his wine, but they were now gathered outside the boundary of Saint Paul's bidding farewell to Fridolf.

'Am I safe with him?' Fridolf asked. 'He thinks I did it.'

'You are in sanctuary,' Hermitage explained. 'No one can do anything to you. And if you come with us you will be open to the attentions of Ranulf de Sauveloy.'

Fridolf could see where his best option lay.

'Go and sit by the fire and drink the wine,' Wat said with obvious unhappiness.

At that moment, the young cleric returned. 'Father Thomas has bid me come and get you,' he said to Fridolf. 'I will take you to your work.'

'Work? What work?'

'Oh, there's a lot to be done here and there.'

'But I've claimed sanctuary.'

'Sanctuary from the accusation of murder, I understand. You now owe the church your life.'

'It is only fair that you make some contribution for your food and drink and shelter,' Hermitage said. 'I'm sure it will be nothing too onerous.'

Fridolf gave a rather hopeless look and turned to follow the cleric.

'I had best get back,' John said. 'Margaret will be sending men to find Fridolf and now we have him, we don't need to bother. And with Brother Hermitage investigating, I am sure it will not be long before our killer is caught.' With an overoptimistic wave, he left them.

Hermitage didn't share John's confidence. It was all very well arguing that Fridolf may not have done it, but finding out who did would present him with the usual difficulties.

Dishonest people would be encountered, shameful actions discovered and disgraceful motivations revealed. All of which would lead to the final identification of a sinner of appalling depth.

And, if the past was anything to go by, that sinner wouldn't even be repentant. It was bad enough having to discover these people, but their resenting Hermitage for uncovering their deed seemed an outrage too far.

Just as he was pondering the next steps, Cwen was shaking her head. 'It must be Fridolf,' she said.

'Really?' Hermitage asked. He thought they'd been over this. 'He seems sincere when he says that he didn't do it.'

'Oh, yes, seems sincere,' Cwen said. 'That's all right then. But think about it. We know all the business of him coming to Hermitage and then Scrydan being dead. Fridolf runs for sanctuary and now we know why.'

'Yes, because people were assuming he'd done it.'

'Or it's because he really did do it. He offered to pay the wergild, didn't he?'

'Well, yes.'

'But then, he comes here, finds the other masters turn him down and so he does the deed.

'But then what? Word comes from the Normans that they want this killer. Fridolf probably even gets his purse out, ready to pay. Only then does he find out that the punishment for murder is now execution.

'Well, that's enough to make anyone run for their lives.'

'But he didn't run,' Siward pointed out. 'He hid in Aunt Mildrith's hovel.'

'Only because no one knew he was there. As soon as you knocked the house down, he was off.'

'We didn't knock the house down,' Bart protested. 'Fridolf did that himself.'

'Whoever knocked the house down,' Cwen was impatient with the details. 'Fridolf ran for sanctuary.'

Hermitage thought about this and had to admit that it did not look good for Fridolf. They had no confession, but all of the information they did have pointed to the young apprentice. 'But he insists that he didn't do it.'

'Oh, that's all right then,' Cwen said. 'As long as he says that he didn't do it, he must be innocent. After all, a murderer wouldn't lie as well as kill people, would he?' She looked hard at Hermitage for an answer to this.

'In the face of overwhelming evidence, I don't know that he would. When we've found other murderers and confronted them with the incontrovertible truth, they've admitted everything. In fact, a few of them have boasted about their actions. Why continue to deny if you really did do it?'

'Avoid execution, perhaps?' Cwen suggested.

'There is that,' Hermitage accepted. 'Or Fridolf could be telling the truth. And we would not want to send an innocent man to his death.'

Cwen shook her head in disappointment. 'I don't know how we're going to find anyone who looks more guilty than Fridolf,' she huffed. 'He is the only one who actually asked if he could kill Scrydan. I assume you didn't have a queue, Hermitage?'

'No, of course not.' He didn't like to think that Cwen had a point. Other than finding someone who was prepared to confess, he didn't know how Fridolf's apparent guilt could be avoided.

144

'We will simply have to find out what we can and see where that leaves Fridolf. In the meantime, we shall simply have to think of him as our, what could you call it?'

'Here we go,' Cwen sighed. 'Here comes the Latin.'

'Prime suspect,' Hermitage announced, very satisfied with the nomenclature; and that it was nomenclature.

'Told you,' Cwen rolled her eyes.

'Now,' he said to Bart and Siward, anxious to move on before any more doubts about Fridolf were raised. 'You mentioned the Shire Reeve, Ansgar?'

'That's right,' Siward confirmed. 'Terrible man, by all accounts.'

'He sent us for execution,' Bart pointed out.

'Only because you confessed,' Cwen reminded them.

'Was he investigating the murder, then?' Hermitage asked.

'Well, he was at Scrydan's workshop and that seemed to be his business.'

'Why are we interested in him?' Wat asked. 'Better to get the goldsmiths direct, I'd have thought. I wouldn't be at all surprised to find one or two of them are a lot closer to Scrydan's death than they ought to be.'

'Bit risky,' Cwen observed. 'Judging other crafts by your own standards.'

Hermitage was used to their to and fro, so carried on as if they hadn't said anything useful. Which they hadn't, anyway. 'The goldsmiths are certainly people we must speak to, but if this Ansgar is investigating, he may already have done so. We could save a lot of time.' Hermitage also held out the hope that Ansgar may have a very good idea who the killer was and so he wouldn't need to do much at all.

'He jumped at the chance of Bart and Siward doing it,' Cwen said. 'I'm not sure he's going to be much help.'

'Nonetheless, he will be a place to start. We just have to find him.'

'Perhaps we could do both,' Wat suggested. 'We could cover more people more quickly.'

'You mean you wouldn't have to go and talk to a sheriff,' Cwen said.

'I don't get on with them,' Wat admitted. 'Always asking questions and sticking their noses where they aren't wanted.'

'Which is their job.'

'I'd be much better dealing with some goldsmiths, you know, craft to craft. They may even have heard of me. And let's be honest, if a monk turns up in a goldsmith's they probably think he's come to buy a plate. And they're not likely to be forthcoming about any murder plans they had.'

'And they will with you?' Bart asked.

'I can tell when someone's hiding something. Especially another craftsman.'

'I suppose the King's Investigator talking to the sheriff could be for the best,' Cwen admitted. 'He might not want to say anything if he found out he was talking to Wat the Weaver.'

'We go to the sheriff and you go to the goldsmiths, then,' Siward said as if it was agreed.

'Erm,' Wat hesitated. 'I was thinking perhaps I'd go to the smiths with Bart and Siward, Hermitage and Cwen can do the sheriff.'

'And why's that?' Cwen demanded.

'You know what these old craftsmen are like,' Wat said as if apologising for them.

'Can't deal with a woman,' Cwen huffed. 'And how do you know they're old?'

'Bound to be.'

'So, why do you want Bart and Siward with you?'

'For one thing, Ansgar probably still thinks they killed Scrydan, so it might not be best if they turn up asking questions. And another, having them with me will be a bit more persuasive, three of us instead of one.'

'It sounds like you know these goldsmiths personally,' Cwen was suspicious.

'Not at all. I've met one or two in my time and they were as soft and slippery as their metal. Just going prepared.'

Cwen didn't say any more and seemed to accept that this was the best plan or the least worst.

'So, how do we find this Ansgar?' Hermitage asked. 'And how do you find the goldsmiths?'

'Oh, they'll be nearby. Nobles and the Church, they're the only people who use goldsmiths. Got to be near your customers.'

'Ansgar said he was the Shire Reeve of Middelseaxe, wherever that is,' Siward said.

'We're in Middelseaxe,' Wat said with a sigh. 'Well, we would be if the Saxons were still in charge. Doubtless, William will change the name to West Normandy, or something. I should just ask anyone you meet. Most people know where the sheriff is, even if it's only to avoid him.'

'Come on then, Hermitage, Cwen said. 'Let's leave the slippery craftsmen to their business.'

Wat gave Siward and Bart a tip of the head, indicating that they should follow him along the street away from the church.

'Pick someone, then, Hermitage,' Cwen said.

Hermitage looked around at the people who were coming and going and wondered what sort of person would know where the sheriff was.

Everyone looked busy about their business and most had the downward gaze of those who did not want to be interrupted.

One fellow was pulling a small cart with a barrel on it and so had to move more slowly through the mud of the street.

'Excuse me?' Hermitage asked as he stepped alongside.

'Ar,' the man replied without looking up.

'Do you know where we might find the sheriff?'

The man did stop now and looked at Hermitage. 'Who?'

'The sheriff. Erm, Shire Reeve, if you will.'

The man considered Hermitage a little more deeply. 'I never touched you,' he said for some reason.

'Erm, no, of course not.'

'What do you want the sheriff for, then?'

'We want to talk to him.'

'About me?' the man asked quite angrily.

'Well, no, not about you at all. I don't even know who you are.'

'Let's keep it that way, then.' The man spat on the ground and trundled on.

'What an extraordinary fellow,' Hermitage commented.

Cwen was simply shaking her head, whether that was in disappointment at the fellow or Hermitage, wasn't too clear.

Another man was walking smartly along the street, clearly with somewhere he had to be. He stopped smartly when Cwen obstructed his passage.

'What, what?' he asked rapidly.

'Where's the sheriff?' Cwen demanded.

'The who?' The man was looking around Cwen, clearly trying to see if there was some way out of this encounter.

'The sheriff. Ansgar. Heard of him?'

'Of course, I've heard of him. He's got a house by the

Crypel Gate, hasn't he?'

'Has he? And where's that?'

'Well, it's north, isn't it?'

'North of here?

'No, go east and then take the Woode Street on the left.'

'There you are. That wasn't hard, was it?'

The man didn't look convinced but at least Cwen now moved out of his way.

'Come on then, Hermitage,' she said cheerfully. 'We find the north.'

'Erm, yes.' He followed her along the street, back away from Saint Paul's and on, looking for a thoroughfare to the left.

Fortunately, there was only one that had to be the Woode Street. This was busy with all manner of people and goods going back and forth and it headed straight north.

A monk and a woman walking together seemed to attract no attention at all, everyone being focused on their own business.

Every now and again, a Norman soldier was spotted, or rather, they were spotted by a Norman soldier. This brought a glare of challenge, although what trouble a monk and a woman were going to cause was a mystery.

It did explain why all the local folk were concentrating on moving along and not giving any cause for concern.

After only a few paces along the road, the wall of London was visible ahead, houses and hovels clustered under its shelter. None of them looked particularly grand or imposing from here, so perhaps Ansgar occupied a normal house.

In amongst these, the road could be seen to wind through a very small gap which presumably took it on to the gate in the wall.

As they drew near they saw that this gate really was small. Hermitage supposed that it would exert a good measure of control as people had to almost stoop to get through and it was more like a tunnel than a gate. On the other hand, it was a point of congestion and the Alders Gate, that they had come through was much easier and not that far away.

It also seemed obvious which was the sheriff's house. One building seemed to be the focus of attention for most of the people milling about in the area. Two Norman soldiers even stood outside, doing nothing other than watching in case anyone started milling inappropriately.

It was quite a grand house now they were up close, although examination revealed that it had fallen into a state of disrepair. Two storeys high, with real glass in some of the windows, it must have been the home of someone of considerable import.

Cwen and Hermitage approached with some trepidation, although, to be accurate, that was only Hermitage. Cwen marched straight up to the front door.

A harassed-looking woman stood just on the inside of the door, talking in an urgent manner to a man who obviously wanted to come in but wasn't being permitted.

As they got close, the end of the conversation could be heard.

'And I've told you, Hartha, the sheriff will attend to your business when he attends to it and not before. There's no point you standing about here because he's not going to see you.'

'How am I supposed to run my tavern without the sheriff's charter?' The fellow who must be Hartha complained.

'The same way you've run it for the last few years,' the woman explained. 'Without the sheriff's charter.'

'And then he'll come and fine me for running a tavern without his charter.'

'It's the risk you run,' the woman explained. 'But between you and me, the last thing the sheriff is worried about is taverns and their charters, now be off with you.'

Hartha grumbled and complained but did turn away and amble down the street.

'We'd like to see the sheriff, Ansgar,' Cwen said.

The woman ignored them and shouted back into the house. 'Culric, if you don't clear that privy I'll come down there and throw you in it.' She turned back to Cwen. 'Now what?'

'We want to see the sheriff.'

'Of course, you do. And you can't, so be off.'

'We want to see the sheriff about the murder of Scrydan.'

'Scrydan? He's all done with now. You're too late for any of that.'

Hermitage wasn't clear what "any of that" might be.

'This is Brother Hermitage, he is King William's investigator.'

The woman looked Hermitage up and down. 'He's a monk.'

'And he is King William's investigator.'

'Well, good for him.'

'And he wants to talk to the sheriff. So, if you'd like to tell Ansgar that the king's own investigator is here, I'm sure that won't be a problem.'

The woman folded her arms at this and seemed to be considering her options. She cast a glance over to the two Norman soldiers who were starting to take an interest in this encounter.

'He's not going to be happy,' the woman explained.

'Oh, dear,' Cwen said without the slightest interest.

With a huff and a tut, the woman turned back to the interior, saving a glance of irritation for Hermitage as she did so.

He tried to look apologetic for causing a fuss and just hoped that Cwen couldn't see.

After a few moments wait, the woman returned to the door and a huge shape followed behind.

Hermitage practised his apologetic look again.

'What's this?' the very large Saxon man who must be Ansgar barked. Even Cwen seemed a little awed by his appearance. 'King's Investigator?' The title sounded like something rather revolting on Ansgar's lips.

'Erm, yes, that's right,' Hermitage had to say.

A deep rumble emerged from somewhere inside the sheriff. 'We didn't defeat the Normans to have their lackeys forced upon us, you know.'

Hermitage's mind filled with only one thing to say; "actually, we didn't defeat the Normans", but he could tell that it would not be welcome.

'I was appointed by Harold,' he managed to say instead. 'Originally.'

'Ha!' This seemed to placate Ansgar somewhat. 'Then you have my sympathy.'

'Thank you.'

'What's an investigator for, anyway?' Ansgar asked. 'It's the second time I've heard that word.'

'I track murders, you know, find out who did it. I am looking into the death of Scrydan.'

'No need to worry there then. His killers confessed. They've been dealt with.'

Hermitage hated to disappoint a man so large and angry as Ansgar. 'Perhaps we could come in and have a word?'

'Is she this investigator as well?' Ansgar glanced at Cwen.

'I'm Cwen,' Cwen said. 'I go where he goes.'

Ansgar considered her for a moment. 'I can see that you do, mistress. Come in then, but I'm a busy man. The sooner we get these Normans out of the place the sooner we can get back to normal.'

Hermitage followed Ansgar into the house, wondering how much disappointment one huge Saxon could take without turning nasty.

Caput XV: Streets of Gold

'Goldsmiths, goldsmiths,' Wat muttered as he, Bart and Siward wound through the narrow streets around Saint Paul's.

'What does their sign look like?' Siward asked. He looked up at the buildings around them and could see the insignia of carpenters, blacksmiths, tanners and leather workers, each indicating to passers-by where they might find the trade they were looking for.

'They tend not to make a display of where they are,' Wat explained.

'How do they do business, then?'

'They're goldsmiths,' Wat sighed his frustration at such ignorance. 'People don't wander the streets thinking, "I wonder where I can get some gold and jewels made into a massively expensive treasure". They know where the goldsmiths are. Or rather their people do.

'The likes of the nobles and the church don't generally go to the goldsmiths, the goldsmiths go to them. Some humble servant will turn up at the workshop and say that the goldsmith is wanted. And off they go.'

'It's a funny way to do business,' Siward observed.

'Very lucrative one,' Wat replied rather wistfully. 'There's nothing the customer of a goldsmith likes more than saying his treasure cost twice as much as anyone else's. If only it was the same for tapestry.'

'So, how do we find them?'

'We look for the indications,' Wat said mysteriously. 'Mind you, they can be well hidden.'

'Wouldn't a goldsmith want to show how wealthy he is?'

154

Siward asked. 'Their workshop would be grander than the others?'

'Not likely.' Wat dismissed that silly idea. 'Sure way of getting yourself robbed. People only steal things from places that look like they've got something worth stealing.'

'What are the indications, then?' Bart asked.

Wat pointed upwards. 'There will be a furnace, so a fire and smoke. Blacksmiths have theirs on display, goldsmiths keep them hidden, so we look for smoke rising from the back of a house instead of the front.

'We also look to see if we can spot anyone far too well-dressed to be wandering the muddy streets. Even the servants who go to the goldsmiths are important.

'And, if all that fails..,' Wat had stopped outside a door that was firmly closed. 'We look for the one closed door in a street of merchants and craftsmen plying their trade.' He hammered on the door.

They all waited while Wat looked confident that his call would be answered.

Eventually, the door creaked open the smallest slice and a cautious head appeared. 'Yes?' It sounded as cautious as it looked, as if it didn't know whether this caller was bringing money or had come to take it away.

'I'd like to see the goldsmith,' Wat said.

The head behind the door considered Wat carefully; very carefully indeed. The appraisal went from top to bottom and back up again. Wat's habitual clothing was given careful examination. His fine jerkin with its embroidered patterns including points picked out in gold thread was looking good, despite their journey.

His leather and fabric belt, with its detailed images of deer parading around his waist, was neat and in good order. The leggings of very fine soft leather were clean and neat and descended into his pride and joy; the pair of leather boots, which, despite having tramped from Derby to London, displayed their quality for all to see.

To add to the show, Wat took the small scented cloth from his belt and dabbed it to his nose.

'Who shall I say is calling?' the face asked, apparently satisfied that this was someone worthy of consideration.

Wat leaned forward and lowered his voice. 'Wat the Weaver.'

The eyes on the cautious face widened. 'Wat the Weaver?' it repeated with some awe.

'The same.'

'The Wat the Weaver?'

'There is only one. As far as I know.'

'Come in, sir,' the face now transformed into a show of interest bordering on avarice. The door was opened and it was plain from the look and the obsequiousness that Wat's dubious reputation for the production of very questionable tapestries was irrelevant. His reputation for having money was all that mattered.

Now holding the door open, the small figure of a workshop drudge or apprentice stood before them. He was a young man with a well-used apron around his front and wooden clogs on his feet, doubtless protection from the sparks and spits of the furnace.

He bowed to Wat. 'Will your slaves stay outside?' he asked.

'My what? Oh, my slaves. No, they can come in. They accompany me everywhere and are quite trustworthy.'

Bart and Siward gave Wat scowls of disapproval but said nothing.

'Come, slaves,' Wat instructed as he stepped forward.

The young man led the way into the house, which was not large, but opened out at the back into the main workshop.

Here, at benches set around the outside of the room, three figures worked diligently, heads bowed over their tasks. A variety of tools could be seen; fine chisels for engraving, small anvils and hammers for bending and forming, touchstones for testing metal, and rabbit fur for polishing. None of the workers looked up at the arrivals.

In the middle of the space sat a modest furnace, and their guide stepped over to this to give the bellows a couple of hearty pumps.

'The master is this way.' Off to the left and out of the main working area there was a much more comfortable spot. Here, a warming fire burned, reed matting covered the earthen floor, and a table with three chairs was sitting idle. This was doubtless the place the goldsmith himself received any visitors.

By the side of the fire, a large wooden chair was drawn up, scattered with expensive-looking feather cushions, in the middle of which slumbered a very large shape indeed. There was no sign that this man visited the workbenches himself, and looking at him, Wat doubted that he could make it that far.

Their escort gave a modest cough.

'Eh, what, what?' the shape in the cushions stirred very quickly.

The boy stepped up in front of what must be his master and spoke quickly and plainly. 'Wat the Weaver calls upon you, master. The Wat the Weaver. And his slaves.' He turned to Wat. 'This is Master Eligius, the goldsmith.'

The one waking up moved seamlessly from anger at being

woken for no good reason, to naked self-interest at being woken for a very good reason. He shifted in his chair to look at Wat but didn't get up.

'Wat the Weaver, eh?' he said with obvious interest.

Wat gave a bow.

'And slaves.' The goldsmith observed. He beckoned Wat to draw close for a confidential word. 'Normans don't approve of slavery, you know,' he informed Wat. 'Take my advice, call them servants. Same thing.'

Wat acknowledged the helpful words with a nod.

'Sit ye, sit ye,' Eligius gestured towards the chairs.

Wat pulled one over and Siward and Bart went to do likewise.

'Not you!' Eligius snapped. 'Good God above. Know your place.'

Wat shook his head. 'They're not used to London ways,' he explained.

Siward and Bart retreated with unhappy looks.

'Hm,' Eligius didn't seem too happy about that.

'Master Eligius, eh?' Wat said.

Eligius waved this away. 'A name of convenience. Most of the goldsmiths of London use them. A sort of tradition, if you like. Patron saint of goldsmiths, Eligius, you see?'

'Ah, very clever.' Wat smiled. 'And keeps your real name from those who might make use of it.'

'Just so, just so,' Eligius chortled. 'Boy! Wine,' he shouted at his drudge, who hurried off to do as he was told. 'Now. What brings Wat the Weaver to my door, eh?'

'Trade, of course,' Wat said reassuringly. 'You may not know this, but I am recently married.'

'Married? Wat the Weaver?' Eligius seemed to have some trouble taking this in.

158

'Married indeed. And it came to me that I would gift my wife something precious. A token of love, if you like.'

'Well, of course, of course.'

'My craft has been successful,' Wat went on. 'Very successful,' he emphasised. 'But what is the point of that success if it cannot be shared, eh?'

'Or displayed, yes?' Eligius suggested.

'You have it exactly. So, I have come to London, searching out the very best.'

'You need search no further.' Eligius held his hands wide as if the excellence of his workshop should be obvious.

'I am sure you are right,' Wat agreed. 'But naturally, I will see many workshops before making a commission.'

Eligius didn't seem put out by this. 'See as many as you will. You will return to Eligius by the end.'

'You could well be right.' Wat plucked a name from the air. 'Scrydan is the only other name I have heard.'

'Scrydan?' There was a moment of hardness in Eligius's voice but it soon softened. 'You have no need to concern yourself with Scrydan. He's dead.'

'Dead?'

'Murdered.'

'No!'

'Just so. He always was a contrary fellow and now he is no more.'

'Not a name of convenience, by the sound of it.'

'Scrydan was not a man of convenience in any way,' Eligius confided.

'Nor of quality?'

'Oh, his quality was good enough, I suppose. If you like that sort of thing.'

'That sort of thing?' Wat asked mildly.

The drudge now appeared with the wine and served a flagon to Wat and Eligius.

'Send Cyneruth over with the armband,' Eligius instructed the boy.

'You will see,' Eligius was confident. 'Of course, this may not be the sort of thing you have in mind, but it will illustrate the quality of my workshop.'

A new young man appeared now and he was plainly an apprentice. He must be about Fridolf's age and wore a full-length apron, which was marked and smeared.

He had a wary look on his face, and in his hands, which trembled slightly, he bore a fine armband.

The body of it was leather, but lined on both edges and evenly studded throughout, elegant gold and small jewels made the thing shine.

'Pass it to master Wat,' Eligius snapped as if his apprentice should have known this.

'Thank you, Cyneruth.' Wat took the piece and examined it. 'Fine work,' he commented. 'Very fine indeed.'

Cyneruth stood slightly straighter and chanced a small smile.

'Be off,' Eligius instructed. 'Back to your work.'

Cyneruth nodded and took half a step to retrieve the armband.

'Well, leave that with master Wat, you idiot,' Eligius barked.

Cyneruth did as he was told but looked slightly confused as to how he was to get back to his work when Wat had it in his hands.

'You see the quality of my work,' Eligius commented on his apprentice's work.

'Just so,' Wat agreed. 'Scrydan did not do so well?'

160

'Crude,' Eligius dismissed the other's work.

'Crude, eh?'

'I have engraved this gold to meld into the leather in a delicate dance with the jewels.'

Wat could see where Cyneruth had done this.

'Scrydan would have done the whole thing in gold. Awful.'

'That would be a lot of gold,' Wat observed.

'Exactly my point. No subtlety, no artistry. Take a slab of gold and stick it on your arm, that was Scrydan. But, as I say, you don't need to be concerned about him as he's dead now.'

'One less goldsmith, eh?' Wat said conspiratorially.

'One less troublesome fellow in general.'

'Really?' Wat sounded as if this was just making conversation as all his attention was on the armband.

'Never a supporter of his fellows,' Eligius gossiped. 'I'm sure you understand. Weavers stand together, goldsmiths stand together.'

'But not Scrydan?' Wat turned the band over in his hand and peered at it intently.

'Only interested in Scrydan,' Eligius complained. 'Take the Normans, for example. Trample over his own children to ingratiate himself, he would.'

'Did he have children?'

'Er, no. But if he did, he would.'

'Trample over his fellow craftsmen though, eh? I know the type.'

'I'm sure you do. So, what do you think?' Eligius nodded towards the armband.

'A fine piece, very fine. I shall certainly bear it in mind as I make my decision. I can see that you have talented apprentices.'

'Hm? Oh, yes, I suppose so.'

'Space for a new master perhaps, now that Scrydan is gone?'

'Oh, I think not. London is well serviced by us. No need to go disturbing the business.'

'I'd do exactly the same myself.' Wat winked. 'Well, I had better be on my way. Don't get up,' he said to Eligius who showed no sign of the intent or ability to get up. 'I shall return this to Cyneruth.' He held the armband out.

'It's been a pleasure meeting you, Wat the Weaver,' Eligius said, holding out a hand to be shaken. 'You'll be back, see if you aren't.'

Wat shook the hand and gestured Siward and Bart to follow him.

He went over to Cyneruth, who was taking the opportunity to tidy his bench, and handed over the armband.

'Very good work, young man,' he said quietly. 'I am sure you will be a master before long.'

The roll of Cyneruth's eyes said all that Wat needed to hear.

'I, erm, hear that the work of Scrydan usually had a lot more gold in it?'

Cyneruth said nothing but cast a glance over towards his master.

'Between you and I,' Wat assured him. 'I have now met your master and I have to say I have no love for him. I've seen his sort before and your best hope is to wait until he dies in that chair. Which may not be long.'

Cyneruth failed to hide the smile at that thought.

'Scrydan?' Wat prompted.

'Murdered,' Cyneruth whispered as he made great play of taking the armband back and searching for the next tool. 'By two strangers.' He gave Siward and Bart a glance at this as if

162

warning them to beware of two strangers.

'But his gold?' Wat asked.

'He had so much of it,' Cyneruth confided. 'It drove the other masters to distraction. The metal is hard to come by these days. If I could have made this armband of gold, I would, but we don't have enough.'

'So? What did they do? I can't imagine they just shrugged and said, good luck to him.'

'They agreed everyone would watch him. All the smiths and apprentices.'

'And the one who discovered something would be rewarded, I wager,' Wat concluded.

Cyneruth didn't answer that.

'But Scrydan continued conjuring up gold?'

'No one knew where he got it from, but the rumour was that the clasp he made for William was solid.'

'That must have annoyed the others no end.'

'They never liked him anyway, but then nobody did. If you think Eligius is bad, you never met Scrydan. But when he let it be known that he had a solid gold clasp for the king..,'

'They weren't happy.'

'To say the least. A lot of gold is something to kill for, isn't it?'

Cyneruth did not deny that but shrugged as if that was the sort of thing he didn't know anything about.

Shaking his head at this sorry tale, Wat gave Cyneruth a pat on the shoulder and assurance that he wouldn't breathe a word to his master. He gave a final wave to Eligius, who couldn't see them anyway. The drudge let them out of the workshop back onto the street and firmly closed the door behind them.

'Well,' Wat said brightly. 'Wasn't that interesting? Not

only did Fridolf want his master dead, but so did the other masters. And they set people to watch him.'

'I can't see Eligius doing it,' Bart said. 'I don't know when he last got out of that chair. It stank.'

'He's a goldsmith,' Wat explained. 'He wouldn't do anything himself, he'd pay someone to do it for him.'

'Including kill Scrydan?'

'Quite possibly,' Wat mused. 'I don't think we need to bother with the other goldsmiths now. Eligius has told us all we need. Let's see if we can find Hermitage and Cwen. Then we can start putting this story together.

'I can see why you didn't want Cwen to come with you to the goldsmiths,' Siward said as they walked along. 'Are you really going to commission a treasure for her? What a lovely idea.'

Wat stopped walking and looked at him. 'Don't be stupid. What gave you that idea?'

'Er, you did. You just said it.'

'That was just to get in with the goldsmith. I can hardly go up and ask him what he knows about Scrydan's murder straight out, can I?' He considered Siward and shook his head. 'Commission a treasure? Ha!'

Siward whispered to Bart as they walked on. 'I don't think we'd better go into the detail of Wat's discussion when we see Cwen.'

'Good God, no,' Bart agreed very quickly.

'We've just got to hope he doesn't.'

Bart looked at Wat with worry on his face. 'He wouldn't be that stupid, would he?'

Caput XVI: The Sheriff's In Town

ermitage and Cwen followed Ansgar into the house and quickly saw that it was a warren of activity. People were bustling in and out, most of them quite oblivious to the presence of the sheriff.

He took them through to a room at the back of the place, pushing aside a cloth that functioned as the door.

Hermitage took one look at the space and didn't know whether to sit down in shock or delight. It was a room of parchment. And not just parchment, whole books were in here of all shapes and sizes, every one of them calling to him to find out what they hid behind their inviting covers.

A table at the back of the room had more material on it and Hermitage could just make out a scribe, sitting behind an outrageously exciting pile.

It was the piles that worried Hermitage. Some of them seemed so tall and precarious that toppling was surely inevitable. And if that happened, damage could ensue.

Perhaps more at risk were the tomes and documents that already lay on the floor, seemingly scattered about as if some great wind had passed through leaving them in its wake. He positively shook as he saw Ansgar step around and over these with horrible carelessness.

Shelves around the walls had haphazard collections seemingly stuffed into every spare bit of space, and he noticed that some of the books even had extra pages sticking out as if being used as bookmarks.

It was either that or, God forbid, the books were falling apart. He put a hand out to the doorway to steady himself.

'This looks like a lot to get through,' Cwen said, Hermitage being quite incapable of speech. His first thought was to rescue this massive body of work from the abuse it was suffering.

'Ha!' Ansgar's cry smacked of long-held desperation.

'Is this what sheriffs do?' Cwen asked. She picked up the nearest piece of parchment and looked at it. She then seemed to wonder why she'd done that and put it down again.

Hermitage, taking her lead, stooped and selected a piece from the floor, where it lay face down, simply crying out for succour.

He scanned this and saw that it was an old Saxon document, granting a right of passage for two cows over London Bridge on the first Sunday after Lent. Even he had to admit that that wasn't very interesting.

'This should not be what sheriffs do,' Ansgar complained. 'But the wretched Normans say everything must be in order.'

Hermitage glanced around and saw that order was still a long way off. 'They do like things that way,' Hermitage observed sympathetically.

'That's why the sooner they're gone, the better,' Ansgar grumbled.

'They do seem to be rather, erm, settled,' Hermitage said politely. 'William has built his castle, after all.'

'It's a damnable insult, that's what it is,' Ansgar swore. 'After their defeat, they come here and start building. It's not right.'

'Yes,' Hermitage said carefully. 'About this defeat. I thought that matters near Hastings rather went the other way?' He tried to sound as if this was an insignificant enquiry from an ill-informed monk.

'Not Hastings.' Ansgar snapped. 'I'm not talking about Hastings and Harold's disaster. I'm talking about

166

Southwark.'

'Southwark?'

Ansgar sighed very impatiently, which did nothing for Hermitage's ease.

The sheriff stated the case very plainly. 'The Normans were defeated at Southwark. By me.'

'Were they? I did not know that.'

Ansgar threw his hands in the air and walked around in a small circle, trampling several documents as he did so. 'Everyone seems intent on forgetting,' he complained loudly.

Hermitage wasn't sure how he could forget something he hadn't known in the first place. He noticed the scribe bury his head further into his work. This was obviously a common topic of conversation.

'The Normans marched here from Hastings, yes?' Ansgar asked.

'Erm, yes, I suppose they would,' Hermitage agreed.

'When they got here, they tried to cross the river by the bridge and enter London, but we were ready for them.

'Try as they might, they couldn't break through. We held them back, me and the nobles, Morcar and Eadwine. We rallied the Saxons and defeated William's forces in mighty battle.'

'Defeated, I see.'

'And they left with their tails between their legs.'

'Very good.'

'It was very good,' Ansgar agreed. 'But then what did they do?'

'I'm not sure I know.'

'They travelled west, crossed the river at Wallingford and came into London from the north. Deceitful cowards.'

Hermitage tutted obligingly.

'And the good people along the way started surrendering.' Ansgar clearly didn't think these were good people at all. 'By the time William got back to London, it was surrounded. Eadwine and Morcar turned out to be nobles without nobility, and fled.'

'But you remained?'

'Of course. I would have defeated them again if anyone had stood at my side.'

'And they started building their castle,' Cwen noted.

'I keep telling them that they were defeated and that they have no right to do that.'

'But they ignored you?'

'Worse than that,' Ansgar complained. 'As a gesture from the new king, William said that I could keep my estates and stay sheriff of Middelseaxe. All I needed to do was sort the place out.'

'Hence all the parchment,' Hermitage observed.

Ansgar glared around the room as if he would rather face a horde of mounted warriors than one small book.

'You mark my words,' he said. 'In years to come no one will remember that the Saxons defeated the Normans at Southwark. It'll all be Harold and the battle near Hastings. You see if I'm right.'

'You could be,' Hermitage sympathised. He wanted to get back to the question at hand, rather than have a discussion about the rights and wrongs of the Norman conquest.

'The Normans do seem to be taking things for granted, rather. And have obviously put a lot onto your shoulders. Hence having to deal with the murder of Scrydan, I assume.'

'Oh, him,' Ansgar dismissed this as the least of his worries. 'I don't know why you're worried about Scrydan, he's done and done. Two idiots turned up saying they'd done it.'

'Two idiots, yes, that would be right,' Cwen agreed.

'It is just an unfortunate part of my duties,' Hermitage said, hoping he could garner some support from Ansgar if he thought they shared the inconvenience of the Normans. 'He was found by the castle, I understand.'

'Aye, that's right. Stabbed with his own gold. The Normans found him and then I get told to discover the killer.'

'I see.'

'Discover the killer? Who do they think I am? Begging your pardon, brother,' Ansgar seemed to recognise the insult.

'Think nothing of it,' Hermitage said. 'You are the sheriff of Middelseaxe, this shouldn't be your task.'

'Damn right. But then, the two idiots turned up, I sent them to the Normans and that was that.'

'Hm,' Hermitage hummed and thought and nodded and tried to look as if he had just come up with a problem. 'From a discussion we had near Saint Paul's earlier, it seems that the two, erm, idiots, may not have done it after all. In fact, one Fridolf appears to be the prime suspect.'

'The what?' Ansgar asked with irritation.

'Oh, erm, the one most likely to have done it.'

'Fridolf?' Ansgar scowled.

'Scrydan's apprentice.'

'Aye, I know of Fridolf.'

'You do?'

'I have been sheriff for many years. You get to know your goldsmiths and their business. Permissions, charters, taxes, that sort of thing.'

Hermitage couldn't stop himself from looking around the mess and wondering what the many years of Ansgar as sheriff must have been like.

'It was all in order,' Ansgar said biting back at the criticism. 'Until the bloody Normans came through and ransacked everything like Vikings in a monastery. Begging your pardon, brother.'

'Ah, of course.'

'What was the point of that?' Ansgar asked bitterly. 'Bring ruination and then tell me to tidy it up?'

'Most unjust,' Hermitage agreed.

Ansgar took a breath and tried to calm himself. 'You say Fridolf did it?'

'It is only a possibility.'

Ansgar shrugged. 'Shame the two idiots have been executed, then. Not that I agreed with that. A simple fine would have been sufficient. But oh, no, not good enough for William and his friends.'

'I also heard that the two, erm, idiots may not have been executed, in fact. They raised the question of Fridolf and their deaths were postponed.'

'Seems fair.' Ansgar didn't seem terribly concerned about the murder of Scrydan at all.

'Do you think Fridolf could have done it, knowing him as you do? And Scrydan, I assume?'

'Always possible, I suppose. To be honest..,' Ansgar was starting to lose interest in this conversation and looked around his room as if trying to spot what it was he was supposed to be getting on with.

'To be honest?' Hermitage prompted.

'What? Oh, yes. To be honest, I'm surprised no one killed Scrydan a long time ago.'

'Really?'

'Awful fellow,' Ansgar explained. 'Hated by everyone. Except for some of the nobles. The likes of Eadwine and

Morcar bought his works, and he kept them happy.'

'But no one else?' Hermitage checked.

'You never bought anything from him?' Cwen asked.

'Me? Ha! What use have I for trinkets and trifles? The blacksmith's forge for a good sword and armour, that's where a man should devote his attention.'

'We hear he was taking a, erm, trinket to King William when he was killed.'

'And that was what killed him,' Ansgar nodded. 'It's justice of a sort, I suppose.'

'What happened to the trinket?' Cwen asked.

'What happened to it?'

'Yes. We thought it odd that he was stabbed with it and it was left in his body. We've, erm, heard that no one took it, so presumably, it was still with him. Did it go to the king in the end?'

'No,' Ansgar said. 'I was summoned to go and look at him. Me? Summoned? I ask you.'

'And it was still in him?'

'That it was.' Ansgar looked around the room. 'I've got it here, somewhere, I think. Bedric, where did that trinket go?' He addressed the scribe who now stood from behind his desk.

This was a young man, looking as harassed and out of sorts as his master. The volume of work before him was obviously a challenge, if they had even sorted out which volume was which yet.

'It's here,' Bedric replied. 'I thought I'd better put it somewhere safe. You know what people are like about gold.'

'Pah,' Ansgar dismissed such petty interests.

Bedric bent down behind his desk, rummaged about and then re-emerged.

'Here you are,' he said nonchalantly as he held the clasp out.

Cwen's mouth dropped open and her breath poured out of her like mist over a waterfall. Hermitage thought that she might have stopped breathing as it didn't seem to go back in again. Even he gazed upon this thing with wonder. He had seen gold pieces on the altar but only from a distance and even they weren't quite as, well, gold as this.

'It's,' Cwen said. She closed her mouth and swallowed. 'Quite big,' she noted, although it came out as a bit of a squeak.

'It is,' Ansgar agreed. 'You can see how it would kill him. The pin is long and the gold is heavy.'

Cwen reached out, obviously to weigh just how heavy this gold was. However, reaching out seemed to have a far deeper motivation; an impetus that almost made her look like Wat.

She took the clasp from Bedric and nearly dropped it straight away. 'Great God,' she said.

'Cwen!' Hermitage reprimanded but she took no notice.

She managed to lift the thing up in front of her, neither Ansgar nor Bedric seeming particularly interested.

'This is,' she seemed to be finding it hard to choose her words. 'Huge.'

'It is a large clasp,' Ansgar agreed. 'Far too big to be of any real use. But then I suppose that's the sort of thing kings want.' He clearly had a very low opinion of kings.

'Is it?' Cwen paused. 'Is it solid? I mean, solid gold? All of it? The whole thing? All the way through?'

'I should think so,' Ansgar even shrugged. 'It's heavy enough, that's for sure. Too soft to be any good for anything, though.'

'I have never seen so much gold,' Cwen breathed deeply

now. 'Never in one piece. Perhaps never in my life when you put it all together.'

'Scrydan always was the best supplied of the goldsmiths.' Ansgar said this as if talking about the blacksmith with the most nails.

Cwen slowly recovered her senses. 'Why would anyone leave this lying around? It must be worth a fortune. Several fortunes, probably. No one in their right mind would leave it lying anywhere, let alone in a dead body in the middle of the street.'

Ansgar frowned slightly as if he hadn't thought of that.

'If you hate Scrydan enough to kill him,' Cwen reasoned. 'You're going to steal his gold, aren't you? Even the two idiots would know to do that.'

Hermitage had a horrible thought. 'Perhaps not Fridolf, though.'

'Not Fridolf?' Ansgar asked, his irritation rising again. 'First, you say it is him, now you say it isn't?'

'No, no,' Hermitage explained. 'I mean that the one person who might not take the gold would be Fridolf.'

'Why?' Cwen asked.

Hermitage went through the reasoning as it occurred to him. 'He couldn't simply take it back to the workshop, that would be as good as a confession. How did he get it from Scrydan if not by doing the deed himself?

'Neither could he melt it down for more gold, as presumably, the sheriff here keeps a close inventory of the gold in the town so that it can be taxed.'

'Well, Bedric does,' Ansgar said.

Bedric nodded that this was the case.

'It would further explain why Fridolf kept watch on Scrydan's body, to make sure the clasp wasn't taken.' He turned to Ansgar. 'What will happen to this now?'

'The clasp?' Ansgar asked as if he didn't care.

'Yes, the clasp.'

'Hadn't thought about it. Go to the king, I suppose.' His brow creased at this. 'Although, as it hadn't been gifted to William, it can't be his, can it?' He seemed to take some small delight in this conclusion. 'Back to Scrydan's workshop, I suppose?'

'The workshop that Fridolf will now be in charge of,' Cwen reached the conclusion. 'He kills Scrydan, watches over the gold and then gets it back anyway. It's very clever.'

'I don't think we should refer to murder as clever,' Hermitage cautioned.

Bedric now came out from behind his desk, as if only just realising that he had been looking after an enormous treasure. 'Can I have another look?' he asked Cwen.

'Of course, you can,' Hermitage said when Cwen showed no sign of handing it over.

Hermitage leaned in and took the clasp from Cwen's hand. He did so with some difficulty as her fingers seemed stuck to the surface. Either that or she had developed a cramp and her hands wouldn't open.

She released a little sigh as the gold left her reluctant grasp.

Bedric simply weighed the gold in his hands and frowned. 'We have some scales, somewhere,' he said.

'I think Medwyn had them in the front,' Ansgar said. 'Weighing a goose.'

'Weighing a goose?' Cwen asked.

'Dispute over who owned a fat goose,' Ansgar explained with a growl. 'I'm a bloody Saxon noble, you know. Ancestors were Danes. Defeated the Normans at Southwark and I'm weighing bloody geese!'

174

Leaving him to his continuing disappointment, Bedric led them into the front of the house where an elderly woman sat with a dead goose at her feet.

'Medwyn?' Bedric asked directly. 'What happened to the goose?'

Medwyn almost jumped at the question. 'Erm, dispute not resolved.'

'What do you mean, not resolved?'

'It didn't weigh what either of them said. So I confiscated it?'

'And was it dead before it got confiscated?'

Medwyn hesitated. 'It was on the way out.'

'We shall speak later,' Bedric warned her. 'Now. Where are the scales?'

Medwyn nodded to a table behind the door, giving Bedric a nasty glare as she did so. When he turned his back to her, she stuck her tongue out.

'Now.' Bedric placed the gold on one side of the scales and took weights from the table for the other side. He progressively added more and more weight until the scales balanced. He looked at the weights.

'Three pounds, near enough.'

'Three pounds of gold,' Cwen breathed.

'Aye, a goodly weight,' Bedric agreed thoughtfully.

'Very goodly,' Cwen nodded.

'Hold this,' Bedric said to Cwen as he offered her the clasp.

'Yes please,' Cwen said.

Bedric led them back into the room at the rear and started looking around. 'I know it's here somewhere,' he muttered to himself. 'It's one of the ones I've already sorted.'

He scoured the shelves, obviously looking for something particular. 'Ah, here we are.'

He took a large and very well-bound volume from the shelf. It was plainly heavy and had an excellent cover, even tooled with fine engraving. This was a book of great value. Not as great a value as the gold that Cwen was now stroking, but of more interest to Hermitage's eye.

Bedric took the book over to his desk and placed it on top of the sheets of parchment that were already there, making Hermitage wince.

He opened the book, and Hermitage saw that it was a list of some sort. A clear tabulation appeared to have names and numbers in a repetitive order. The numbers in two of the columns were plainly money, the others weren't so clear.

Ansgar came over to peer at the volume.

Cwen now appeared to be explaining something to the gold clasp and looked as if she didn't want to be disturbed.

Bedric turned over several pages until he got to the section he was looking for. He then ran his fingers down the columns and turned two or three more pages as he worked his way through.

He reached a certain point and frowned. He then went back to the beginning and did it all over again.

Hermitage nodded approvingly at his diligence.

He then turned and looked at the gold clasp once more. He closed the book with a thump and turned to Hermitage and Ansgar.

'There's a problem,' he said. 'With the clasp.'

'Which is?' Hermitage asked.

'It weighs three pounds.'

'It is a huge amount of gold,' Hermitage agreed.

'It is. And there is one thing I can say for certain.' He held their gazes and tapped the pages of his book. 'In the last five years, there hasn't been enough gold in London to make it.'

Caput XVII: Simply Too Much

'Scrydan had too much gold,' Wat and Hermitage blurted the words at each other when Wat appeared at the sheriff's house with Bart and Siward.

'Well, exactly,' Hermitage agreed with himself.

The woman at the front door very reluctantly agreed that they could come in, but they weren't to settle or make themselves comfortable.

They all gathered in the front room, Medwyn having gone off on urgent goose business. Ansgar and Bedric came through from the back at the noise and Ansgar scowled hard at Bart and Siward, clearly disappointed that they were still alive. He also scowled at Wat, as if he was trying to put a name to the face.

Cwen came behind bearing her precious cargo.

'My God above,' Wat breathed when he saw the clasp. Siward and Bart looked stunned by its presence.

'I do wish people would stop taking the name of the Lord in vain every time they see a bit of gold,' Hermitage grumbled.

'That's not a bit of gold, Hermitage.' Wat's expression was a confusion of awe, greed and disbelief. 'That is a, erm, it's a, what is it? Lump is too rude. Weight isn't respectful enough. Lot. That's a lot of gold, Hermitage.'

'It is large, yes.'

'A lot. It's a lot of a lot of gold.' He stepped reverently forward and held his hands out.

There was a moment's hesitation in Cwen's eyes, but she allowed him to take it from her. Not that she didn't keep a very close eye in case he tried anything.

'Good, erm, gracious,' Wat was struggling to speak. 'This is incredible. I have never seen anything like it.'

'A work of high quality?' Hermitage checked.

'A work of high weight,' Wat explained. 'Never mind the quality.'

'Three pounds,' Hermitage said. 'The clasp weighs three pounds, doesn't it, Cwen?'

'Three pounds,' Cwen agreed in a rather peculiar voice.

'We checked it with the sheriff's own scales,' Hermitage said quite proudly.

Wat just nodded at this. 'I didn't know gold even came in pounds. I held an ounce of it, once. And I was being watched when I did that. This is, just, unbelievable.'

Hermitage was hoping Wat would move on from admiring the gold.

'We had it from one of the goldsmith's apprentices that Scrydan had more gold than the others,' Wat explained. 'Which made them hate him even more than they hated him anyway, but this is something else.'

'Yes, and..,' Hermitage began.

'And he was using it to ingratiate himself with the king. He could have a flock of kings with this thing. And a Pope.'

'I know, and..,'

'If this thing isn't a reason to want someone dead, I don't know what is.'

'We've been looking at the sheriff's records,' Hermitage managed to get in.

'Oh, yes?' Nice.' Wat didn't sound at all interested in the sheriff's records.

'And they show something even more interesting.'

'Which is?'

'Scrydan shouldn't have had the gold in the first place.

There's no record of it coming into London.' Hermitage was disappointed at Wat's continuing lack of interest.

'Very interesting.'

'Well, it is,' Hermitage insisted. 'Where did three pounds of gold come from?'

'Someone who had three pounds of gold.'

'Very helpful. The city under Ansgar was well managed.' He nodded at Ansgar. 'This is Bedric, the scribe, and he has records of all the gold brought into the town. There has simply never been enough to make the clasp. This raises serious questions about where Scrydan got the gold. It could have some connection to his death.'

'Hm,' Wat was thoughtful. 'I think I need a bit of fresh air after that,' he said, which seemed odd. 'Perhaps we'll just go outside for a moment.' He was obviously apologising to Ansgar.

The sheriff clearly had more important business, but he still frowned at Wat as he left. 'I'd better keep this,' he said, taking the gold from Wat. Cwen released a sigh at its departure.

Once outside, Wat beckoned that they should all draw near to hear his explanation.

'You can get anything you want if you know the right ways,' he said.

'Right ways?' Hermitage worried about that expression.

'Yes.' Wat spoke in a quiet voice and cast his eyes to the house as if making sure no one else was listening. 'Look, if you want to do a bit of trade without the sheriff or the local lord knowing, where's the harm?'

'Where's the harm?' Hermitage asked. 'Apart from evading the taxes?'

'Evading tax isn't really doing harm. It's doing good when

you think about it.'

'Is it?' Hermitage said these words quite firmly, hoping to make it clear that it wasn't doing good at all.

'If the king or the lord gets the taxes, what are they going to do with it? They'll probably go and have a war, or buy some weapons or something, which is bad, obviously. If the money is kept in trade, it goes around and does good for more people.

'Tradesmen don't have wars, they spend their money on one another. Everyone gains.'

'Or they turn it into gold and silver and simply keep it to themselves,' Hermitage said. 'They never spread it around, much less do they do good works, like endowing monasteries or giving alms to the poor. For some of these tradesmen, wealth seems to be an end in itself.'

'My point is,' Wat was obviously avoiding the moral issues. 'That if you need some gold that isn't in the sheriff's records, it can probably be done.'

'Three pounds of it?' Hermitage asked. 'That's a lot of gold.'

'And it wouldn't be without its problems, would it?' Bart spoke up.

They looked at him.

'Well, it's just that my old master once thought it would be a good idea to make his own coin.'

'His own coin?' Hermitage didn't understand how that would work.

'That's it. Then everyone around would have to use his coin for their trade. And he'd be able to make it and use it like everyone else.'

'Risky.' Even Wat seemed concerned about a scheme like that.

'Exactly. The king controls the coin, and he doesn't like people interfering. Nevertheless, my master found a smith who was up for making a small mint and a supplier who could get the metal.'

'Why do people put so much effort into dishonesty?' Hermitage despaired.

'It all started off all right,' Bart went on. 'But soon, the metal supplier decided he wasn't being paid enough. When the master refused to pay, he said he'd tell the king.

'Then my master said he could go ahead, as who was the king going to believe, a noble master or some crooked tradesman?'

'Awful.' Hermitage shook his head.

'That led to threats of death, come to think of it.'

'How do you know all this?' Siward asked.

'Oh, all the servants listened to everything they could. You never knew what might be useful.'

'And how was it worked out?'

'Well, it wasn't really. My master had to give it up as the king's men were sniffing about. The tradesman just disappeared.'

'Disappeared?' Hermitage asked with concern.

'Yes, with a ship full of coin, apparently. Not that he'd be able to spend it anywhere.'

'Melt it down and use it for something else,' Wat suggested. 'Which is exactly the sort of thing I'm talking about.'

'I know it is,' Hermitage said pointedly.

Wat didn't get the point. 'If Scrydan wanted to get gold, there would be someone out there to get it for him.'

'I'm obviously not the expert in this area,' Hermitage said. 'Thank goodness. But I would think that anyone who can supply three pounds of gold without it being taxed, is not

181

someone to cross.'

'And why Scrydan?' Wat asked. 'Yes, he's a goldsmith in London and has a new king to impress, but three pounds of gold is beyond most mortal men.

'If a merchant had three pounds of gold available, he'd go to someone much more important than any goldsmith. That is, if he didn't want to buy a small country and settle down.'

'But if Scrydan had the money?' Hermitage asked. 'Being one of those who had accumulated wealth through dishonest means?'

Wat nodded slowly at this but didn't seem convinced. 'It would still be more money than most can imagine.' He seemed to be working the situation through in his head.

'Scrydan takes the gold on the promise of payment. He uses it to impress the king and get commissions, after which he'll pay. But if the time came and he refused to pay, or couldn't, or didn't cooperate, or something, he might be removed from the situation.'

'It sounds horribly possible,' Hermitage said. 'But this makes the fact that the clasp was left behind even more of a problem. If this dishonest gold merchant is prepared to kill Scrydan, he would most certainly take his gold back after he'd done it.'

'Hm.' Wat could see the problem.

Hermitage pressed on. 'Which, quite apart from the question about where the gold came from, made me wonder again about Fridolf. He would want the gold returned to the workshop, which he is now in line to be master of.'

'Not if the other masters have anything to do with it,' Wat said. 'They don't see the need for a new master in London. With the short supply of gold in the first place, they want to keep what business there is to themselves.'

Hermitage sighed. 'We are creating more problems than solutions. First, we had Fridolf as our prime suspect. Now we have jealous goldsmiths and dishonest merchants to consider. What do we do, ask them all if they killed Scrydan?'

'When no one is going to say yes, anyway,' Siward observed.

No one had anything helpful to offer.

'We have to see Fridolf again,' Wat concluded. 'What can he tell us about the gold? Does he know where it came from? Who was Scrydan dealing with? Were any of the other goldsmiths really in the mood to kill him?'

'Or we press him further and find that he did do it,' Hermitage said.

'You were the one who said he was sincere when he said he didn't,' Wat pointed out.

'I was,' Hermitage admitted. 'But, I suppose his sincerity could have simply been sincere dishonesty.'

'Careful, Hermitage.' Wat said. 'You're in danger of becoming as cynical as the rest of us.'

As they started to head back to Saint Paul's, Hermitage thought that an investigation was supposed to start with a lot of people who might have done it and worked until there was only one left. This one seemed to be going in the opposite direction. He hoped that it wouldn't carry on like this or they'd soon have most of the people of London as suspects.

Cwen kindly offered to stay and guard the gold while the others all went off to find the killer, even doubting that the sheriff could do as good a job at this as she would.

Assuring her that Ansgar would be able to manage on his own, they persuaded her to go, although she cast longing backward looks quite frequently.

'We need something to eat,' Wat said. 'It's way past noon

and no one's fed us.'

There were several stalls offering food and drink along the road, and Wat delved into his purse and bought something for them all with very little complaint.

Hermitage wondered if the sight of all that gold had affected him somehow.

Back at the door of the church once more, Hermitage was left to push it open and lead the way in.

There was no Mass taking place, but he spotted a figure in clerical robes up towards the altar. He indicated that the others might stay at the door while he went over.

'Forgive me, but I am looking for Fridolf.'

The figure turned, and it was a rather elderly fellow with a pinched face who did not look happy at being disturbed. Uncharitably, Hermitage doubted that he had looked happy at anything for some years.

'What do you want him for?' the man asked quite rudely.

'I am Brother Hermitage, the King's Investigator. I am looking into the death of Scrydan and need to ask him some questions.'

'Brother what, the what?'

'King's Investigator,' Hermitage thought this was a man who would respond better to the king's title.

The man sniffed as if this was a poor reason for anything. 'He's busy.'

'That is good to hear. I can ask my questions and then he can get back to work.'

The fellow made no move to do anything.

'Perhaps Father Thomas could assist?' Hermitage asked as politely and rudely as he could.

The man huffed at this unwarranted threat. 'Oh, very well.' He beckoned that Hermitage could follow. In turn,

Hermitage beckoned that the others should come up now.

'What's this crowd?' the man asked with irritation. 'Do they all want to ask questions? We'll be here all day.'

'We shall be as quick as we can.' Hermitage tried to sound decisive, but he knew it never came across that way.

With more grumbling, the man led them off to the left of the altar and pointed to a small door. 'He's in there. Don't be long.' And with that, he was gone.

Inside was a simple room containing a cot, a table and chair and a small fireplace set in the wall. The floor was flagstones, and it was here they found Fridolf.

'That old man grabbed me and has got me scrubbing his floor,' Fridolf complained.

'I can see that,' Hermitage agreed.

'I'm a goldsmith's apprentice. What am I doing scrubbing floors?'

'You're a goldsmith's apprentice claiming sanctuary for murder,' Cwen reminded him. 'The alternative being execution for it.'

'Yes, but scrubbing floors,' Fridolf moaned. 'I could be put to better use, surely. I thought they'd want me to repair some of their gold or silver, but oh no. Scrub the floor.'

'And you're not even doing that very well,' Cwen observed. 'You've missed a bit.'

'We need to ask you some further questions, Fridolf,' Hermitage said. 'About Scrydan's gold.'

'What about it?' Fridolf whined rather, but he did stop scrubbing the floor.

'Where did he get it?' Wat asked. 'That clasp weighed three pounds.'

'Three pounds, two ounces,' Fridolf corrected. 'Without the jewels.'

'All right, three pounds, two ounces. Where did Scrydan get three pounds and two ounces of gold from?'

'According to the city records,' Hermitage said, 'there hasn't been that much gold in London for many years.'

'So where did it come from?' Wat repeated.

Fridolf looked at them all and sat back on his haunches. 'I don't know.'

'You don't know,' Wat did not sound ready to accept this as an answer. 'You don't know where enough gold to buy an army came from.'

'No, I don't.'

'But you happily turned it into a clasp,' Cwen said.

'Of course. What else was I supposed to do?'

'You're seriously telling us that you didn't know where all that gold came from and you didn't wonder?'

'Of course, I wondered. Who wouldn't? It's a huge amount, I know that. But it didn't pay to question Scrydan. He simply gave me the gold and told me what to do. I did it.'

Wat sat on the cot. 'What was the gold like when he gave it to you?'

'What was it like? It was like gold.'

'I mean what form was it in? Was it a solid mass? Like when it comes out of the ground? Was it coins to be melted? Was it already a clasp?'

'No, it was just a raw piece to be worked. It had obviously been melted down, but Scrydan did that himself.'

'The master worked his own furnace?' Wat asked. 'Now that is suspicious.'

'Did you see anyone else? Was there anyone who came around and had a private discussion with Scrydan?' Bart now asked.

'You mean a dishonest merchant who sold Scrydan the

186

gold? No, there wasn't.'

'Why would you think about a dishonest merchant?' Wat pressed.

'Because we all wondered where Scrydan got his gold. It was the gossip of the town, so we all joined in. And what sort of dishonest merchant has access to three pounds, two ounces of gold? Let alone one who would sell it to Scrydan?'

'And none of you had any ideas. Not even his own apprentices?'

'I've told you,' Fridolf insisted. 'If I knew where he got his gold, I could have got some myself. Or at least I might have some hold over him. He'd have make me up to master.' '

'Did he go anywhere and come back with it?' Cwen asked.

'Not that we saw. Mind you, Scrydan could always vanish when he wanted to.'

'We're no further forward,' Hermitage moaned.

'If we believe Fridolf,' Cwen replied.

'Listen,' Fridolf explained. 'If I knew where I could get my hands on three pounds, two ounces of gold, I wouldn't be here scrubbing floors, would I? I'd have bribed the Pope to make me king of somewhere. England, probably.'

'All right,' Wat said. 'Who are the gold merchants? Where do all the smiths get their material?'

'There's only one,' Fridolf said.

'Only one? In the whole of London?'

'Horik.'

'Horik, eh? And how did Horik get to be the only gold merchant?'

'There used to be others, but they've sort of gone.'

'Sort of gone? What do you mean, sort of gone?'

'You know. Gone. Left, died.'

'Died? The other gold merchants died? How did they die?'

'Not all of them died, but a few did,' Fridolf said. Then he frowned. 'Oh, I say, that sounds a bit suspicious, doesn't it?'

Caput XVIII: Going To The Source

'm not sure how much more of this I can manage,' Hermitage said when they stood outside Saint Paul's once more. 'First Fridolf says that he wants to kill Scrydan. The goldsmiths want him dead, now we have a gold merchant who's killed all the others.'

'We don't know that he's killed any,' Cwen said with some impatience at the rash conclusion. 'Some left and some died. People do just die.'

Hermitage sighed. 'I don't think anyone just dies anymore.'

'At least he should know about any gold,' Bart said. 'Being the only merchant.'

'Where do we find him?' Siward asked. 'I imagine gold merchants live in nice houses.'

'Oh, I'm sure they do,' Wat agreed.

'Perhaps we could have asked Fridolf.'

They all glanced back at Saint Paul's and decided that they didn't want to go there again.

'Lots of people will know where the gold merchant lives,' Wat assured him. 'The rich will know because they stick together and everyone else will know because he'll show them. No point having a better house than anyone else if no one can see it.'

As if to prove his point, Wat stopped the first person who came within reach. 'Can you tell me where Horik's home is. Horik the gold merchant.'

The person stopped was a woman who was carrying a sack over her shoulder that looked like it might be full of bread. She looked at Wat and considered his dress in some detail, from the fine jerkin to the expensive boots.

'Ha,' she said and walked off.

'What was that about?' Siward asked.

'No idea.' Wat stopped a young boy who was hurrying on some errand. 'Can you tell us where the gold merchant's house is?'

'The gold merchant?' the boy checked.

'That's right.'

'It's on Goldsmith Street, isn't it?'

This merchant even had his own street.

'And where's that?'

'Where's Goldsmith Street?'

'Yes,' Wat ground out the confirmation. 'Gold merchant on Goldsmith Street. That's what we're looking for.'

The boy seemed very puzzled by the question. 'You go up towards the Crypel Gate and it's on the left, isn't it?'

'Is it?'

'Of course, it is. Everyone knows that.'

'Except people who ask, perhaps?' Wat suggested.

The boy turned up his nose at this, shook his head at the idiots he had to deal with and continued his journey.

'Right,' Wat said. 'Goldsmith's Street. Can't be far.'

In fact, Goldsmith's Street was the road that ran along the rear of Scrydan's workshop, which Wat pointed out as they arrived.

'A bit too close for comfort, eh?' he said. 'Handy for passing gold from one to the other, though.'

They turned into Goldsmith's Street, and it was immediately obvious which house belonged to the merchant.

This was the house of a man who knew modesty, and how to avoid it.

It was two storeys high, which was impressive enough, but it was neat, clean and in the very best of order. And it was obviously kept that way by the small army of people who were at this moment, cleaning it and keeping it in the best of order.

One woman on a precarious ladder was cleaning the windows with a rag, something Hermitage hadn't even thought could be done.

A carpenter, his tools laid about him, was working on the main door, either repairing it or making some improvement.

Up on the roof, thatchers were throwing down old straw and hauling up bundles of fresh on a rope and pulley. The stuff that landed on the street looked perfectly serviceable, even if it was a bit dirty.

Leading up to the door from the street, three fine stone steps were scrubbed to a gleaming shine never found in nature.

Most peculiar of all, on either side of the bottom step, stood old Roman statues. One seemed to be of a woman carrying a large jug on her shoulders which were draped with vines, probably indicating that she was a wine-bearer.

On the other side, a large man appeared to be fighting a huge cat of some sort and was winning. The cat's teeth were sunk deep into the arm of the man, but it didn't seem to bother him. He hefted a spear ready to finish the battle.

Hermitage had seen Roman statues before, everyone had. But these looked like they'd only been made yesterday. Horik the gold merchant obviously liked everything clean. He must be a very peculiar fellow.

Of more concern were the two living men who stood by the statues. They were very well dressed and neatly presented and looked like they could spear a big cat as well if they had to.

'Move on,' one of them said in a deep and demanding sort

of voice.

Wat stepped forward confidently. 'We've come to see Horik.'

'Move on,' the second man repeated as if irritated that they hadn't listened the first time.

Wat didn't seem put out by this. 'As I say,' he continued as if no one had said anything. 'We've come to see Horik. I'm Wat the Weaver.'

The first man now explained exactly what they had meant slowly and precisely. 'Move on.'

'You can tell Horik that Wat the Weaver is here.'

The tone now became blatantly threatening. 'Move on.' The first man now took a step towards them.

'I can take my business elsewhere,' Wat offered.

'You do that.' At least this was a change from "move on".

'And I'll take my three pounds, two ounces of gold with me.'

The two large men exchanged glances. It seemed that Wat had said the magic word.

'You have gold?' the first one asked suspiciously.

'I do.'

The mood of the men changed instantaneously. 'Well, why didn't you say so? Come in, come in.' They beckoned happily.

To Hermitage's mind, this welcome was akin to that of old Abbot Andrew, who used to beckon brothers into his study like this. Fortunately, the brothers knew better than to go.

'I'm not sure their welcome is sincere, Wat,' Hermitage whispered.

'I'm absolutely certain that it isn't,' Wat replied quite happily. 'That's why it's just you and me, this time.'

'You and me?' Hermitage wasn't following.

Wat turned to Cwen and spoke quickly. 'You three wait

here. If we're not out in an hour, say, go to Ansgar.'

'Fetch the sheriff?' Siward checked with some concern.

'That's it. I'm sure we'll be fine. After all, we don't have any gold with us and that's what Horik will want to see.

'However, if these are the men he has stopping people getting in, I dread to think what the ones will be like who stop people getting out.'

'Why the two of you, then?' Cwen asked.

'Are you coming, or not?' One of the big men at the door asked.

'Yes, yes,' Wat called back. 'Just a moment.' He turned back to Cwen. 'Because I am Wat the Weaver, and while I might not be as rich as a gold merchant, at least he'll give me a hearing. And Brother Hermitage is King William's investigator. If this Horik has any sense at all, he won't want to be upsetting the king.'

'How would he upset the king?' Hermitage asked, having a horrible idea just how he might do it.

'No idea,' Wat said disingenuously. 'But I can already tell that this Horik is not a man to be trusted. Now, we've got to go. Be back before you know it.' He took Hermitage by the arm and propelled him towards the house where the two men now stood smiling a welcome.

Hermitage couldn't help but think of them as gargoyles, and he was the one going to be spat out.

One man led the way up the steps, while the other followed as if making sure that the two of them didn't change their mind.

Inside the home of Horik, the twin themes continued. Utmost cleanliness and workers striving to keep it that way.

The construction was all wood with wattle and daub walls, which was perfectly normal. What wasn't quite so normal was the number of people in here.

The front door had opened into a single large room that spanned the house with two large windows at the front. To the back of the room, a dark door led into the interior.

Two figures were cleaning the wooden floor, one leading with a scrubbing brush and bucket, the other following up with a rag to dry and polish.

Two men had buckets of whitewash and were painting the walls with horsehair brushes. One more was cleaning the windows inside.

Hermitage considered all this effort and wondered if the place had just been built, that was why everyone was still working on it. It didn't explain the thatch being replaced, but this level of activity couldn't possibly be the daily routine, could it?

'Wait here,' one of the men said as he made for the door at the back.

The second nodded his agreement that this was what they should do before he left and returned to his post outside.

'Nice place,' Wat commented, looking around. 'Very, erm, clean.'

'Very,' Hermitage agreed.

One of the men whitewashing the walls turned to them and rolled his eyes in a very extravagant manner. He had a look that said whitewashing Horik's walls was his life's work.

The door at the back of the room opened and the man from the front stood holding it like he was announcing the arrival of some prince.

After a moment a new figure appeared from the darkness. This must be Horik.

It was easy to make an immediate judgement about Horik the person, as the clothes made a declaration like a pair of trumpets.

Huge volumes of brightly coloured silk wafted into the room as if they had been blown by a magnanimous breeze. Hermitage couldn't quite understand what he was looking at. Were Horik's clothes being brought in before him, or was this some decoration about to be hung on the walls?

Then he saw that in the middle of the swathes of colour, there was a face. It was a mature face and one that said that it had seen much in the world and had dealt with it all. There was one feature that was such a shock that he took a sharp breath and couldn't contain his response.

'You're Horik?' he asked in complete surprise.

'I am,' Horik replied as the small mountain of silk drifted into the room.

'Oh, I see. Only, I thought, erm, that is to say, I was expecting, erm..,'

'A man?' Horik asked.

'Well, yes.'

'Hm.' Horik did not sound pleased to hear this. She cast a gaze heavy with disdain at Hermitage, and he immediately felt small and ashamed of his world-worn habit.

The gaze moved on to Wat, who was much better presented. He gave Horik a formal bow.

'Mistress Horik,' Wat acknowledged.

Mistress Horik blinked slowly. 'You have gold?' With a simple narrowing of her eyes, she directed her guard to go and stand by the door. It was clear that this was what the large man was, and now he was guarding in case Hermitage and Wat got any ideas about leaving.

'I am Wat the Weaver,' Wat announced. 'And this is Brother Hermitage, King William's investigator.'

'You have gold?' Horik repeated with absolutely no interest

in the introductions.

'We do,' Wat confirmed. 'Not with us, obviously. That would be rash. Walking the streets with gold about us.' He chanced a smile.

Mistress Horik did not smile. 'A weight was mentioned.'

'That's right,' Wat confirmed. 'A very significant weight, for gold.'

'Three pounds, two ounces,' Horik said.

For all her fine appearance and meticulous cleanliness, Hermitage thought he saw her dribble slightly at this. She soon licked her lips clean, but it wasn't in a nice way.

'A weight of gold previously in the possession of Scrydan,' Wat went on. 'The now dead Scrydan.'

Dead Scrydan was clearly of less interest to Horik than three pounds, two ounces of gold.

'And where is this gold now?' Horik asked with horrible coldness.

'Oh, it's with Ansgar, the sheriff.'

Horik's face hardened at this, and it had been hard, to begin with.

'And why do you come to me? Simply with news? Where's the value in that?'

'It's a lot of gold,' Wat remarked. 'And we hear that you are the only gold merchant in London.'

Horik's face was completely blank at this and she showed no sign of responding in any way whatsoever.

'Did I mention that Brother Hermitage is King William's investigator?' Wat asked brightly. 'I think I did. That means he looks into murders for the king. Who killed who, that sort of thing.' Wat sounded perfectly nonchalant about this as if he was only making conversation.

Horik did not look in the mood for a chat.

'And Scrydan has been murdered,' Wat added. 'Although I'm sure you knew that. Everyone does. So, here's the problem.' Wat took half a step closer to Horik, which was accompanied by the guard taking half a step closer to Wat.

'The king, William, and his noble lord, Ranulph de Sauveloy, are very keen to find out who killed Scrydan. Apparently, they don't want murders happening in town. Well, not without their approval, I imagine. Ha, ha.'

If Wat was trying to cajole Horik into any sort of constructive engagement, it wasn't working.

'They've even changed the punishment from a fine to execution. Seems a bit harsh to me, but there we are, they're in charge now.

'And Scrydan created a mighty clasp as a gift to the king. He had these three pounds, two ounces of gold on him when he was murdered.

'Then, after he was murdered, he had it in him.

'Oh, by the way, I'm helping the King's Investigator with this, if you wondered. And we're asking ourselves, where did three pounds, two ounces of gold come from? How did Scrydan get it?

'According to the sheriff's man, there hasn't been that much gold in London for years. Hence we come to you. You might be able to help clear up the question.'

Horik's expression hadn't changed one iota. Hermitage suspected that it wouldn't change if the archangel Gabriel appeared in the room.

'For the king,' Wat added with a smile.

Horik took one simple breath and looked as if she might be thinking about her reply.

'No,' she said. If she had thought about it, it hadn't taken long.

'I'm a merchant myself, of sorts,' Wat said, apparently ignoring Horik's reply. 'Tapestry, that's my business. You may have heard of Wat the Weaver, many people have.'

Horik showed no recognition.

'And I know how it is. There's no need for the local lords to get involved in every little trade. Taxing this and taxing that, I don't know where it will end. If we want to move some goods around without those in authority interfering, where's the harm, eh?'

'No,' Horik said blankly.

'I see,' Wat said.

Hermitage would have to wait for Wat to explain what he saw. He almost jumped out of his skin when Wat clapped his hands together.

'Well, you've been most helpful,' he said with a grateful bow.

Hermitage couldn't see that at all.

'We'll not detain you further.'

Horik gave the merest hint of an eye movement to her guard, and he moved away from the door.

'Come, Hermitage,' Wat said. 'Let's not keep Mistress Horik from her business.'

Hermitage followed Wat out in a bit of a daze. He wasn't at all sure what had just happened, but he knew that he hadn't enjoyed it.

'That was quick,' Cwen said when they got back on the street.

'It was, and very useful too,' Wat said.

'Was it?' Hermitage asked.

'You were there, you heard her.'

'I was, and I did,' Hermitage reported. 'First of all, Horik is a woman.'

'Good,' Cwen said.

'Secondly, she said about four things, and two of them were "no".'

'Yes, but they were very informative, weren't they?'

'How?' Hermitage asked plainly.

Wat shook his head that Hermitage can't have been paying attention.

'First of all, no, she doesn't know where Scrydan got his gold and no, she didn't sneak any gold into the city, for Scrydan or anyone else. She was furious about his clasp and would very much like to know where he got the gold.'

'Was she?' Hermitage wondered if his mind had wandered during the meeting and Wat and Horik had had some private conversation without him.

'And, yes,' Wat confirmed. 'She would have killed Scrydan herself at the drop of a jewel or had one of her large men do it for her, but she didn't.'

Hermitage gaped. 'She didn't say any of that.'

'She didn't have to say it, did she?'

Hermitage thought that yes she did. How was anyone to understand things if people didn't say them out loud?

'And we believe her, do we?' Cwen asked. 'We asked the woman cleaning the windows, and apparently, it gets done every day. Who has their windows cleaned at all? Let alone daily? Then she has statues outside her door as well as big men to keep people out? There's something wrong with her.'

'I don't think she was lying,' Wat said. 'If she had killed Scrydan, or had him killed, the first thing she would have done is take the clasp for herself, not leave it sticking out of Scrydan.'

Caput XIX: Unusual Steps

'What do we do now, then?' Siward asked as they stood outside Horik's house being scowled at by the large men. 'We seem to have a list of people who would like Scrydan dead, but we're no closer to working out who did it.

'And if we don't get close pretty quickly, I have a horrible feeling Lord Ranulph de Sauveloy will want to pick up his execution where he left off.'

'Don't worry,' Cwen responded. 'This is quite normal, isn't it Hermitage?'

'What is?' Hermitage couldn't think of anything normal at all.

'Not knowing who did it, or having lots of possibilities. You'll just have a good old think about it and say "aha". Then we'll all be impressed about how you worked it out.'

Hermitage shook his head. 'I don't feel any closer to working out anything at the moment.

'Yes, we have a lot of people who didn't like Scrydan and would like him dead.'

'We have Fridolf, who was actually planning to kill him,' Cwen pointed out. She then noticed that the two large men outside Horik's house were paying close attention to their discussion. 'Perhaps we had better go back to Ansgar's.' She tipped her head towards the two listeners. 'Get some privacy.'

They all moved off and Cwen continued to state her case. 'After all, he is the apprentice who came and gave you advanced notice.'

'Yes,' Hermitage admitted. 'But presumably, all these people, Fridolf included, have wanted Scrydan dead for some time. Why kill him now?'

'A huge gold clasp going to the king?' Wat suggested. 'The goldsmiths risked losing the king's business and Fridolf was having his work stolen, in effect.'

'Yes, that's all good motivation, but killing someone requires a bit more than that.'

'Method and opportunity,' Bart announced.

'Yes, but even something beyond.' Hermitage pondered this. 'Anyone might have the method, motive and opportunity to kill someone, but they still don't do it. Take me, for instance.'

'You?' Cwen asked. 'I can't see you even thrusting a rude word at someone, let alone a deadly weapon.'

'Exactly. Consider Abbot Athan. I had many motivations for killing that man. He made my life a misery.'

'And he tried to kill you,' Wat reminded them.[9]

'Yes, he did. What more could you ask for to justify some attack on him? And of course, I had opportunity. I was alone with him on many occasions. For method, I could easily have struck him from behind with something heavy.' He felt a burst of shame as the thought of hitting Athan from behind with something heavy crossed his mind and lingered there.

'But I still wouldn't do it.'

'You're too good,' Cwen said as if not killing people was some sort of failing.

'Ability,' Hermitage said. 'On top of all the usual factors, the killer has to have the ability to do it.'

'I can see that murder by accident might be possible for anyone, but that doesn't seem the case here.'

'Accident?' Siward asked.

'Yes, you know, you're having an argument with someone you wish dead, you push them and they bang their head on a

---

[9] *A Murder for Brother Hermitage:* (for, not of)

rock, or something.'

'And that's all right, is it?' Siward checked.

'No,' Hermitage said quickly. 'It is not all right. My point is that is not a deliberate act. Sticking a gold clasp into someone and killing them is hardly an accident. It would take ability. The ability to stick something into another human being with the intent of doing them harm.'

'Doing them to death,' Siward said.

'Quite. And I don't honestly think that the goldsmiths or Fridolf have the ability.'

'Fridolf said he was going to do it,' Cwen insisted.

'Yes, said,' Hermitage agreed. 'I still can't see him actually pushing that clasp into Scrydan's chest. It's a horrible thing to do. Talking about killing someone is bad enough, but doing it is a completely different deed. Courage is entirely the wrong word to use, but I don't think he would have it when the moment came.'

'The only one we've come across who I think could do it is Horik,' Wat said. 'And I don't doubt for a moment that she could order someone else to do it. Someone who wasn't lacking in ability.

'But, as we've said, she would have taken the gold. Leave three pounds, two ounces of gold sticking out of a man on the street? She really wouldn't have the ability to do that.'

'Presumably,' Siward said thoughtfully. 'You have to kill someone first.'

'I beg your pardon?' Hermitage asked. 'If no one is killed, there isn't a murder.'

'No, no,' Siward corrected himself. 'I mean there has to be a first time you kill someone. Before that, you didn't have the ability, afterwards, you do. Then you might do it again and it would be a bit easier. Like practice, I suppose.'

'Is this rambling helpful in any way?' Cwen enquired.

'I'm just thinking that the people who don't have the ability, the goldsmiths and Fridolf, might acquire it. Every murderer has to have a first murder, I imagine.

'The goldsmiths and Fridolf have wanted Scrydan dead for a long time, but now he's pushed them too far. He's going to the king with the clasp that Fridolf made. That might raise their anger to a point that they do it.'

'Greed, anger, revenge,' Wat said.

'All of them?' Siward asked.

'No. It's what we've said on other occasions about what actually drives someone to murder. They might have all the method, motivation and opportunity they need, but Hermitage is right; it needs ability. And that ability can come from greed, anger or revenge. Get a goldsmith angry enough and he might just do it. A Fridolf wants revenge for being slighted. A Horik is greedy for a big bit of gold.'

'Money.' Cwen's face was thoughtful.

'Yes, three pounds, two ounces of it,' Wat agreed.

'No, the other thing that persuades someone to actually kill another person. You pay them to do it.'

'Someone who already has lots of ability, you mean?'

'Exactly. Consider the Normans. Most of them are well-versed in making other people dead. Give one of them some money and they'd probably do it for you.'

'Oh dear,' Hermitage fretted. 'You mean the person who did it might not be the one who wanted to do it. It was just a job?'

'Could be.'

'We'll never find them.'

Wat was shaking his head. 'I'm not so sure. We've still got the problem of the gold being left in Scrydan. If a paid killer had done the deed, the clasp would be gone.'

'Unless it was left there as a message,' Cwen speculated.

'What sort of message?' Wat asked. 'Clasps can be dangerous?'

'No, you idiot. Scrydan was killed with his gold clasp to show other people that, erm..,'

'To show them what?'

'I don't know,' Cwen huffed. 'Don't try to impress the king. Don't get above yourself. This is what happens to men who try to ingratiate themselves with the Normans. Oh, that's a thought.'

'Yes, it is,' Wat agreed. 'It's definitely a thought. What's it a thought about?'

'Saxons,' Cwen said.

'What about them, I mean, us?' Bart asked.

'Could this be Saxon resistance to the Normans?'

'What?' Wat clearly thought that was ridiculous. 'Let's show the Normans that we will fight them to the death by killing a goldsmith? Yes, very impressive, that'll show them.'

'It's not to show the Normans, is it? It's to show the Saxons.'

'So, now we're adding another whole band of people to the list of those who might have done it?' Hermitage asked with despair.

'Or the Normans could have done it to show people not to try and get on their good side,' Siward offered.

'We're going backwards,' Hermitage complained. 'We've been at this all day and we now have more possibilities instead of fewer.'

'How to narrow them down, that's the question?' Wat mused.

'I don't suppose it could have been an accident?' Bart

suggested. 'You know, Scrydan's walking along with his precious clasp, he trips and falls on it?'

'That would be too easy,' Wat said. 'Men with three pounds, two ounces of solid gold do not trip over and kill themselves with it.'

'How do we know?'

'Because it's ridiculous.'

'Doesn't mean it couldn't happen,' Bart sulked.

'It's the gold,' Wat insisted. 'That's the key to this, I'm sure. Where did Scrydan get it? Someone must know something. You don't find that much gold just lying around. It must have come from somewhere.'

They were back at Ansgar's now, and the woman on the door gave them a very weary look, as she had dearly hoped never to see them again. 'What do you want now?' she asked.

'We've come back,' Cwen replied.

'I can see that, but it doesn't answer the question, does it?'

'We haven't got anywhere else to go,' Bart said.

That clearly wasn't the right answer either.

'We are helping the sheriff resolve the murder that he's managed not to do,' Cwen said plainly. 'And if his house has no room for King William's investigator, perhaps we'll just go to the Tower of London and tell them we're not getting any cooperation.'

The woman thought long and hard about a response to this but couldn't come up with one. Instead, she moved aside with her arms folded and muttered to herself about the things she had to put up with and how unhelpful people were these days.

'Evening is drawing on now,' Siward observed as they settled themselves in the front room. They didn't have anything useful to say to Ansgar, so no one was anxious to even let him know they were here.

'Where are we going to spend the night?'

'Here, probably,' Cwen said.

'If they'll have us.'

'Oh, they'll have us,' she said with certainty.

'But then what do we do?' Bart asked. 'Start again in the morning? Who else is there to ask about this murder? Or the gold?'

'We just haven't found the right person yet,' Siward said. 'Wat is right, someone must have seen something.'

No one had any suggestions as to who might have seen what or how they might be found.

'Does Scrydan have any family?' Bart asked.

Hermitage shook his head. 'Fridolf reported that he did have a wife, but she died in childbirth.'

'Everyone else seems to have hated him to a greater or lesser degree,' Cwen observed. 'Could there be anyone he confided in?'

'He didn't travel to the east or Wales and get three pounds, two ounces of gold out of the ground,' Wat said. 'That's for sure. So, someone knows where he got it. They must do.'

'What do we do? Ask everyone in London?'

Hermitage gazed out of the window at the encroaching darkness and thought that it was on just such an evening that Scrydan took his final walk. This thought took a path of its own and led to a very peculiar conclusion.

'I've just had an idea,' he said. 'You will tell me if it's ridiculous, won't you?'

'We will,' Cwen assured him.

Hermitage tipped his head from side to side as he considered the most important feature of his idea; the etymology. 'Re-enactment,' he said.

'I'm not sure that's even a word,' Cwen said. 'Never mind an idea.'

'From the Latin.'

'It would be.'

'*Agere*, originally, obviously. To do something, perform, that sort of thing.'

'How lovely.'

'And adding *re*, for repeat.'

'It all becomes clear,' Cwen said, which meant it wasn't clear at all.

'Let me explain.'

'That would be helpful.'

Hermitage was reasonably confident that this was a good idea, but he knew that talking about his ideas frequently made them go bad, somehow. He would just have to see what happened with this one.

'It was an evening such as this that Scrydan was murdered, yes?'

'It was an evening, yes,' Cwen agreed. 'And this is another one. They tend to come along this time most days.'

'The people out and about at this time of day, particularly in the streets that Scrydan travelled, may well be out tonight. Doing the same thing in the same place.'

Wat got it and clicked his fingers. 'We go and ask along the streets if anyone saw Scrydan or his actual attack.'

'More than that.' Hermitage was enthused by someone taking one of his ideas seriously. 'We get someone to play the part of Scrydan. They dress as he did, walk as he did and follow his route. By this means their memories may be prompted.'

Cwen sounded surprised. 'That's actually a good idea.'

Hermitage was quite surprised as well.

'Who plays Scrydan?' Bart asked. 'Do we even know what he looked like?'

'We ask Ansgar. He'll know.'

'Ask Ansgar what?" Ansgar said as he came through from the back room. He frowned at them all, clearly wondering what they were doing back here. He looked at Wat once more and his eyes widened.

'Wat the Weaver,' he accused.

'Erm, yes?' Wat agreed.

'You are Wat the Weaver.' Ansgar didn't sound happy to have realised this.

'Always have been.'

'I thought I recognised you and now it's come to me. Wat the Weaver.'

Wat couldn't really confirm it a third time.

'You've got some impudence, turning up here.'

'Here? Have I?'

'London.'

'What, the whole of it?'

'You know what I mean. The incident at Alders Gate market.'

Ansgar's glare was very direct. Everyone else looked lost.

'Oh, that,' Wat said sheepishly.

'Yes, that,' Ansgar confirmed.

'That was all a misunderstanding. I'm a changed man.'

'He is,' Hermitage confirmed.

Ansgar considered the room and pointed a large finger on the end of a large sword hand at Wat. 'You had better be.'

Wat nodded confirmation.

'One suggestion of an incident like that again, and we'll be having an extra execution. Clear?'

'Oh, very clear,' Wat agreed.

The ensuing silence was painful, and Hermitage was dearly hoping that no one would ask what happened at Alders Gate market, much less that someone would explain. If they did, he would try not to listen.

'We wondered what Scrydan actually looked like?' he asked, hoping to move the subject on from Wat's unpleasantness.

'What he looked like?' Ansgar asked.

'That's it.'

'What do you think he looked like?' The sheriff's anger was rising. 'He was lying on the floor with a lump of gold sticking out of him.'

'No, no. I mean, what did he look like when he was alive? Was he short, tall, thin, fat?'

The sheriff obviously didn't understand why he was being asked, but he answered anyway, perhaps just to stop these people talking to him. 'He was about fifty, short and stout. Bald head, no beard. Well dressed, like most of the goldsmiths.'

Hermitage had a horrible thought. 'You haven't, erm, got him here, have you?' Only now did it occur to him that this was one murder where he hadn't seen the body. He'd been so grateful for that, that he hadn't thought to ask.

'Got him here?' Ansgar was outraged. 'No, of course, I haven't got him here. What do you think this is? I had him taken away and buried.'

'Oh, dear.'

'Oh, dear? What do you mean oh, dear? What else are you suggesting I should have done with him?'

'It's just that it is sometimes useful in these situations to see the body.'

'He died days ago,' Ansgar reminded them. 'Do you really

want to see him?'

'I suppose not,' Hermitage admitted. 'At least we have a description now.'

'And what good is that going to do?' Ansgar clearly thought this band was made up entirely of idiots.

'We're going to re-enact his murder,' Hermitage announced.

'You're going to what?' Ansgar sounded quite disgusted.

'We'll be mummers if you will. We shall perform Scrydan's final journey and ask people along the way if they recall anything from the fatal night.' Hermitage thought it sounded positively, erm, dramatic - which was obviously from the Greek, so perhaps best not to confuse everyone too much.

'The question is, who do we get to play Scrydan?' Hermitage said. 'None of us fit his description.'

In the silence that said no one had any suggestion, Cwen slowly raised her arm.

Everyone looked at her and followed her eyes as they moved over to one individual.

'What are you all looking at me for?' the woman who guarded the sheriff's door asked.

Caput XX: Re-enactment

'You think I look like who?' The woman was more than mightily offended. In terms of mightiness, her reaction could probably have fought off the Normans and the Danes in the same afternoon.

Wat stepped quickly forward. 'She didn't mean you looked like Scrydan, did you, Cwen?' He made this comment as pointed as a fish hook and hoped that it bit.

Cwen gave a nonchalant shrug.

'What did she mean, then?'

Hermitage wondered how Wat was going to get out of this. If the description of Scrydan had been true to life, this woman did bear a remarkable similarity. True, she wasn't bald, but she was short and round.

'She meant that, erm, you'd be perfect to play the part of Scrydan.'

'I'm not playing anyone's parts,' the woman folded her arms, probably to hold all her indignation.

'We're doing a, what did you call it, Hermitage?'

'Oh, erm, re-enactment.'

'You're all disgusting,' the woman announced.

'No, no, it's like mumming,' Hermitage explained.

'That's it,' Wat picked up. 'We're going to have a procession through the streets, and you'd be the most important person in it.'

That did seem to calm the reaction. 'A procession with Scrydan?' she asked.

'Exactly.'

'But he's dead.'

'So he can't do it himself, can he? And you'd dress up,

211

obviously. I mean, you don't look like Scrydan at all, that's clear.'

Cwen coughed at this.

'But you do have the same, erm, height,' Wat said with a glare for Cwen.

'Obviously, we'd have to put some padding on you. You're much slimmer than Scrydan. And we'd have to cover up your lovely hair, erm..?'

'Aeva.' Aeva introduced herself, and Hermitage thought he caught the glimmer of a smile.

Wat chanced taking a step closer. 'And we'd get you a fine robe. I understand Scrydan dressed very well.'

'Which I could keep?' Aeva asked very quickly.

'Oh, I'm sure you could keep it.'

Aeva was now in that state of having decided to do whatever this was, but not wanting anyone to know that. 'Why are you doing a procession for Scrydan anyway? He was a horrible man, or so I've heard.'

'Did you ever meet him?' Hermitage asked.

'He came by now and again. In the old days. Just to talk with the sheriff.'

Hermitage looked to Ansgar who nodded his agreement. 'Goldsmith's charter, that sort of thing,' the sheriff explained.

'So, you know what he was like. How he walked?' Wat checked.

'How he walked?' Aeva was sounding offended again.

Hermitage thought a proper explanation might be helpful.

'Mistress Aeva. As you say, Scrydan is dead. He was stabbed with the gold clasp he was carrying.'

'Aye, the town knows that.'

'My task, er, our task is to find out who did it. That's where you can help.'

'It wasn't me,' Aeva now howled. 'I didn't kill him, I didn't.'

'No, no, of course, you didn't.' Hermitage said with a little irritation at a ridiculous conclusion. 'No one is saying that you did. What we want to do is see if anyone around the streets on the evening he was killed remembers anything.

'To help them do that, we will dress someone up as Scrydan, you, and walk along the same street.'

Aeva regarded him with obvious horror. 'You want me to be murdered?' she screeched.

'No one wants you to be murdered. You won't be murdered.' This was worse than trying to teach that novice Loric to read. Hermitage had written the word, God, and explained what it was. Loric then concluded that God was in the ink and wouldn't go near it.

'You're going to pretend to be Scrydan and walk down the street. We will be with you and will ask people if they remember Scrydan himself being there. And if they do, did they see anything?'

'Like him being murdered?' Aeva checked.

'Well, that would be good, but unlikely, I think. They may have seen someone following him, that sort of thing.'

'And this killer's going to follow me?'

Wat sighed. 'Just dress up as Scrydan, walk down the street and get a good robe for your trouble.'

Aeva looked at him with a steely gaze. 'Oh, all right.'

'God above,' Wat muttered as he turned away. 'Ansgar, does anyone have a robe such as Scrydan would have worn?'

'Such as he would have worn?' Ansgar repeated the request.

'Yes, so that Mistress Aeva here can wear it and look as much like Scrydan as possible.'

'A robe such as he would have worn,' Ansgar said again

213

slowly.

'Yes.' Wat was clearly wondering why this was so complicated.

'I don't know,' Ansgar was thoughtful. 'Scrydan was very particular about his clothing. I'm not sure anyone would have one exactly the same.'

'Near enough would do,' Wat said.

Ansgar nodded. 'I've got the one he was wearing if that'd be all right?'

'You've got what?'

'I've got Scrydan's own robe. Is that the sort of thing you're looking for?'

Wat took a very deep breath. 'Yes, that would be fine.'

'Why have you got his own robe?' Siward asked with some worry.

'It's a fine robe,' Ansgar explained. 'Too good to bury him in it.'

'You're giving me dead Scrydan's own robe?' Aeva asked sounding a bit shocked at the suggestion.

'It seems that we are,' Ansgar said with some reluctance.

'Oh,' Aeva said. 'That's a good one that is. I seen him about in it.'

'Can we get on then?' Hermitage said. 'The evening is drawing near, and we need to be ready. Do we have something that can cover Mistress Aeva's hair?'

'Like a hat?' Cwen suggested somewhat sarcastically.

'I don't suppose you have Scrydan's hat as well as his robe?' Siward asked Ansgar.

'Of course. A dead man doesn't need a warm head, does he?'

'Do I get to keep the hat as well?'

Ansgar grumbled something as he went into the back room.

He emerged a moment later bearing a robe and a large floppy hat.

Aeva slipped the robe over her head, and it was a remarkably good fit.

'No need for any padding, then,' Cwen muttered under her breath.

Aeva tucked her hair up into the hat, adjusted everything and then waddled around the room.

'Aha,' Ansgar almost laughed. 'It could be old Scrydan himself.'

Aeva cackled at her performance.

'Good,' Hermitage said. 'Now. We need to go to Scrydan's workshop and then follow the path straight from there to the point his body was found.'

'Always assuming that was the way he went,' Bart put in.

'There aren't many choices,' Ansgar explained. 'Unless he wandered around the town for a bit, which is not a sensible thing for a goldsmith to do at all, let alone one carrying a weight of gold.'

'Let us assume that he went straight there,' Hermitage said. 'Of course, we're also assuming that he was on his way to the castle with the clasp.' He suddenly wondered if they might have got a fundamental element of this investigation completely wrong. He felt like he got fundamental elements of most of his investigations wrong, but they all worked out in the end.

'Don't know where else he'd be going with it,' Ansgar said. 'There's only one king now, and that's where he lives.'

'We have no other information to go on,' Hermitage concluded. 'To the workshop, then.'

The procession set off from the sheriff's house and was such a line of people that the locals passing by stopped to see what was going on.

Some large woman dressed as a man was being followed by a monk. Two boys then came along, with a girl and a well-dressed something-or-other at her side. At the back, the sheriff walked as if herding the lot of them along.

'Bloody Normans,' someone muttered as they were passed. 'The things they get up to are disgusting.'

'You know where Scrydan's workshop is?' Hermitage checked with Aeva.

'Oh, yes,' she said. 'It's a small place and all the goldsmiths keep together. Not that I've ever had the wherewithal to visit before.'

They returned to Ceapen Street and got even more odd looks as they made their way to Scrydan's workshop.

'I suppose we had better start inside,' Hermitage said to the others. 'That's where Scrydan would have come from. And we probably need a few moments to talk to people in the street, you know, see if they were here, get them to watch the re-enactment.'

No one had anything else to offer.

Hermitage looked up and down the street. 'Which is the door?' he asked.

Bart came forward and walked the few steps to Scrydan's door. 'This is the one.' He didn't seem to know what to do with it now it was in front of him.

Wat pushed forward and hammered on it with his fist and they all gathered round to wait for admittance, Hermitage and Aeva at the front.

Only when the door was opened and the workshop drudge screamed and fainted, did it occur to Hermitage that perhaps having someone dressed as Scrydan might not have been wise.

'Oh, for heaven's sake,' Cwen complained. 'Get him up.'

Bart and Wat bent forward and helped the stricken drudge from the floor.

He slowly came to his senses and opened his eyes. He took in Wat and Bart and simply seemed puzzled at what was going on. When he caught sight of Mistress Aeva he tried to climb backwards out of his skin.

'It's not Scrydan,' Wat assured him. 'It's only someone dressed as him.'

The drudge peered hard and seemed to accept that the one in Scrydan's robe and hat might not be the goldsmith.

'What's wrong with you? the drudge asked angrily. 'Do you think this is funny? Turning up at the door scaring the life out of honest folk.'

'Sorry about that,' Hermitage spoke up. 'It's a long story, unfortunately, but we can explain. Might we come in?'

'You want to come in? With him dressed like that?'

Aeva took her hat off.

'Good God, it's a woman. What's a woman doing dressing up as Scrydan?'

Ansgar stepped up. 'Just open the door and let us in,' he instructed.

The drudge obviously recognised the sheriff but seemed even more concerned about what he was doing involved in all this.

Nevertheless, he did as he was told and held the door wide for them all to enter.

Once inside, they saw that the space was a workshop, but it was a cold and dead one. No furnace burned and no apprentices worked at their craft.

Hermitage looked around. 'Have you had to stop work now that your smith is no more?'

At his words, two nervous faces appeared towards the back of the room.

'Who is it?' A trembling voice asked.

'It's the sheriff,' the drudge replied. 'And some idiot dressed as Scrydan.'

'Come forward,' Ansgar ordered.

Two thin figures emerged from the darkness, no more than boys really.

'Who are you?' Ansgar peered hard at them. 'You're Scrydan's apprentices,' he said.

'We are.' one of them replied. 'I'm Brod and this is Gythred.'

'And I'm Caelwin,' the drudge introduced himself.

'You stay here?' Hermitage asked.

'Nowhere else to go,' Brod replied. 'Fridolf should be here. He came back before Scrydan died, but we haven't seen him since.'

Hermitage wondered about telling them that Fridolf was safe in sanctuary, but for some reason, he decided that it was best to keep the information private for now. He didn't really know why, he just thought it might be sensible. He moved quickly on, hoping that the others would pick up on his caution.

'You have no work to do?' he asked.

'None,' Gythred confirmed. 'Scrydan kept all the commissions to himself so we wouldn't know what to do. Fridolf might have some ideas, but we're still early in our apprenticeships.'

'In any case,' Brod said. 'We don't have any metal at all, let alone gold or silver.

'You could at least light the furnace,' Wat suggested. 'Keep yourselves warm.'

'No fuel,' Caelwin said.

'Why don't you go out and get some?' Cwen asked, impatiently.

'No money either, Scrydan kept all of that.'

'You're hopeless,' Cwen concluded. 'You can't simply hide in here. Scrydan's dead, what do you think is going to happen?'

'Fridolf might come back?' Brod suggested.

'Or you might have to go out of the door and sort yourselves out,' Cwen said. 'Go to the other goldsmiths, you'll have to get work sometime soon.'

The three lads seemed to accept this but obviously weren't inclined to do anything about it.

Brod looked at them all. 'What are you doing here anyway, with her dressed up like Scrydan?'

'We are trying to discover who killed him,' Hermitage explained.

'What? You get someone to dress up like him and see if he gets killed as well. Sorry, she.' Brod acknowledged Aeva.

'You said I wasn't going to get killed,' Aeva complained loudly.

'And you aren't,' Hermitage assured her. He held his hands up hoping that everyone would take this as a sign to keep calm and not draw their own conclusions.

'We are going to walk down the street, as Scrydan did, and see if this prompts anyone to remember seeing him on the fatal night.'

'Fatal night?' Gythred asked as if he didn't understand the term.

'The night that was fatal for Scrydan,' Cwen explained.

'Oh, right.'

'You saw him leave here, I assume,' Hermitage asked,

wondering if he shouldn't have come and spoken to these boys some time ago.

'We did. He went off with the clasp in its box.'

'To the king.'

'He said he was going to court, that was all. He never said what he was doing or why.'

'Had he had any visitors recently? In the days before he was killed?'

'He never had visitors,' Brod explained. 'No one would spend time with Scrydan if they could avoid it.'

'He was a successful goldsmith,' Ansgar said. 'People must have visited him.'

'He visited them, mainly. At least we assume that was what he was doing.'

'The one thing you could say for Scrydan,' Gythred said plainly. 'Was that he was never here.'

'Never here?' Hermitage checked.

'Always off somewhere doing something.'

'And nobody asked what he was doing?'

'You didn't ask Scrydan anything,' Brod cautioned.

'Interesting,' Wat said thoughtfully. 'A gold merchant who doesn't have visitors. Must be very rich customers if he goes to them.'

Brod shrugged that he supposed that must be the case.

'Did Horik ever come by? The gold merchant?'

'Oh, God, no,' Brod said urgently. 'You don't want to mess with Horik. You don't want her anywhere near you.'

'Yes, we got that impression. Did Scrydan go to her to get his gold, then?'

'Again, we just assume he did. There's nowhere else to get gold in London.'

'Yet Scrydan had three pounds, two ounces of it,' Wat

mused. 'Three pounds, two ounces that didn't come from Horik.'

The apprentices looked as confused about this as everyone was. 'Where did he get it, then?' Gythred asked.

'That, we do not know,' Wat said. 'Would he just go out and come back with pounds of gold?'

'Not exactly. He'd go out, but then he did that all the time. Sometimes he'd come back and work at the furnace. Next thing is, he's giving us some gold to work. Well, Fridolf, mainly.'

'Where did it come from?' Wat asked the question of the air. 'If this supply of gold isn't connected to Scrydan's death, I'm a goldsmith.'

No one had any more to offer.

'So,' Cwen prompted. 'Do we get on with this re-enactment, thing?'

'Oh, yes, right,' Hermitage remembered why they were here. There didn't seem any more to get out of these boys. They were obviously lost and confused by Scrydan's death and couldn't even bring themselves to go out of the door. 'Put your hat back on, if you would, Mistress Aeva.' He turned to Brod. 'What time of day did Scrydan leave on his last journey?'

Brod peered out of the door. 'Would have been about now, I suppose.'

'Good. Off we go then. We will go out first, to engage with people in the street. Everyone spread out and try to talk to anyone you come across. Ask them if they recall seeing Scrydan and whether there was anything unusual.'

Aeva put her hat back on. 'And you're sure I'm not going to get murdered or nothing.

'No, you are not going to get murdered. We will all be here

to protect you.'

With nods all around, Hermitage stepped out into the street.

There was a good gaggle of people passing by and he selected one who didn't look too intent on not being disturbed. He was a reasonably well-dressed fellow, but not too rich. Probably a simple tradesman of some sort.

'Excuse me, sir, I wonder if I might trouble you for a moment.'

'I gave at the church,' the man replied, quickly considering the monk before him.

'No, no. I'm not seeking alms. I just wondered if you frequent this area around this time of day?'

'You wonder if I what?' the man now looked quite worried about Hermitage and took a step back.

'If you might have been around at the time Scrydan the goldsmith left his workshop, and whether you saw anything that could be helpful in knowing what happened to him?'

'I don't know, do I?' the man protested. 'I don't watch other people about their business.'

'Perhaps this might help.'

Hermitage gestured over to the door of Scrydan's workshop, through which Mistress Aeva now appeared.

'Oh, dear,' Hermitage said as he watched the man disappear down the street screaming about spirits and the dead rising from their graves. 'This isn't going at all as I planned.'

Caput XXI: The Talk On The Street

'This is doing wonders, then, Hermitage,' Cwen came over and stood at his side. 'We've terrified half the people of London, who now think Scrydan has come back to haunt them.'

Hermitage considered the length of the street, which now seemed to be in a complete panic.

The man he had stopped had told everyone he passed that Scrydan was back from the dead to take them all to hell. Naturally, people believed this instantly, instead of making their own enquiries as to its veracity.

Over on the other side of the road, where Aeva walked, people were screaming, and those who had doors and windows were shutting them. Several passers-by had even laid down on the ground with their hands over their heads, perhaps hoping that the spirits of the dead ignored people with their hands over their heads.

Anyone a reasonable distance away, simply pointed, shouted alarm and got even further away as fast as they could.

'It could be good when you think about it,' Hermitage tried.

'I am thinking about it.' Cwen clearly couldn't see the good.

'It means people knew Scrydan. They knew what he looked like and were aware of him passing along the street.'

'So?'

'So, now we explain to them that this is not Scrydan, and ask them to recall the last time they saw him.'

'If we can catch them,' Cwen said as another local ran by.

'What have you done?' Ansgar now demanded as he strode

up.

Hermitage trembled in the face of the large, angry Saxon.

'He's prompted people to think about Scrydan,' Cwen bit back. 'Which was exactly what we set out to do.'

Well, that was kind of her.

Ansgar frowned at the panic in the street and obviously couldn't recall setting out to do any of this.

'Stop someone and ask them,' Cwen instructed. 'You're the sheriff.'

Ansgar scowled at her but did look around before stepping in front of a woman who was scurrying along as if the devil was after her, which she obviously thought was the case.

'Stop, stop,' Ansgar held his arms up.

With such a large obstruction in her path, the woman could do nothing but stop. She looked hither and thither as if trying to identify a way round, but Ansgar moved with her, and she soon realised her escape had been thwarted.

'What do you want?' she asked urgently.

'Why are you running?' Ansgar demanded, still angry.

'What he means,' Cwen stepped in with a disappointed glance for Ansgar. 'Is what made you run?' She asked this gently and with interest.

'It's Scrydan, isn't it?' the woman explained something that should need no explanation. 'He's back from the dead.'

'No, he isn't,' Cwen assured her. 'That's mistress Aeva dressed up as Scrydan.'

The woman was not convinced.

'I promise you. It's just Scrydan's robe and hat.'

A nervous glance was cast back down the road towards Aeva who was still waddling along with the others nearby, unable to do anything other than watch all the potential witnesses run away.

Like Ansgar, they were trying to stop people who passed by but weren't having any luck. But then, they didn't have a large Saxon sheriff on their side.

Upon closer inspection, the woman seemed to doubt whether this really was the shade of dead Scrydan returned to earth.

'Scrydan's been buried,' Cwen explained. 'He'd look a lot worse than that if he'd risen, wouldn't he?'

When Mistress Aeva trod in something and howled that she'd ruined her shoes, the deceit was undone.

'What's Aeva doing dressed as Scrydan?' The woman now demanded. 'What sort of thing is that to do? And you the sheriff.' She directed her considerable ire at Ansgar, who backed off slightly.

'We are trying to find out if anyone saw Scrydan before he was killed,' Cwen explained.

The woman looked at Cwen with frank disappointment. 'And you couldn't just ask?'

'This has helped restore memories,' Hermitage explained. 'A simple question would not have had the same effect.'

'Oh, really?' The woman was not convinced. 'And what's a monk got to do with this? Ought to know better than to get involved in this sort of thing. Tricking people with spirits. That's not what a monk should do. Is it?'

Hermitage could only bow under the onslaught.

'Did you see Scrydan out and about then?' Cwen asked directly. 'The day he was killed?'

The woman seemed to be considering whether she was willing to answer any of these questions at all, having been tricked by these heartless people.

'It's important,' Ansgar said.

'Might have done,' the woman admitted.

'That's good,' Cwen encouraged. 'So, Mistress erm..?'

'I'll keep my name to myself, if it's all the same to you,' Mistress Erm huffed.

'Very well, mistress. You saw Scrydan?'

'I saw him a lot. He was always out and about.' It was clear that always being out and about was not the sort of thing decent people did.

'Always?' Cwen pressed.

'Every day. Coming here and going there. You'd think a man with a trade would stick to his task, not go wandering the streets at all times of day and night.'

'Interesting,' Hermitage muttered.

'It might be interesting to you, brother monk, but this is a nice part of town. We have goldsmiths and all sorts.'

'Well, quite,' Hermitage agreed, although he wasn't quite sure why.

'But Scrydan was always out?' Cwen checked. 'Going places or just wandering. Gossiping, that sort of thing?'

'Him? He didn't have the time of day for no one. Intent, that's what he had.'

'Intent?'

'Going somewhere. You can tell when someone's going somewhere, can't you? Got something to do, somewhere to be, someone to meet.'

'Er, yes, I suppose so.'

'Well, that was Scrydan. Full of intent, he was.' This obviously wasn't right either.

'Did you ever know where he was going?'

'Certainly not. Who do you take me for?'

Cwen seemed to consider the woman for a moment with thoughtful eyes.

'Of course, you wouldn't,' she agreed. 'But I can imagine

that some less scrupulous people might gossip.'

'Less what?'

'Scrupulous. It's one of the words Hermitage uses.'

'What's a Hermitage?'

'This is. This is Brother Hermitage and it's the sort of thing he says all the time.'

Hermitage didn't recall saying it all the time, or much at all, really. He thought about embarking on the Latin origins but decided not. 'Erm, it means to make fine distinctions.'

'Exactly,' Cwen agreed quickly. 'Less fine people than you might gossip.'

'That they would,' the woman agreed with some relish. 'That Mistress Elnor's no better than she ought to be.'

Cwen nodded encouragingly. 'And what does Mistress Elnor say Scrydan was up to?'

'She didn't know either. Said he'd just disappear.'

'Disappear?'

'Like magic. One moment he was here, and then he was gone. Couldn't be found if you looked for him.'

'And where will we find Mistress Elnor?'

The unnamed mistress looked up and down the street. 'That's her.' She pointed to a woman who was standing further along, apparently berating Aeva with some vigour.

The words could not be heard, but Aeva was giving as good as she got, by the look of it. Both women waved arms and gesticulated, and it was clear that this would soon descend to pushing and shoving.

'Thank you, mistress.' Cwen gave a quick nod and beckoned Hermitage and Ansgar to follow her over to Aeva.

'Well, really,' the woman huffed. 'Don't mind me, will you?' She waited for a moment and then slowly followed along, her right ear leading the way.

'Mistress Elnor?' Cwen asked quite loudly to interrupt the dispute.

Elnor was confused by the new arrival but was happy to turn her anger on Cwen 'Is this your doing? Getting people dressed up as the dead to parade up and down the street frightening God-fearing people out of their wits?'

Cwen held her gaze. 'Yes, that's me.' The addition of "and what are you going to do about it" was unnecessary.

Elnor quickly glanced from Cwen to Hermitage to the sheriff and recognised when she might be facing a greater force. 'Well, it's not right.'

'You should have heard the things she called me,' Aeva complained. 'And me helping the sheriff and a monk. She's got no call.' Aeva folded her arms. 'Mind you, she always was a busybody.'

'How dare you? Elnor responded quickly.

'Oh, be quiet, the pair of you,' Cwen instructed. 'We're dealing with the death of Scrydan here.'

'Dealing with it?' Elnor seemed happy to change the subject. 'What do you mean, dealing with it?'

'Finding out who did it.' Cwen explained.

'We know who did it. It was two strangers,' Elnor explained condescendingly. 'They confessed to the sheriff and the Normans executed them.'

'Yes,' Cwen said knowingly as she pointed over the road to Siward and Bart. 'That would be those two strangers.'

Elnor followed the direction. 'Are they risen from the dead as well?' she asked with renewed worry.

'No, they never died.'

'Well, that's remarkable,' Elnor commented with interest. 'Executed but didn't die, eh?' This was obviously a fascinating topic for future gossip.

Cwen took a breath. 'They didn't die because they weren't executed because they didn't do it.'

'Oh.' Elnor sounded disappointed that something as interesting as an execution had been put off for such a flimsy reason.

'And so we're trying to find out who did do it. Brother Hermitage here is King William's own investigator. It's what he does, finds out who killed people.'

Elnor appraised Hermitage who gave a nod of the head.

'Funny job for a monk,' she observed.

'That's as may be,' Cwen said. 'But we hear that you might know about Scrydan's comings and goings?'

'Me? Who told you that?' She scanned the street and fixed the source of the information, who was now loitering within earshot, with a hard gaze.

'Never mind who told..,'

'We only heard that you are a reliable source of information,' Hermitage interrupted. 'And may have seen Scrydan as he went out and about.' He looked to Cwen and hoped to suggest that encouragement might work better than threat in this situation.

Elnor looked rather haughty as if she was not going to be taken in by such flattery. 'I might have done,' she admitted.

'He was frequently out of his workshop, we hear,' Hermitage went on. 'Even his apprentices report that he was seldom there.'

'That's right,' Elnor confirmed. 'The other goldsmiths are barely seen. Old Eligius hardly stirs from his chair and the others are no better. And when they do gather, it's only with one another. Too good for the likes of us.'

'Where did Scrydan go?'

'He vanished,' Elnor reported.

'Vanished?' Hermitage knew that people couldn't really vanish, but he didn't know what Elnor meant.

'One moment he'd be walking off down the street, then, when you look around the corner, he's gone.'

'Following him, then, eh?' Aeva enquired nastily.

'Going in the same direction,' Elnor sniffed. 'About my business, which is mine to know of.'

'He can't really have vanished, can he?' Hermitage asked. 'He came back, I assume.'

'Well, he did until he didn't come back at all anymore.'

'So, he must have gone somewhere. Just somewhere you didn't know.'

'Could be,' Elnor admitted.

'Was it always in the same direction that he vanished?'

'Aye, it was.'

Hermitage waited but there was no further explanation. 'And which direction was that?'

'Well, it was towards the church, wasn't it?'

'Was it?'

'It was.'

'And on the night he died?' Cwen asked. 'Did you see him then? And did he vanish?'

'He was going the other way, off towards the castle carrying something.'

'You didn't see him attacked?'

'No, of course, I didn't. If I'd seen that I'd have raised a cry, wouldn't I?'

'Was there anything else remarkable?'

'Such as?'

'I don't know. People following him. Strangers looking suspicious?'

'There were a lot of people about. Some were going that

way, how would I know if they were following him?'

'As if you can't spot someone following,' Aeva snorted. 'What people?' she asked directly.

Hermitage and Cwen looked at her wondering at this intervention.

'Come on, Mistress Elnor of Ceapen Street,' Aeva encouraged. 'If you don't know who the people were, I don't know who would.'

Elnor seemed to take this as a compliment. 'The usual,' she said. 'Mistress Bote off to see that ferryman she thinks no one knows about. Master Frithstan going about his business, which is best not talked about at all. A few others.'

'No strangers at all?'

'Not strangers, as such, I'd say.'

'What would you say, then?'

'Well, it's not really for me to comment,' Elnor said, which was strange considering that was exactly what she was doing. 'But that Fridolf, the apprentice, was out. And I'd not seen him for a long time.'

'Was he?' Cwen asked with serious interest.

'And one of the apprentices from Eligius's workshop. Cyneruth. He was out for a walk or something.'

'Another goldsmith's apprentice,' Hermitage noted.

'Then there was that fellow of Horik's, you know the big one. They call him Grun, but I don't think that's his real name.'

'This is getting to be quite a crowd,' Cwen observed.

'And young Wilf and his aunt from over Alders Gate way.'

'How do you know some Wilf from Alders Gate?' Aeva asked.

Elnor simply looked at her as if she should know better than to ask questions like that. 'They used to live not far from here, but then the Normans came and knocked their house down.'

'What did they do that for? Was she a rebel?'

'No, they said there was a castle going up and her home was in the way. Down it came, without a by-your-leave. She said she was moving as far away from them as she could get. But they're everywhere now.'

'What were they doing back here? Loitering about?'

'Young Wilf's got eyes on being a goldsmith's apprentice. He was always about, pestering the goldsmiths.'

'Was he?' Cwen asked with interest. 'Pestering Scrydan as well.'

'No one would go near Scrydan unless they had to,' Elnor reported. 'But as everyone expected Fridolf to be made up to master soon, there might be a vacancy for a new apprentice.'

'Good luck with that,' Aeva snorted. 'Goldsmithing doesn't seem like a trade for decent folk.'

'Anyone else?' Cwen urged, wanting to move from simple gossip.

'Then there was the old carpenter, Todwulf. Drunk as normal.'

'Any more?' Cwen asked as if expecting a list of the whole population.

'Just the usual churchmen. Although Father Thomas was out of his bounds as well, which was unusual.'

'Father Thomas?' Hermitage repeated the name. 'And all these people were following Scrydan?'

'Well, I can't say that for certain, can I?' Elnor replied. 'They was all going in the same direction, but that doesn't mean anything, does it?'

'It may not mean anything,' Hermitage agreed. 'But then again, it may.'

'Very helpful,' Cwen observed.

At this moment, Wat, Siward and Bart arrived. 'I hope you're having better luck than we are,' Wat said. 'All we get asked is when we're going to bury Scrydan again and will he stay down this time.'

'We've got Mistress Elnor,' Cwen boasted. 'Who saw every single person on the street and knows them by name.'

'Excellent,' Wat said rubbing his hands. 'Who killed Scrydan then?'

'Well,' Cwen was thoughtful. 'By the sound of it, we could have narrowed it down to a dozen or so.'

Caput XXII: Going In Disguise

Having extracted as much as was possible from Mistress Elnor, they all returned to the sheriff's house. Full evening had drawn on, and most of the streets flickered with the flames of torches put up on the sides of the buildings to help people extend the working day.

Of course, flaming torches on the sides of thatched buildings carried their own risk and every now and then a bucket of water was thrown to prevent a conflagration.

They hadn't extracted everything from Mistress Elnor, which would have taken days, but they had stopped her when the recollections drifted too far from the matter in hand.

Knowing why the second cousin of the man who used to own the house on the corner had gone to France, seemed to have nothing whatsoever to do with the death of Scrydan. Even then, it was hard to escape Elnor, who looked dangerously like following them at one stage.

It was only when Wat told her that she should stay on the street and keep watch, that they could get away.

Aeva said that she had had enough of dressing up as dead people and was going home. She would keep the robe and the hat for her trouble, and if they ever wanted anyone to pretend to be Scrydan again, they could find someone else.

At the house, Bedric, the scribe, was still hard at work sorting out the records of the town, which seemed to be an endless task. Medwyn was nowhere to be seen. Doubtless, the goose demanded her attention.

At least Ansgar seemed to be taking the question of Scrydan's death a little more seriously now. Hitherto, it had just seemed to be a nuisance, the biggest part of which was his perpetrators escaping their execution.

He brought a jug of ale into the front room, and everyone found a spot to rest.

Hermitage could detect that all the gazes were to him, so he thought that he might summarise the situation. He hoped to goodness that they didn't expect him to name the killer. He hadn't got a clue about that.

'First then, we still have Fridolf. We know that he wanted to kill Scrydan as he's been the only one so far to announce the fact. Now we hear that he was in the street, possibly following Scrydan the night he was killed.'

'Which he did say he was,' Wat pointed out. 'Just that Scrydan was dead by the time he got to him.'

Hermitage nodded at that. 'But that seems problematic, now that we know he was in the street when Scrydan was still alive.'

'He did do it, then? Siward asked.

'Oh, it's far too soon to say that,' Hermitage cautioned. 'Next, we have the goldsmith's apprentice Cyneruth. He was there and seemed to be going in the same direction as Scrydan.'

'And we know that the goldsmiths wanted Scrydan out of the way as well,' Wat reminded them.

'So, that's another possibility,' Hermitage acknowledged. 'Then we have this Grun fellow. Presumably one of the large men who works for Horik.'

'Who really would want Scrydan dead,' Wat said. 'And, in my opinion, wouldn't hesitate to do it. Or get it done.'

'We also have Father Thomas,' Hermitage added thoughtfully.

'You don't think he had anything to do with this?' Ansgar asked in a worried tone.

'I can't imagine it,' Hermitage said because he couldn't.

'It doesn't pay to mess with the church. Difficult people. Begging your pardon, Brother.'

'And then there's Wilf and his aunt who were over from Alders Gate,' Cwen added.

'Now they really don't have anything to do with it,' Bart said. 'They probably didn't even know Scrydan and were only in the street by coincidence.'

'It was the night Scrydan was murdered,' Cwen said. 'There's no coincidence. And anyway, young Wilf wanted to be a goldsmith's apprentice, apparently, so he certainly did know Scrydan.'

'Good luck with that,' Wat snorted. 'Goldsmiths are a very protective band. Like most craftsmen. You can't just turn up and ask to be an apprentice.'

'And if we're worried about people who were there, we can add Mistress Elnor herself,' Siward pointed out.

'Too busy watching everyone else to do any killing, I'd have thought.' Wat said.

'And a drunken carpenter, Todwulf,' Hermitage added for completeness. 'And they are only the ones Mistress Elnor noticed. I suppose we could speak to each of them and ask directly what they know.'

"One of them's going to say, "oh yes, Scrydan's murder. Now you ask, that was me", are they?' Cwen snorted.

'Watching,' Wat repeated in an odd tone.

'Yes, she was,' Hermitage confirmed. 'Not really an appropriate way to behave, but a useful one on this occasion.'

'What is it?' Cwen asked Wat.

Hermitage glanced over and saw that Wat was now looking odd as well as sounding it. He was staring fixedly at the wall, and it was clear that significant thoughts were running through his head.

'Elnor was watching, and Father Thomas was watching Scrydan. The church,' he announced.

'Keep away from them,' Ansgar warned.

'It all fits.' Wat was excited.

Hermitage didn't know what fitted where, but Wat sounded convinced.

'The gold and Scrydan's disappearances,' Wat said.

'Are you going to explain?' Cwen enquired.

'All along, we've wondered where Scrydan got three pounds, two ounces of gold,' Wat began. 'It didn't come from Horik, and it wasn't registered as entering London at all.

'It's also a huge amount of gold for anyone to have. He must have got it from somewhere.'

'That seems reasonable,' Cwen agreed.

'So, he stole it.'

'Stole it?' Hermitage asked.

'Of course. He must have done. You don't just find that quantity of gold lying around. You have to take it from someone who already has it.' He seemed to wait for them all to catch up, which they failed to do.

'And who has pounds and pounds of gold?'

'Erm,' Hermitage tried to think.

'The church!' Wat was positively bubbling.

'Oh, well, I suppose they might.'

'And Saint Paul's seems a particularly wealthy church. I imagine they've got a treasury stacked with gold and silver. Plates, jugs, all the stuff churches have.'

'Well, I suppose it's possible,' Hermitage admitted. 'But as you say, it would be in the treasury. Safe and secure.'

'You would think,' Wat said. 'But where did Scrydan disappear? Which corner did he vanish around? The one by

Saint Paul's.'

Hermitage put the picture together. 'You think Scrydan was stealing the gold from the church?' It was a truly appalling idea. If it was true, perhaps God put the clasp in Scrydan's chest.

'Where else?' Wat asked. 'The church has the gold. Scrydan disappears near the church? I think he had a secret way into the treasury.'

'Surely, the church would notice if pounds of their gold went missing?'

'Not if they've got so much of it,' Wat said. 'And it could be that they just discovered the fact, which would explain Father Thomas being after Scrydan.'

'We don't know that he was after him,' Hermitage said.

'We don't know that he wasn't.'

'What do we do now, then?' Bart asked. 'Go and ask Father Thomas if we can have a look in his treasury?' He clearly intended this as a ridiculous suggestion.

'Exactly,' Wat agreed.

'I don't think he's likely to agree,' Hermitage said. 'Most churchmen wouldn't be allowed in the treasury, never mind us.'

Wat thought about this. 'Either he knows there is gold missing, in which case, he'd probably prefer it if no one found out. Can't be good, having your gold taken when you're supposed to be looking after it.

'Or he doesn't know there's gold missing, in which case he might be quite grateful. And him being in the street really was a coincidence.'

'Or he simply doesn't believe any of this,' Cwen said. 'And politely invites us to leave. Or impolitely.'

'Got to be worth a try,' Wat said.

Ansgar was shaking his head. 'Very difficult, churchmen. Even in Harold's time and Edward before him. You could never get the church to cooperate over anything.

'I wanted to build a bridge over the River Fleet from their land and they said no. So, I said I'd put a ferry in. They said no to that because they'd decided to build a bridge. Impossible.'

'We can but ask,' Wat persisted. 'And I don't know that any of the other passers-by on the night of Scrydan's death would have three pounds, two ounces of gold in their treasury.'

'It's late now,' Hermitage said. 'Perhaps this would be best for the morning.' He was optimistically hoping that something else would occur to them and when the morning came, they wouldn't need to bother Father Thomas at all.

'You could be right,' Cwen agreed, much to his relief.

'Although,' Wat said slowly. 'Sneaking into the church treasury at night might be easier than turning up at the front door.'

'Sneaking in?' Hermitage hoped he wasn't serious while knowing that he was.

'I can't imagine Scrydan knocked on the door nicely and asked for some pounds of gold,' Wat said.

'It'll be as dark as a cave,' Cwen said. 'Scrydan knew his secret way, how are we going to find it?'

'There are torches. It can't do any harm to look, can it? And if it's dark as a cave, we might not be spotted?'

'Or you are spotted and get hauled away,' Cwen said.

'Who by?' Wat asked. 'The sheriff?' he nodded towards Ansgar.

'Don't get me involved in this,' Ansgar warned. 'I'm not messing about with the church.'

'Who's with me, then?' Wat asked. 'It probably is best if we don't all go. A crowd trying to break into the treasury might be noticed.'

'I thought you said you were going to sneak?' Hermitage asked.

'Sneak, break? Who's to know?'

'And what is it you're going to discover if you do get in, eh? Tell me that.' Cwen sounded as if she had identified a major problem.

'We'll find the gold,' Wat assured her.

'Excellent. And you'll find there's some missing?'

'Could be.'

'You can spot missing gold in the dark, can you?'

Wat opened his mouth to answer quickly but found that he couldn't.

'We'll find out if there's a way in, that will help,' Wat tried.

'Until we get Father Thomas to say whether any is missing, it won't help at all,' Cwen said.

'Hermitage,' Wat pleaded. 'What are treasuries like?'

'What are they like?'

'Yes. Knowing you, I imagine they'd be organised neatly. Probably a separate box for every piece, or a special shelf, that sort of thing.'

'Oh, yes,' Hermitage agreed. 'The church will know every piece of plate it has and what function it performs.'

'So, if there are gaps in the place, we'll know that some has gone.'

'Oh, could be, I suppose. You could always consult the record, as well.' Even as he said these words, his stomach dropped to his shoes, letting him know that if he was forced into this awful mission, it was staying here.

'The record?' Wat asked with interest.

Hermitage sighed. 'There will be a book. It will have a record of every piece in the treasury. It will also note when it is taken out, by whom and when it is returned.'

Wat gloated like a goat with a lamp on its head. 'We'll need someone who can read, then.'

For a hopeless moment, Hermitage thought that Bedric might be the man for the job but he could not shirk his responsibilities.

'That would be me, then,' Hermitage sagged.

'Excellent. And a monk in a church might go unnoticed.'

'Two monks would be better,' Ansgar said.

'Have we got another one?' Bart looked around the room.

'No, but I have a monk's habit that Master Wat might wear.'

'How many robes and clothes have you got?' Cwen asked.

'Things get handed into the sheriff,' Ansgar explained.

'Monks' habits? Who hands in a monk's habit?'

'A monk who's changed his mind?' Wat suggested.

'There are those who turn from their calling,' Hermitage said.

'And leave their clothes behind?' Cwen grimaced at the thought.

'They find others,' Hermitage didn't think he should have to explain that.

Ansgar returned to the back room and came back with a weight of dark cloth across his arms.

Wat went over to take it. He took a cautious sniff. 'Good Lord. What did the last monk do in this?'

'It has been lying around for some time,' Ansgar explained. 'It's probably a bit stale.'

'I can't put this on,' Wat complained.

'Of course, you can,' Cwen urged. 'Just don't breathe.'

'And think of Alders Gate market,' Ansgar warned in a fearsome tone.

Wat looked most uncomfortable and closed his eyes as Cwen and Ansgar slid the habit over his head.

As he stood in it, he looked as if he would like to move his head a bit farther away from his body.

'Stop making such a fuss,' Cwen instructed.

'It doesn't look quite right.' Hermitage appraised the cloth. 'There are lumps.'

'Well, they're not mine,' Wat replied.

'Of course, you're not supposed to have your clothes on underneath,' Hermitage said. 'This is all you wear.'

Wat was clear. 'I am not letting my bare flesh anywhere near this thing. I'm only safe because I think the smell must have killed all the fleas.'

'You look just the part,' Cwen stood back admiringly. 'And the smell will keep everyone away. Perfect for sneaking.'

'I suppose people may think you an anchorite,' Hermitage mused.

'I am not.'

'A monk who retreats from life and lives alone in a world of prayer.' He thought wistfully of such a life. 'They tend not to wash.'

'Come on,' Wat said reluctantly. 'Let's get this over with. The sooner we check the treasure, the sooner I can get out of this thing. I just hope I don't see anyone I know.'

Cwen waved them off into the night with unnecessary humour, and Wat led the way back towards Saint Paul's.

'Of course,' Wat admitted. 'We may not find Scrydan's way in at all. It wouldn't be much of a treasury if anyone could help themselves.'

'How long do we look?' Hermitage hoped that not long at

all, would be the answer.

'We'll see when we get there. Where's this treasury likely to be?'

'In a church the size of Saint Paul's, I'd say it would be underground, in a crypt of some sort.'

Wat nodded to himself. 'So, we look for some sort of opening at ground level. A low window or a hatch of some sort. Anything out of the ordinary.'

They were already at the back of the church building, where there was nothing of any note at all. Simple solid walls stretched away above them, with only high windows punctuating the bare stone face.

'It's a bit dark,' Wat commented as he looked along the ground as they walked.

Hermitage didn't like to point out that that's what Cwen had said.

Wat stood upright, looked around and went and helped himself to a torch from the wall of a nearby building.

'Wat, you can't just take a torch,' Hermitage insisted.

'No one was using it,' Wat replied.

'Everyone was using it to see their way along the street.'

'They should all be at home.' Wat ignored the problem and now looked along the ground with his torch in hand.

'Nothing, nothing,' he muttered as he went.

Hermitage followed along, not looking for a way in, but rather keeping an eye out for passers-by, in case he needed to apologise.

'Ah, what have we here?' Wat called out.

Hermitage went over to him.

In the ground at the foot of the wall about halfway along the length of the church, a small wooden door was sunk halfway into the ground. Two steps led down from the road and even then, a crouch would be needed to get through.

'It doesn't look very secret,' Hermitage observed. 'It looks like a perfectly normal door.'

Wat stepped quickly down and tried it. 'Locked.'

'Not Scrydan's way in, then.'

'Not tonight,' Wat agreed. He examined the door as closely as he could. 'Unless Scrydan had a key?' He directed Hermitage's attention to a keyhole, quite an extravagance for a normal door.

'Why would he have a key?' Hermitage asked.

'To get in and help himself to the gold.'

'I don't mean what would he use a key for, I mean why would Scrydan have a key to a door in the wall of the church? How did he get it?'

'He's a metal smith. He could make one, they're simple things.'

'A key out of gold?' Hermitage wondered how such a thing would work. He knew that Saint Peter had a golden key, but that was different.

'No, not gold,' Wat snorted. 'He could work any metal if he was a competent smith.'

'Do we look for his key, then? In his workshop. Perhaps Ansgar found it?'

'We carry on looking for now. There could be other ways in.'

Wat proceeded on along the walls of the church with his torch in hand.

Hermitage was just thinking that if anyone did ask, he would say that they were walking the bounds by torchlight as part of their devotion. It would be a pretty odd devotion, but then many of them were.

They were more discreet when they walked across the

front of the church, but thought it unlikely that Scrydan had crept in that way.

The far side of the church revealed no more entrances.

'That has to be it, then,' Wat concluded.

'If Scrydan did take gold from the treasury at all,' Hermitage said.

'Where else, Hermitage?' Wat sounded impatient. 'We've been through this. The only other people who might have gold would be the Normans. And stealing from the church is bad enough, stealing from the Normans would be really stupid. Particularly if the point of stealing it was to give it back.'

'We look for a key, then?'

'We do. We also come back and ask Thomas about the contents of his treasury.'

They had walked back around the church and were passing the sunken door once more when Hermitage was sure he heard a voice.

'Hello?' he asked. 'Is someone there?' He didn't know where "there" would be, as no one was in sight.

'It's me, Fridolf.'

'Fridolf? Where are you?' Hermitage looked around.

'I'm in the church.'

'Well, that's good That's where you should be.'

Wat stepped down to the door. 'Are you behind the door?'

'No,' Fridolf replied. 'You're behind the door. I'm up here.'

Hermitage looked up and peering out from one of the high windows, he could just make out the shape of a head.

He and Wat stepped back from the building and looked up.

'What's that smell?' Fridolf asked.

'Never mind the smell,' Wat replied. 'What do you want?

And what are you doing up there?'

'You've got to get me out of here.'

'You were the one who claimed sanctuary.'

'I want to unclaim it now. They're all mad. I had to sneak away and climb up here to get away from them.'

'Why do you think they're mad?' Hermitage asked.

'It's that Father Thomas,' Fridolf said. 'the old man had me cleaning his floor, but then Thomas came and found me. He keeps asking where the gold is and telling me that I've got to give it back. Does he mean the clasp? I haven't got it. What's he talking about?'

'Oh, he wants it back, does he?' Wat asked. 'That is interesting. We definitely need to have a word with Father Thomas.'

'Now?' Fridolf pleaded. 'You'll come now?'

'We'll have to come in the morning,' Wat said. 'There's something very important that I've got to attend to first.'

'What's that?'

'Change my clothes.'

Caput XXIII: Time For Church

'We've got him,' Wat reported as he got out of the habit as quickly as possible. 'Father Thomas.'

Ansgar grumbled some more about the church but took the habit, seemingly without being affected by its odour.

'What did he say?' Cwen asked.

'We didn't see him.'

'I see.'

'We heard from Fridolf.'

'You heard from Fridolf? And this means that you've got Father Thomas.'

'It does.'

Wat shivered as if still recovering from the awful experience with the habit.

'Hermitage,' Cwen said. 'You explain.'

'Oh, right, well. Let's see. We found a door that appeared to lead beneath the church but it was locked. It is possible that Scrydan had a key, so we must look for that.

'When we were coming back, we heard a voice from a window, and it was Fridolf. He asked us to get him out of there as Father Thomas kept asking him where the gold was and saying that he had to give it back.'

'You see,' Wat said. 'Father Thomas.'

'Unless, of course, Father Thomas has only just discovered that some of his gold is missing. He has worked out where it went and wants Fridolf to return it,' Cwen suggested.

'Yes,' Wat admitted reluctantly. 'Or, he knows that Scrydan took it, had him killed and now wants the gold back from Fridolf.'

'If he had Scrydan killed,' Bart thought out loud.

'Wouldn't he have taken the clasp back?'

'Yes,' Siward agreed. 'You'd hardly have someone killed for taking your gold and then leave them with the gold. I'd have thought.'

'All right.' Wat was irritated. 'There may still be some details to sort out, but Father Thomas knows about the gold, however you look at it.'

'So, we ask him,' Cwen said.

'We do,' Wat agreed. 'In the morning. I need to do something about the stink from that habit.'

'What about poor Fridolf locked up in the church with the mad people?'

'Oh, he'll be fine,' Wat dismissed the problem. 'I don't think they'll let him go anywhere.'

. . .

The following dawn saw everyone still in the front room. As they'd spent the entire night in there, this was hardly surprising. Various collections of straw had been located but it still made for a very uncomfortable and unsatisfactory rest.

Of them all, only Wat seemed at all refreshed.

'I've slept in worse places than this,' he explained without going any further.

'Now,' he rubbed his hands with happy anticipation. 'Father Thomas.'

Ansgar appeared from his chamber somewhere off in the house and seemed slightly disappointed that they were all still here.

'We're off to church,' Wat said.

'You go, then,' Ansgar replied. 'And tell me what you find.'

'And if we find that it was Father Thomas?' Bart asked.

Ansgar shrugged. 'Don't know what we do. I can't see even the Normans wanting to execute a churchman, even if they were allowed to do it. They can't get at Fridolf, so they certainly won't get at a priest.'

'There is something you could do,' Hermitage said.

'And what might that be?' Ansgar did not sound happy at the suggestion.

'The other people who were in the street that night. The ones who seemed to have an interest in Scrydan.'

'What about them?' Ansgar sounded suspicious that he was going to be asked to do something he didn't want to do.

'We need to hear from them all.'

'It's Father Thomas,' Wat assured the room.

'It could well be,' Hermitage agreed. 'But we still need all the other tales. From Cyneruth, Wilf, Grun and Todwulf. We need to know what they saw.'

'Todwulf can't usually see anything,' Ansgar grumbled.

'But they might know something of use to us. They may even have seen Father Thomas and what he was really up to.'

'I can't go wandering the town talking to that lot,' Ansgar complained. 'I'm the Shire Reeve of Middelseaxe, I've got more important things to do.'

'Like dead geese and leftover clothes?' Cwen asked.

Ansgar's face darkened. 'It doesn't take five of you to question one priest,' he said as if it was an instruction. 'Those two can go and find the others.' He pointed at Siward and Bart.

'Oh,' Bart complained. 'We want to see the gold.'

'That's my command,' Ansgar said and it did not sound like a command to be questioned.

Hermitage could tell that they were not going to move the sheriff, and, when he thought about it, he saw that they had gone about asking him in entirely the wrong way.

'You will have to go,' he told Bart and Siward who moaned in response. 'It is an important part of the investigation.'

'It's not the bit with gold in it,' Siward muttered.

'That is my decision.' Ansgar seemed to say this primarily for Cwen's benefit.

She gave a "please yourself" sort of shrug.

'Right, time to go.' Wat seemed very keen to leave the sheriff's house now.

'Where do we find these people?' Siward moaned as they filed out of the door past Mistress Medwyn who was just arriving, bearing what looked like fresh goose fat stains down her front.

'Investigate,' Cwen told them simply.

'You already know where Cyneruth is,' Wat said. 'Go and start with him.'

'They think we're your slaves,' Bart complained.

'How did that come about?' Cwen asked.

'Long story,' Wat clearly didn't have the time for a long story. 'That's only Eligius. It's Cyneruth you need. And if Wilf is trying to be an apprentice, Cyneruth will probably know where to find him.

'As for a drunk carpenter, ask anyone. It sounds like he has a reputation.

'You also know where to find Grun.'

'He's probably one of the big men who guard Horik's house,' Siward moaned. 'How are we supposed to ask him anything?'

'You open your mouths and some questions come out,' Cwen explained.

'And if he doesn't like us opening our mouths in front of him?' Bart asked seriously. 'If he decides to hit us in our

250

mouths?'

'Duck,' Cwen said. 'You want to be an investigator, work it out.'

With no more helpful or unhelpful advice to impart, they walked on. When they came down Ceapen Street, Wat extravagantly indicated where Eligius's workshop was, and that Siward and Bart were going that way.

Still looking very reluctant about it, Bart went over and knocked timidly on the door of the workshop.

The others walked on.

'We could come back in a few hours and find they're still there,' Cwen complained.

Only when they crossed into the bounds of Saint Paul's did Hermitage wonder what they were actually going to do. Asking to see Father Thomas would be easy enough, getting him to talk about the gold might be a very different matter.

His experiences of dealing with senior figures in the church were universally bad. As priest of Saint Paul's, Thomas would be one of those figures and either Hermitage had a problem with them, or they did with him. They always seemed to talk at cross-purposes, confuse one another and part on poor terms.

Perhaps Wat would have better luck. He could deal with all sorts of people, but Thomas might be one of those who disapproved of the weaver's earlier works.

Of course, everyone disapproved of Wat's earlier works when they were asked about them. It seemed to be an entirely different matter in private.

They were walking up the steps to the church now, so whatever was going to happen had become inevitable and out of Hermitage's control.

He knew that he frequently avoided dealing with issues

until they became inevitable, by which time it was too late. It wasn't really the best way of getting through life.

The main door to the church was already open for the first Order of the day, although Lauds was probably over now. If only Hermitage had got up earlier, he could have taken part.

There was no one about when they entered the church, which seemed a little odd for such a large place.

Hermitage led the way on down towards the altar, looking to left and right to see if anyone could be spotted in the aisles. The place was completely empty, and the only thing he could think to do was return to the chamber where they had originally discussed all this with Thomas.

With a shrug to the others, he nodded towards the small door, and they followed his direction.

Once at the door, he gave a light tap and waited for the invitation to enter; or the instruction to go away.

Cwen leaned around him, thumped hard on the door and turned the handle to go in.

Three faces turned towards them.

Fridolf was seated in a chair in the middle of the room and looked at them with a distinctly worried face.

In front of him, clearly caught in the middle of pacing up and down, Father Thomas did not look at all happy.

Standing off to one side, the cleric they had met before stood as if observing whatever was going on.

'Thank God you're here,' Fridolf called. 'They caught me,' he explained with a pained look towards Father Thomas.

'Taking the name of the Lord in vain will not aid you,' Father Thomas snapped. 'What do you want?' he turned his irritation to the new arrivals.

'Ah,' Father Thomas,' Wat said. 'Just the priest we were looking for.'

This got no response.

'We've come about the gold.' Wat sounded as if he had come about a hole in the roof.

'The gold?' Thomas snapped. 'What do you know about it?'

Well, that was something, to Hermitage's mind. At least Thomas wasn't denying that there was any gold, or even that he knew what gold was.

'Scrydan's gold,' Cwen clarified.

'The gold that was made into that massive clasp for the king.'

'Yes, yes. Where is it?' Thomas demanded.

'It's in safe hands.'

'What's that supposed to mean? Who has safe hands?'

'The sheriff. Sorry, Shire Reeve,' Wat explained.

Thomas breathed heavily and appeared to be mightily relieved. 'Then it must be returned.'

'I suppose it should,' Wat didn't sound convinced.

'What do you mean, you suppose it should?' Thomas asked. 'There is no question. It must go back.'

'To the treasury?' Cwen enquired.

'How do you know about that?' Thomas now demanded. 'In fact, how do you know about any of this?'

'Brother Hermitage is the King's Investigator,' Wat said. 'It's the sort of thing he does.'

Hermitage gave a weak smile.

'The gold and the murder of Scrydan, that sort of thing,' Cwen explained.

'Scrydan's gold clasp was huge,' Wat said. 'Three pounds, two ounces, no less. We have also discovered that he didn't get it from the only gold merchant in town.'

'Horik,' Thomas said. 'Awful, sinful woman.'

'She certainly seems so. But she both supplies gold for London and makes sure that no one else does.

'So, where could Scrydan get his hands on that quantity of gold?'

'And you worked out where he had?' Thomas sounded quite impressed.

'We did,' Cwen said.

'Perhaps we'd better go and look?' Wat suggested. 'To see just how much is missing?'

'Really?' The priest seemed somewhat surprised by this idea.

'Of course. Hermitage likes evidence, don't you, Hermitage?'

Hermitage nodded that he did.

'It's best if we see it for ourselves before we draw all this to a close.'

'If you wish.' Thomas sounded more confused than anything by this request, which made Hermitage worry that they were about to discover some new problem. 'Come then. Scrydan's apprentice here persists in claiming to know nothing about this. If he sees the scale of his master's sin, he might change his tale.'

'I didn't know,' Fridolf said plaintively.

'It is quite possible that he didn't,' Hermitage said. 'We have discovered that Scrydan was a secretive fellow who told no one of his business. Not even his apprentices.'

'See.' Fridolf gloated. 'I told you I didn't know.'

'Hm.' Father Thomas was not convinced but gestured that they should all leave the room.

Once back in the main body of the church, Thomas led them over to the left of the altar and into a dark corridor beyond.

A little way along this, he came to another small door on the left which had a great lock set in the wood. From his belt, he lifted a key and put it into the lock.

It turned with some ease, and he pushed the door open. On the other side of it, small steps led down in a tight spiral.

Halfway down these stairs, a door was set into the wall. 'The other door on the outside?' Wat checked. 'Into the street?'

'It is,' Thomas confirmed. 'One that had never been used, and which, as far as we knew, was sealed fast.'

'But Scrydan had a key,' Wat said. 'Probably made himself.'

'He certainly didn't get one from me,' Thomas confirmed.

'Then how did he know this was here at all?' Cwen asked.

Thomas explained as he went down the stairs. 'We had a gold chalice that was damaged during a festival. Dropped by some careless hand. We commissioned Scrydan to repair it.'

'I remember that,' Fridolf spoke up. 'He brought it back and I repaired it. He never did say where it had come from.'

'So, he knew the treasury was here,' Wat said. 'And he worked out how to get in.'

'It must be so,' Thomas agreed.

'You didn't know he was helping himself to the gold?' Cwen asked.

'What?' Thomas was appalled. 'How dare you? Of course, I didn't know.'

'Only asking,' Cwen defended herself. 'Scrydan was making a great clasp to impress the king. You sounded pretty keen to keep on the good side of the Normans when Fridolf came here for sanctuary. You could have come up with this plan between you. You supply the gold and he makes the clasp.'

'I make the clasp, you mean,' Fridolf muttered.

Father Thomas stopped at the bottom of the stairs.

'That is the most disgusting and disgraceful accusation,' he said fiercely. 'It was only just before Scrydan's death that I discovered where the gold had come from.'

'You don't come down here often, then?' Wat asked. 'It must have taken Fridolf quite a while to make that clasp.'

'It did,' Fridolf confirmed.

'Which means Scrydan took the gold some time ago And you're seriously saying that you didn't notice?'

'Of course, I didn't,' Thomas protested. 'How would I?'

'Let's have a look then' Wat prompted. 'See how easy it is not to notice that three pounds, two ounces of gold have gone.'

Thomas turned away, clearly still angry.

It was very dark now that they were at the bottom of the steps and Thomas took an unlit torch that was sitting in a sconce on the wall. He handed it back to his cleric, who took a flint and striker from his robe, and expertly produced a bright flame. He also produced quite a quantity of smoke, which, being in a small underground chamber, would soon become uncomfortable.

He handed the torch back to Thomas who held it up.

They were in a small and unremarkable room. The stairway was now behind them and a crude table sat against the wall to their right. Ahead of them, a very large wooden cupboard occupied the whole wall. It was closed, its wooden doors clamped shut with another lock.

Off to the left, a dark opening went on, presumably into the foundations of the church.

'Is this it, then?' Wat asked, nodding towards the cupboard. 'Is this the treasury of Saint Paul's?'

Hermitage noticed that the table had quite a modest book

on it, doubtless the treasury record.

'It is,' Thomas confirmed.

'Let's have a look, then.'

'Let's have a look, then?' Father Thomas sounded quite appalled by the idea.

Hermitage could understand this. The treasury would be full of sacred items and should not be thrown open for just anyone, but these were remarkable circumstances.

'I fear it is necessary, Father,' he said.

Thomas looked at them all and shook his head at the things he was having to deal with. He nodded towards his cleric who stepped forward.

'I carry the key to the door,' Thomas explained gruffly. 'Mark here carries the key to the treasury. That way, neither of us has direct access to the treasure itself. If either of us were taken, the church's property would be safe.'

'A very sound arrangement,' Hermitage commented.

'Hm,' Thomas huffed. 'If you would, Mark?'

The cleric stepped forward, giving everyone a hard look in support of his master. He took his key and put it in the lock of the cupboard. He gave it a turn and stepped back.

It was clearly Father Thomas's role to open the doors which he now did, with a bow of respect to the contents.

With the treasure of Saint Paul's now revealed in all its glory, Hermitage could see why Thomas was so angry.

On one shelf stood a chalice, doubtless the one Fridolf had repaired. It was a magnificent piece, being so large that it would need two hands to lift it. It was simple in design but shone in the light of the torch.

On the next shelf down was a plate. This too was a large and impressive piece of gold, being at least two feet wide and embossed all over with religious images and decoration.

And that was it.

One chalice, one plate. It wasn't much of a treasury anymore.

'Oh dear,' Wat said.

'Oh, dear?' Thomas demanded, angry once more. 'What do you mean, oh dear?'

'Well,' Wat gestured with little interest toward the chalice and plate sitting in a cupboard that was capable of holding so much more. 'It's not much of a treasury, is it?'

'Not much of a treasury? These are revered items.'

'I'm sure they are,' Cwen sympathised. 'So, erm, what's missing?'

'Missing?' Thomas didn't seem to follow.

'Yes. What's missing? What did Scrydan take?'

Thomas looked at them all and frowned. 'This is the Treasure of Saint Paul's. The great chalice and the plate of Saint Augustine.' His frown lifted and he now looked at them with horrible superiority.

'Oh, I say.' He now smiled calmly. 'You didn't think Scrydan had got his gold from our treasury, did you? No, no, no.' He sounded positively smug and happy. 'I'm afraid you've got it completely wrong.'

Caput XXIV: Priestly Secrets

'But,' Wat said and then stopped. 'Scrydan got down here, yes?'

'He did. After showing him our treasury and getting the chalice repaired, he obviously came back.' Thomas nodded to Mark who now closed up the cupboard once more, putting the wealth of the church away from prying eyes.

'You saw him?'

'Mark did.'

Mark nodded that this was correct. 'Father Thomas and I had been down here to return the chalice following our rehearsal for the festival of Saint Adomnan.

Wat and Cwen looked to Hermitage who nodded that this was reasonable.

'I was just closing up the cupboard when I heard a noise and went to see. I thought it must be rats.' Mark nodded towards the dark entrance on the left of the chamber. I had only gone a few paces when someone came out and almost knocked me over. He dashed up the stairs and out of the side door.'

'Scrydan?' Hermitage checked.

'It was all a rush, but it was definitely Scrydan. Everyone knows what he looks like. Sorry, looked like.'

'So,' Thomas continued. 'Mark reported this to me, and we came down to see what Scrydan was up to. Like you, we feared that he had eyes on our treasure.'

'What was he doing, then, if not taking your gold?'

Father Thomas appeared to be considering them carefully. 'You obviously thought the gold had come from our treasury. So, if I am to show you more, I need to swear you all to secrecy.'

'Secrecy?' Wat didn't sound very keen.

'I can show you something that will explain much, but you must share it with no one.'

Hermitage didn't have a problem with that, but he could see that Wat and Cwen did.

'We don't know what it is now,' he said. 'Do we?'

'Obviously not,' Cwen replied.

'Then what is the harm in swearing secrecy? If we do, Father Thomas will show us but we can tell no one. If we do not swear, he won't show us. And then we won't be able to tell anyone anyway.'

Cwen looked at him and frowned. 'What?'

'Yes, we swear secrecy,' Wat said with a sigh.

'Do we?' Cwen asked.

'Like Hermitage said, what do we have to lose?'

'Is that what he said?'

'Near enough. We swear secrecy,' Wat confirmed.

'I'm not so sure,' Fridolf said and everyone looked at him. 'I've learned that it pays not to know secrets, they only cause trouble. People always want you to tell them. People like Horik.'

'And so you do tell them?' Cwen asked pointedly. 'Not being able to keep a secret?'

Fridolf didn't reply but looked a little chastened. 'Horik's not one to lie to. Best not to know in the first place.'

'You can return up the stairs if you wish,' Thomas said.

Fridolf looked torn between wanting to know what this secret was and not wanting to have to keep a secret. He turned back to the steps. 'If you don't know, you can't tell, Fridolf,' he muttered to himself.

'Very well,' Thomas spoke to the rest of them. Let us go

and see, then,' He gestured towards the end of the chamber. 'Mark can lead the way with the torch.'

'The smoke is getting a bit thick,' Cwen commented. 'Are we going to be able to breathe in there?'

'Oh, you will,' Thomas confirmed in a very knowing manner.

Mark led the way with Thomas bringing up the rear.

Hermitage could only think of this passage as a tunnel, for that was what it felt like. A small tunnel. A small tunnel with five people and a smoky torch in it. His trepidations weren't at their full power yet, but they were waking.

'How long is this tunnel?' he asked, trying to sound only mildly interested instead of increasingly terrified.

'It soon opens out,' Thomas replied. 'You'll see.'

They walked on without any sign of anything opening up.

'What is this place?' Cwen asked.

'Originally, it would have been for the builders,' Mark explained. 'The foundation timbers of the church go deep into the ground. They would have started down here and then built the church upwards.

'It could be that they left this tunnel here to allow access, or that they simply couldn't be bothered to fill it in.'

Hermitage noticed that the floor was sloping downwards. Which was not at all helpful to his worry. 'We must be feet below the ground, now,' he observed shakily.

'Yes,' Mark agreed. 'And beyond the bounds of the church. Which makes understanding this even more puzzling.'

The torch in Mark's hand suddenly burned bright and the choking smoke blew away as if they had stepped into the open.

They all filed up behind him and looked out at what his light revealed.

'My God,' Wat breathed.

For once, Hermitage did not comment on his language. He was too awestruck by the sight before them.

He spun around and tried to comprehend what had just happened.

Behind them, it looked as if they had come through a break in the wall. The tunnel at this end had no door, or neat entrance, rather a pile of rubble lay off to one side. At some point, someone had broken through the end of the passage into this place. And what a place it was.

In front of him was nothing less than a street. An underground street. It was such a ridiculous concept that Hermitage's mind tried to tell him that there must be some trick to this.

The road beneath their feet was cobbled with neatly laid stones and on either side, low stone buildings lined the way. Many of these had pillars to their front, holding up triangular pediments, meticulously carved into even shapes and patterns.

Others had friezes depicting figures in exquisite detail, with words laid in both top and bottom.

As his eyes got used to the light, Hermitage saw that this was not a long street. In fact, the squat buildings seemed to form a square of some sort, as more could be made out towards the back of the space.

'Romans,' he whispered. His voice hissed around the void and almost seemed to invite the Romans to return to their street and greet these visitors.

'So it seems,' Thomas agreed. He had obviously been here before and so was less overawed by the sight.

'What were they doing down here?' Cwen asked as she looked up to the roof of this cave.

Hermitage still couldn't hold the ideas of being in a cave and on a street in his mind at the same time. For now, he would try to concentrate on the street.

'And they must have been small,' Cwen observed. 'Those houses are tiny.'

'They are not houses,' Thomas explained.

Cwen looked at him and frowned.

'Tombs,' he said.

She didn't react immediately. 'Oh,' she said eventually, but it sounded like a very worried, oh. 'We're in a street full of dead Romans in a cave, then.'

'It's a lot of trouble to go to for dead people,' Wat observed.

'I have heard of Roman tombs,' Hermitage said. 'But they're in Rome. And usually, they're for important people. They had emperors, that sort of thing.'

'We can only imagine that the Romans dealt with their dead in the same way, wherever they were,' Thomas said.

'It would explain why we're underground,' Wat noted.

'We have explored a little further,' Mark spoke up. 'The ground is loose in parts, and it seems the street goes on around the back of the tombs. It is ridiculous, but Roman London must have been lower than the current one.'

'How did that happen?' Cwen asked.

Father Thomas explained with authority. 'We have surmised that because of their ungodly ways, the Lord struck them down and buried them, putting good Christian folk on top.'

'Which seems the only reasonable explanation,' Mark added.

No one could object to that very sound conclusion.

'So, we've got a street full of dead Romans in their tombs,'

Wat said.

'In their spoiled tombs,' Father Thomas specified with all seriousness.

'Spoiled?' Cwen asked. 'Who spoiled them?'

Hermitage explained. 'I imagine Father Thomas means spoiled in its original Latin form.'

'Oh, I'm sure he does,' Cwen sighed.

'Robbed.'

There was a pause in the street at this. The place was so remarkable, so unexpected and frankly magnificent, that everyone felt disgusted that a place like this should be robbed.

'By Scrydan,' Wat concluded.

'Exactly,' Thomas concurred. 'From what little he left behind, it seems that the Romans took their gold to their graves with them.'

'And Scrydan took it out again,' Wat said sadly. 'Which explains just where he got his three pounds, two ounces from. Has he been through them all?'

'No.' Thomas shook his head. 'As far as we can tell there are still some that are untouched. Which is how Mark came upon him.

'He must have been down here replenishing his stock just when Mark was putting the chalice back. If it were not for that coincidence, we might never have discovered his appalling act.'

'Being discovered must have annoyed him no end. No more gold.'

'And the gold he had taken should be put back,' Thomas said firmly.

'Put back?' Cwen asked. 'It sounds like he melted it all down.'

'When I say put back, it should be put back in the church. It should add to the treasury of Saint Paul's, not increase the wealth and standing of a grave robber.'

'Not be given back to the Romans then, eh?' Wat observed. 'I can imagine what Scrydan's response to that suggestion was. I assume you went and saw him.'

'I most certainly did,' Thomas confirmed. 'And he behaved in the most dreadful manner. He said he had found the gold and so it was his to do with as he liked.'

'Found it by breaking into a Roman tomb,' Hermitage pointed out.

'Exactly. And I suspect that this was not his first occasion.'

'Good heavens, really?'

'How did he know to explore the depths of the church?' Thomas asked. 'We all know there are Roman graves outside of the city walls. They are common in the eastern cemetery. I suspect Scrydan started there.

'Then, when he was brought down here to look at the chalice, he spotted the tunnel and the door and decided to come back and see what he could find.'

'When was this?' Wat asked.

'Mark only encountered him two days before he was killed. We suspect he had been down here long before that.'

'What an awful man,' Hermitage summarised.

'An awful man who said that he was not going to give you the gold back and that he had used it to make something for the king,' Wat speculated.

'I even threatened him with ex-communication for his actions.'

'To which he said?'

'That he had enough gold to buy a church of his own.'

Hermitage shook his head. It seemed that Scrydan really

was a man beyond decency. Now they had seen the things he was prepared to do, it might be no surprise that someone had killed him, but they were still no nearer finding out who.

'So,' Cwen said thoughtfully. 'On the night of the murder you were out in the street, following Scrydan,' Cwen added.

'Me?' Thomas asked.

'Yes. There's only one Father Thomas, I assume. And you were seen by someone who knows everyone.'

'Mistress Elnor,' Thomas concluded with some sadness. 'That woman needs to turn her thoughts to higher things.'

'It's a good job she hasn't. She saw you following Scrydan.'

'I was,' Thomas confessed. 'I still thought I could persuade him to return the gold, if only for the saving of his immortal soul.'

'I'll wager he thought he could buy another one of those, as well,' Wat said.

'And did you see what happened to him?' Cwen pressed.

'I did not,' Thomas confirmed. 'There were too many people about for me to discuss anything with him. I even thought that some others might be watching Scrydan, and so I left.'

'Yes, Elnor told us others were following.'

'But Scrydan was on his way to the king with the gold,' Wat said. 'It was about to be too late to stop him.'

'You mistake me for a merchant,' Thomas said. 'I had no interest in whether Scrydan gave gold to the king or not. I already have regular discussions with the Normans, and it would be easy to let them have word about the gold. Doubtless, they would have returned it once they knew.'

'Oh, doubtless,' Wat said, although it sounded as if he didn't believe it.

'Is there anything else we need to do down here?' Cwen

asked. 'I think I'd quite like to see the daylight again.'

Hermitage thought that he would quite like to be out of this place as well, despite the fact that there were clear Latin inscriptions on some of the tombs and he hadn't read them.

'We can go back up,' Thomas confirmed. 'But you will all recall your promise of secrecy concerning all this.'

'We won't tell,' Hermitage promised before anyone else could respond.

'Who'd believe us?' Cwen asked.

'I can see why Horik should never hear about it,' Wat said. 'If you think Scrydan is bad, I suspect that woman would tear the church down to get at any gold.'

Mark held the torch by the exit, and when they were all gathered, led the way back into the treasury chamber.

'You built a cupboard down here to hold your fine cup and plate,' Wat observed. 'When a few yards away, a whole cave full of gold was just sitting there.'

'Gold in the tombs of the dead,' Thomas said. 'Where it should have been left.'

Back at the top of the stairs again, Hermitage felt as if the pressure of the world had been lifted from his head. Simply standing under the magnificent roof of the church made him feel as if he could fly, compared to the oppression of the dark realm beneath his feet.

Fridolf was waiting for them and looked as if he was itching to know what the secret was now.

'You've been gone a while,' he observed.

'Yes, we have,' Cwen agreed mischievously. 'But it's a secret.'

They all made their way over to the chamber where they had first met.

'What will you do now?' Father Thomas asked Hermitage

when they were settled comfortably.

'We have to ask the others who were on the street what they may have seen. Mistress Elnor has given us some names.'

At that moment, the door to the chamber burst open and Siward almost fell into the room.

Everyone stood at this intrusion.

'Siward?' Hermitage asked. 'What's amiss?'

'It's the others,' Siward explained nothing at all.

'What others?' Cwen asked.

'The ones you asked us to go and get.'

'Go and get? No one asked you to go and get anyone.'

'Wilf and Cyneruth and Grun and Todwulf.'

'We didn't ask you to go and get them,' Cwen said with some impatience. 'Hermitage asked you to go and find out what they saw.'

'Did he?' Siward suddenly sounded very unsure of himself.

'Yes, he did. What have you done instead?'

'Well, we found them.' This sounded like it was a good thing, but it might also be the only good thing. 'And we, erm, sort of asked them to come along.'

'Come along where?'

'To the sheriff's.'

'You asked Grun to come with you to the sheriff's?' Wat checked. 'And he came?'

'We had to say we were only acting on the sheriff's orders, which we were. Sort of.'

'Well, I suppose it's one way of talking to them,' Cwen said. 'We'd better go and see what they have to say for themselves.'

'Good,' Siward breathed more freely and smiled. 'Only..,'

'Only what?' Cwen asked with resignation.

'The sheriff's sort of locked them up.'

'Locked them up. What, all of them? Where's he locked

them up?'

'In the lock-up,' Siward explained, plainly wondering why this was a question. 'It's a little house he has around the back for the troublesome drunks.'

'And why?' Wat asked.

'Well, they got a bit troublesome.'

'Troublesome?'

'It was hard to follow, but they all deny killing Scrydan. Said someone else did it.'

'They said what?' Hermitage asked. 'Who? Fridolf?'

'Do you mind?' Fridolf complained.

'They didn't give a name. But then they all started arguing and got into a bit of a fight. The sheriff locked them up.'

'I think we really had better go and see what this is all about,' Hermitage urged.

They all stood to leave, including Father Thomas.

'If this has to do with Scrydan, I need to know what it is,' he explained to Hermitage's questioning look.'

'And try to get your gold back,' Cwen muttered.

'And perhaps Fridolf had better come along as well if he's willing to step out of sanctuary?' Hermitage suggested.

Fridolf didn't look too happy at the prospect.

'If they're all accusing someone else,' Cwen said. 'What have you got to worry about?'

Caput XXV: The Gathering

Sheriff Ansgar did not look happy to see them. He hadn't looked happy from the moment Hermitage met him, but now he had an urgency to his unhappiness as if he expected someone to do something about it immediately.

He also seemed quite shocked at the number of people who were crowding into his house.

'You know,' he said to Hermitage. 'It used to be me, Bedric, Medwyn and Aeva and we managed perfectly well. A couple of men for errands and we were done. Now we've got dozens of you cluttering the place up.'

Hermitage's first reaction was to point out that it wasn't dozens, but he could see that a touch of pedantry would not make things better. And he was quite pleased to have seen that.

'There is a complicated and significant murder to be resolved,' Hermitage said politely.

Ansgar started growling but went very quiet when Father Thomas and Mark entered at the back of the line.

'Shire Reeve,' Thomas acknowledged quite stiffly.

'Father,' Ansgar responded.

There was clearly some problem between these two men, but that was the least of the problems at the moment.

'I understand you have locked up a number of people?' Hermitage enquired.

'Troublemakers,' Ansgar summed them up. 'And it was your two who brought them in here.' He glared at Siward and Bart.

'Yes,' Hermitage acknowledged. 'But they were only doing their best in trying to determine who killed Scrydan.'

270

'You think it was one of them?' Ansgar sounded disbelieving. 'They're all mad. Or drunk.'

'I understand that they all claim not to have done it.'

'It's the sort of thing idiots like that do when they're trying to get out of trouble.'

'So you think one of them might have done it?'

'I think they've all heard that the Normans execute people for murder, now. The best thing to do in those circumstances is to make sure someone else takes the blame, whether you had anything to do with it or not.'

'But from what you have seen, do you think one of them could have done it?'

'I thought those two had done it,' Ansgar gave Siward and Bart his favourite look. 'In fact, they told me they had. Since then, the whole thing has got ridiculous. Still, at least you can take the other lot away now.'

'Take them away?'

'Of course. I don't want them.'

'Erm,' Hermitage had no idea what he was supposed to do with them.

'You are the Shire Reeve, yes?' Cwen asked.

Hermitage winced slightly as he could see where this conversation might end up.

'I am,' Ansgar confirmed in a positively threatening manner.

'Excellent,' Cwen smiled disarmingly. 'So normally, it's your job to find out who killed who and deal with them. Brother Hermitage is the King's Investigator, he only does murders the king wants him to look into. You're lucky he's here.

'Once this one is all done, you can get on with them yourself again.' She took a breath. 'In fact, come to think of it, perhaps you can take over now and we'll be on our way. After all, it's probably one of the people you've got locked up. You just have to work out which one.'

Ansgar looked as if there was another Ansgar inside, desperate to get out. That one wanted to run to the hills and do battle with mighty foes, and not be bothered with working out who did things. He clenched his fists and gritted his teeth. 'What do you suggest then, mistress?' he asked, making it very plain that Cwen had better have something helpful to suggest.

'We do what we always do on these occasions.'

'And that is?'

'We get everyone in a room together. Hermitage walks up and down in front of them explaining everything and then says who did it.'

Hermitage was suddenly very keen to visit those hills with Ansgar.

'I do what?' he asked shakily.

'What you always do.'

'But, we've got no idea who killed Scrydan. Even after all this time and all these people.'

'You've got a lockup full of people who were there at the time. We get them all and talk to them. It'll come to you.'

'It'll come to me?'

'It always does.'

Hermitage looked to Wat for some aid in this awful situation, but the weaver only shrugged, seeming to say that it was worth a try.

'We've got a lot of information now, Hermitage,' he said. 'Talking to this lot might well reveal the truth of it all.'

'And if it doesn't?'

'What have we lost?'

This wasn't what Hermitage had had in mind at all. 'Perhaps we could talk to them one at a time. You know, get their stories and see where the contradictions lie. Then, we confront each with the specific details of the questions raised.

'A further round of interrogations will narrow this down further until we reach a point at which we have a reasonable level of confidence that one or other of them is the most likely perpetrator.'

Ansgar was looking completely lost. 'And how long is all that going to take?'

'As long as it needs.'

'Medwyn,' Ansgar called. 'Clear the space, I'm bringing that lot in from the lock-up. The monk here is going to spot the killer.'

'Right oh,' Medwyn called happily.

'No, I..,' Hermitage tried, but Ansgar was already off.

'It'll be fine, Hermitage,' Cwen encouraged. 'You'll see. Something will occur to you.'

Hermitage didn't like relying on things occurring to him. He wanted to know what they were in advance.

Medwyn pushed the chairs and table to the side and looked around the room as if making sure that she had tidied properly for some important guests.

'This is jolly, isn't it?' she said.

'What's going on?' Bedric appeared from the back room.

'Hermitage is going to say who the murderer is,' Bart explained enthusiastically.

'Oh, right.' Bedric pulled up a chair and made himself comfortable.

Even Aeva now came in from the front door. 'I'm not dressing up as Scrydan again,' she said, having plainly overheard. 'Not with the killer in the room.'

Father Thomas stepped in and gestured that Mark should get him a chair. There were going to be so many people, it would be standing room only.

Hermitage wondered for a moment whether, given that Aeva was now away from the door, he could make a run for it. He didn't know where he would run to, or what the consequences of his running would be, but anything had to be better than this.

Wat, Cwen, Bart and Siward now joined the growing throng, while Fridolf loitered by the door. It put his own thoughts of escape to one side as he realised that the young man would soon be caught if he did try to leave.

The clattering by the door made Hermitage's stomach drop several inches and Ansgar reappeared.

He was shepherding a peculiar flock into the house, and Hermitage did his best to appraise them as they arrived.

Grun came first, and he was the man from Horik's door. If Hermitage were to conclude guilt based on who looked most guilty, it would be him.

He was big enough to murder anyone without hindrance, and the look on his face said that he was ready to do it to someone now. It was only the size and presence of the sheriff that seemed to be keeping him under control.

Next was Todwulf. This had to be Todwulf. He was an old man and was the only one of the number who was plainly drunk. How he managed to be so after being locked up was a mystery. He must have been drunk when he came in.

His bleary eyes looked around the room as if trying to make it stop moving, and he swayed precariously on his own feet.

Hermitage immediately found it hard to believe Todwulf could have done the deed unless it was an accident. And accident was a distinct possibility. But with the pin of a huge gold clasp? Only a fool would trust Todwulf with anything sharp. If he really was a carpenter, it was a wonder he managed to saw any wood without taking his own fingers off.

Behind him must be Cyneruth, the goldsmith's apprentice. He was a slight young man, but he had an intelligent look about him. He was obviously appraising the room as he came in and making quick judgements about the people before him.

There was something scheming about this, but he gave Hermitage the impression that he was too clever to be caught doing something so crude as stabbing a goldsmith to death.

Finally, there was Wilf. And, like Todwulf, there was no mistaking him. He was by far the youngest of the group, perhaps being only fourteen or so. Despite those years, he carried himself into the room with a confidence that was almost overbearing. He was also the best-dressed of the band, wearing a fine robe that hung neatly around a rather large frame.

There must be some wealth in Wilf's family as he clearly dressed and ate very well indeed.

His look was one of rather condescending willingness to put up with all of this.

Add Fridolf to the band and Hermitage still had not the first idea who might have done the deed.

He supposed he should add Father Thomas, as he only had the priest's word that he had turned back and not followed Scrydan. And if there was one thing he had learned, it was that murderer's words were seldom to be trusted.

'Right,' Ansgar commanded. 'This monk here is going to tell us who killed Scrydan. So shut up and listen.' He nodded to Hermitage that he could now proceed.

'What's a monk got to do with it?' Wilf asked.

Cwen held him with a gaze. 'This monk is King William's own investigator of murder. That's what he's got to do with it. All right?'

Wilf muttered to himself but didn't say that it wasn't all right.

Hermitage looked at everyone in turn. Then he pursed his lips and nodded a couple of times. After that, he put his hands behind his back and took a couple of paces up and down. Still, nothing occurred to him.

'Well?' Wilf asked impudently. 'I don't know what we're doing here anyway. This is nothing to do with me.'

Hermitage knew that he had to say something. He never usually had a problem saying something. Whether it would be any use was a different question.

'I gather you all deny the murder of Scrydan,' Hermitage said.

'I know it wasn't me,' Wilf replied. 'In which case, it was probably one of them, wasn't it? '

'Or someone else completely?' Hermitage suggested.

'What have we been dragged here for, then?'

'You were on the street the night Scrydan was murdered.'

'I imagine lots of people were.'

'But you were all following Scrydan.'

'Says who?' Wilf sneered.

'Says someone who saw you,' Cwen snapped. 'So it's time to shut up now.'

Wilf looked ready to respond but satisfied himself with a sulk instead.

'And you all had reason to be following Scrydan,' Hermitage continued. 'Including Fridolf, here.'

Fridolf looked offended that he was being brought into this

again.

Hermitage now voiced his own thoughts, which at least sounded as if he was getting somewhere.

'Fridolf had been turned down for master by Scrydan and there was no sign of his being able to progress. He approached the other masters, to see if one of them would take him on, but they refused. He wished Scrydan dead, he even said so. And he was on the street the day of the murder, yet he claims not to have done it.'

'I didn't,' Fridolf insisted.

'If there was a fine at the end of this, instead of execution by the Normans, you might not be so sure,' Cwen pointed out.

'I did not kill Scrydan,' Fridolf repeated.

'So you say,' Hermitage agreed that he had said it. 'Next, we have Master Grun. Master Grun who works for Horik the gold merchant.

'We know that Horik was most put out that Scrydan had his own supply of gold. As the only merchant in London, a position perhaps secured through the removal of any opposition, she could not have him undermining her. She might well wish him dead and in Grun had the means to make it so.'

'I didn't,' Grun said simply.

'Everyone says they didn't,' Hermitage noted. He looked to the room. 'I assume no one wants to confess?' he said hopefully.

No one did.

'Cyneruth, then? Another apprentice goldsmith following Scrydan?'

'Another apprentice who thinks he should be a master but who isn't,' Wat added. 'This time for Master Eligius, who also hated Scrydan with some passion.'

Hermitage considered this. 'Perhaps sent on a mission by your master? To make sure Scrydan never made it to the king?'

'Nothing of the sort,' Cyneruth protested loudly.

Hermitage was losing hope that anyone was going to say anything that might give a hint as to who had done this deed.

'Master Todwulf, the carpenter,' he now tried. 'You are a puzzle. I ask myself what on earth you are doing in this band? Why were you following Scrydan?'

Todwulf didn't look capable of giving a sensible answer to where he was now, never mind what he'd been doing days ago.

He swayed about a bit and thumped himself on the chest. 'My box,' he seemed to say.

'Your box?' Hermitage asked.

'S'right. And it's not right.'

Hermitage couldn't make any sense of this but then realised where a box fitted.

'The box that the clasp was in. The one Gythred and Brod told us about. You made the box for Scrydan's clasp?' He asked Todwulf loudly.

'Aye,' Todwulf said proudly. 'And a finer piece of work you'll not find in London.'

'Did Scrydan pay you for it?' Wat asked.

'Ha!' Todwulf answered that question.

'So you were following Scrydan to get payment for your box?' Hermitage checked.

'Said he'd tell the king,' Todwulf slurred.

'Tell the king? Oh, you mean he would tell the king that you made the box. In case William wanted any nice boxes made.'

'That's it. And then he says no.'

'No?'

Todwulf struggled to get his thoughts and words in order. 'This was the day he was going to the king. I comes around and tells him not to forget old Todwulf and he says no.'

'He said he wouldn't forget you?'

'No,' Todwulf protested loudly. 'He said no, he wasn't going to tell the king about me. He was going to be goldsmith to the Normans and he wouldn't have need of the likes of me.'

'So you followed him. What were you going to do?'

Todwulf clearly thought this should be obvious. 'Take me box back.'

'And did you try? Was there a struggle? The clasp came out of the box and Scrydan got stabbed by the pin?'

'What?' No,' Todwulf protested.

'What did happen, then?'

Todwulf drew himself up to his full height, which wasn't great and which caused him to wobble alarmingly.

'It was them,' he said, waving his arms to take in the others, including Fridolf.

Caput XXVI: Dissent In the Ranks

The subsequent fight broke out very quickly indeed.

Cyneruth took a pace into the middle of the room, protesting loudly at this outrageous suggestion.

Wilf was the first to leap forward and head straight for Todwulf, hands stretched out to reach the carpenter's throat.

Grun, obviously being used to this sort of thing, stepped quickly up and barged Wilf aside. Before he could make contact with Todwulf, Ansgar strode into the middle of the fray, his wide arms keeping the parties apart.

'Hold your peace,' he roared. 'Or by God, there will be more murders in this place.'

The warring factions grumbled and complained and continued to stand and stare at one another like dogs waiting to be released.

'This one decided to go for a walk,' Wat announced as he came back into the room holding Fridolf by the scruff of his neck.

Hermitage hadn't noticed him leave. It was a good job someone was paying attention.

'Oh, dear, oh, dear,' Hermitage fretted. 'What is the matter with you people?

'Scrydan has been murdered, yet here you are, trying to injure one another. What is this all about?' He tried to think what it was all about.

'An accusation of murder is a serious matter, yes, but one does not attack one's accuser. And Todwulf is barely capable of standing, let alone defending himself.

'Furthermore, as one who is well into his cups, are you seriously threatened by his suggestion?' As he said this, it was clear that yes, they were threatened by the accusation, otherwise, why would they have responded in this manner?

'Is there truth in what Todwulf says?' he asked seriously. 'Is that why you try to silence him? Is that why you were fighting one another before Ansgar locked you up?'

A bizarre thought occurred to him as he considered the shameful scene. He ran a hand across his face absent mindedly as he thought through the possibility.

'Aha?' Cwen asked, looking at him intently.

'I'm not yet sure,' Hermitage said slowly. 'But it is a possibility.'

'What is?' Ansgar asked. 'I'd really like this nonsense sorted out in short order.'

'They all had reason to wish Scrydan harm,' Hermitage said. 'The only one we haven't mentioned thus far is Wilf.'

Wilf looked as if this was nothing to do with him, and it was positively impudent to say so.

'He wants to be a goldsmith's apprentice, and we have heard he was pestering Scrydan. Everyone assumed that Fridolf was about to be made up and so there would be a vacancy.

'Did Scrydan finally make it clear that he was not going to elevate Fridolf and so Wilf's hopes were dashed? That would give reason for an attack.'

Wilf still appeared to be largely disinterested.

Hermitage mused further. 'Wat said that becoming a goldsmith's apprentice was not an easy task. They are protective of their craft. Why would Wilf think he could join?'

Hermitage looked at Wilf and appraised him quite openly. 'Unless, of course, he was Scrydan's son.'

'What?' Siward was the one to break the silence with the

obvious question.

'Scrydan's son,' Hermitage repeated. 'We have been told that Scrydan's wife died in childbirth. Nothing was said of the child.'

'His son?' Ansgar sounded completely confused at this idea.

'Does he look like Scrydan?' Hermitage asked.

The sheriff looked at Wilf with fresh eyes. 'I suppose he does, a bit. But his son?'

'Living with his aunt nearby before they had to move to make way for the castle,' Hermitage said. 'From what we have heard of Scrydan, I would not be surprised to hear that he disowned his son. With no mother to care for him, Scrydan would not want the burden.'

'Is this true?' Father Thomas asked of Wilf.

Wilf said nothing.

Hermitage went on. 'We now have a little band of people who would all be better off with Scrydan out of the way. They all follow him on that night and he is murdered.

'And, with the goldsmith out of the way, who stood to inherit his place and position.'

'We have no record of Wilf as Scrydan's son,' Father Thomas said.

'I am sure that his aunt would swear before the authorities that he was,' Hermitage said. 'Furthermore, if Wilf took ownership of the workshop, he would reward those who supported him.

'He is no goldsmith, but he would own a workshop. Presumably, he could make Fridolf up.' He looked to Wat who nodded.

'He could also make sure that Mistress Horik was placated. I imagine he expected to discover the source of Scrydan's gold if he got possession of the workshop.'

'And of course, he would not,' Father Thomas said simply.

'And the other goldsmiths,' Hermitage went on. 'We know they would be very happy to see Scrydan removed, and if his son was prepared to make it happen, so much the better.'

'All well and good, Hermitage,' Cwen said. 'But who actually killed Scrydan?'

'There are two possibilities in my mind. One is that they all did.'

'All of them?'

'They all set out to do Scrydan harm that night and so they may all have had a hand on the fatal clasp. It occurred to me that only a goldsmith would know that the pin had to be steel instead of gold, and so would make an ideal weapon. A goldsmith or one's apprentice had to be involved.'

All eyes turned to Fridolf.

'Don't look at me,' Fridolf responded.

'The other possibility?' Cwen asked.

'This I think is more likely, seeing how these people behave. They were all prepared to kill Scrydan and, thinking that all they would get is a fine, they all wanted to do it.

'On the way, they started arguing again. Perhaps Wilf said he should do it as he was the son. Grun said he should, as he was used to this sort of thing.

'Fridolf was probably desperate to do it after all Scrydan had put him through. Cyneruth might have wanted to so that he could report back to Eligius and get credit for it.

'The only one probably incapable of it was Todwulf. But even he doubtless wanted to, having been slighted over his box.

'Pushing turned to shoving turned to fighting. We know that happens as soon as they get in a room together.

'They caught up with Scrydan, perhaps grabbed the box and clasp from him and started squabbling over who would get to do it.' Hermitage shook his head at this appalling behaviour. 'I have had to deal with individual killers. I have dealt with conspiracies to kill. Never have I dealt with a band of murderers who fought one another over who got to do the deed.'

At least Cyneruth and Fridolf hung their heads.

Wilf and Grun looked defiant and Todwulf looked confused.

'Scrydan would be horrified as his precious gold was handled and even thrown about,' Hermitage continued. 'And in the confusion, someone managed to stab him in the chest.'

'Yes, but who?' Cwen pressed.

'That's where execution comes in. We now know that the Normans plan to execute murderers. Naturally, none of them wants to be executed.'

'Seems reasonable,' Cwen agreed.

'But why won't they give up the one who did do it?' Hermitage asked the room.

There was a moment of silent thought.

'Because it was Wilf,' Wat said.

'Because it was Wilf,' Hermitage agreed. 'Who was the one member of the group who had to be protected? The son who was going to inherit the workshop and spread his largesse far and wide.

'I assume, if Wilf were dead, the workshop would simply close?'

Wat nodded. 'Probably be taken by the other goldsmiths as it had no master of its own.'

'Which they would be perfectly happy about, but if Wilf was prepared to kill Scrydan, that would do.'

Hermitage looked to Wilf, hoping to see contrition in his face. None of Wilf looked very contrite.

'An interesting tale, brother monk,' he said confidently. 'If only you had been there at the time, we would know whether any of this was true or not. As you weren't and we don't, it is just that, an interesting tale.'

'But that's the problem, isn't it?' Cwen asked, equally confident. 'Brother Hermitage is King William's investigator and the king takes his tales very seriously. So seriously, that Lord de Sauveloy will rely on it for his execution schedule.'

For the first time, Wilf's expression faltered. 'You wouldn't.' This was half instruction, half plea.

'What else can we do? The Normans want to execute the murderer. That looks like you.'

'Of course,' Wat suggested, 'if Hermitage has to conclude that it was one of you, but he doesn't know which, de Sauveloy can execute the lot. I'm sure he won't have a problem with that.'

'It was him,' Fridolf blurted out.

'You dog!' Wilf snapped.

'It was as you said. We all went up there to deal with him, there was an argument between us, and Wilf grabbed the clasp. Scrydan demanded it back and we all grabbed for it. Wilf was waving it about and that's when he stuck it in him.'

'That's right,' Cyneruth confirmed.

Hermitage looked to Grun, who, strangely, might be the only reliable witness. The man nodded once.

'So, why did you keep watch all night?' Hermitage asked Fridolf.

'We needed the clasp to come back to the workshop by the proper means. If we just took it, there would be all sorts of trouble.'

'More trouble than murder?' Hermitage asked with disbelief.

'It was only Scrydan,' Fridolf said. 'I told you in Derby that he was horrible. Now you know it.'

'There is no lesser punishment for killing horrible people,' Hermitage pointed out.

Wilf looked around the room and there was desperation in his eyes. No one was dragging him away to his death, but they had effectively sent him to it.

His fellows in the crime avoided his look. Ansgar gazed down on him with some satisfaction, probably that everyone would leave now.

Bedric was nodding with interest as if he would go away and make a note of all this.

Aeva was clearly delighted to have some gossip of the very highest quality and interest.

Father Thomas sat with his head bowed.

'Sanctuary,' Wilf said.

'I beg your pardon?' Thomas asked.

'Sanctuary. I claim sanctuary.'

The priest was confused for a moment. 'You can't claim sanctuary, you aren't within the bounds of the church.'

'I could be. In a moment,' Wilf offered.

'I don't think you'll get that far,' Cwen observed.

'I could have Fridolf's sanctuary,' Wilf suggested. 'He doesn't need it anymore.'

'It doesn't work like that,' Mark explained.

Wilf appeared to be trying to think desperately of another option.

Ansgar stepped into the middle of the room. 'Come with me,' he said sombrely, taking Wilf by the arm.

'No, no,' Wilf pleaded. 'You can't do this. You don't

believe them, do you? It was Fridolf, he did it. I never touched him. I loved my father.'

'Come along,' Ansgar prompted with some sadness.

'No, it wasn't Fridolf, it was Grun. He's killed lots of people, you ask.'

Grun gave no response at all to this accusation.

Eventually, Ansgar started to drag him across the floor.

'Please,' Wilf wailed at the room.

As they got to the door, Ansgar bent and whispered something into the boy's ear. The struggling stopped and Wilf seemed suddenly broken and resigned to his fate as he let himself be taken.

'It is awful,' Hermitage said when they'd gone. 'A young lad like that should not suffer execution.'

'But then he probably shouldn't murder people,' Cwen said.

'It sounds as if it was a confusing situation. If Scrydan had surrendered some of his pride, he might still be alive.'

'It was Wilf who put the pin in his chest, there seems no doubt,' Wat said. 'And if the Normans have decided execution is the thing..,' he left the thought to end itself.

Everyone cleared away now, Fridolf, Cyneruth and Grun slipped out, probably before anyone could change their mind about the murderer.

'Do I get my box back?' Todwulf asked as he swayed towards the exit.

'I should ask Fridolf,' Wat suggested. 'It sounds like he was guarding the clasp.'

'And the clasp can come back to the church,' Father Thomas said.

'Back to the church?' Bedric asked with interest.

'A long tale for the sheriff's ear, I think,' Thomas

condescended.

'What's for the sheriff's ear?' Ansgar asked as he came back into the room.

'Oh, nothing, nothing,' Thomas said to the room. 'Perhaps we can have a word in private.'

Ansgar shrugged.

'Locked him up already?' Cwen asked. 'I suppose we had better let the Normans know what happened. We can tell John, and he can let de Sauveloy know. We certainly don't want to see that man if we can avoid it.'

'Hm,' Ansgar was hesitant, which was not like him. 'Funny thing happened on the way to the lock-up,' he said.

'Oh, yes?' Hermitage asked, thinking this was not really the time for jokes.

'Yes. Just as I went for my keys, Wilf slipped away.'

'He slipped away?' Hermitage didn't understand what was being said.

'He did. And by the time I caught up with him, he'd got over the boundary into Saint Paul's.'

'I see.' Cwen now stood before the sheriff with her arms folded. 'In the moment since you left the room, you've chased Wilf all the way to Saint Paul's and walked back?'

'I have,' Ansgar dared her to question it.

'I don't suppose he claimed sanctuary, did he?'

'You know, I think he might have done.'

'And you, the great big sheriff with big, long legs, couldn't catch up with little Wilf at all?'

'That's right.'

Bart stepped up. 'You were prepared to let us be executed, why let him get away?'

Ansgar roused himself. 'You are strangers. Wilf, whatever his faults, is under my protection. I never approved of the

Normans executing people. It should be Saxon law, a fine. That's been enough in the past, it should be enough now.' He took a breath. 'Anyway, I didn't let him get away, he escaped.'

'Of course, he did.' Cwen was not convinced.

'He did do a terrible deed,' Hermitage said. 'And now he will not reap its rewards. Perhaps a lifelong sanctuary at toil in the church is the appropriate conclusion.'

'I can't see young Wilf letting sanctuary last that long,' Wat said. 'Still, he's Ansgar and Father Thomas's problem now. They can tell the Normans while we go home. London's a nice place to visit, but I wouldn't want to live here.'

Hermitage would be pleased to get away as well. The Normans really were too close for comfort.

'We just might manage to get a bit of weaving in before the next person gets murdered,' Cwen said.

'You did find out who did it,' Ansgar observed.

'Well, in a way,' Hermitage agreed. 'But Wilf was right, we never really knew for sure. Until the others accused him and he pretty much confessed, of course.'

'I'm not sure I'm cut out for business like this,' the sheriff confessed. 'You can't grab it and throw it in the lock-up.'

Hermitage didn't know what to say.

'I need an investigator,' Ansgar said.

'Oh, right,' Hermitage blustered. 'Well, I'm sort of spoken for, if you will.' He didn't want to be King's Investigator but he certainly didn't want to be Ansgar's. In a place like London, with all these people, there could be murders day and night.

'What about these two?' Ansgar nodded towards Siward and Bart. 'They seem to know about it.'

'I suppose they do, a bit.' Hermitage felt awkward talking about the two as if they weren't there.

'You were the one who accused us of murder,' Siward complained.

'Only because I thought you said you'd done it. That's why I need someone. Sheriff's Investigators, if you like.'

Siward and Bart exchanged questioning looks.

Ansgar took a breath and spoke plainly. 'I'll give you a room and a penny a week. That's it.'

'Each,' Bart said.

Ansgar thought. 'Aye,' he confirmed.

'What do you reckon?' Bart asked Siward.

'Come to London and be paid for it? Now, let me think.'

'All right, we'll do it,' Bart agreed.

'First murder you don't solve, you're out,' Ansgar warned.

'Fair enough.' Bart turned to Hermitage. 'Looks like the apprenticeship is over, Hermitage.'

'Oh, erm, yes, I suppose so.' It was only Bart who called himself the investigator's apprentice anyway, so Hermitage didn't feel any great change.

However, it did seem as if Bart and Siward had only just arrived and become members of the family of a sort. To have them suddenly leave like this was a bit of a shock.

'What?' Cwen said. 'You're staying here?'

'That's it,' Bart confirmed.

'You're not coming back with us?'

'That too.'

'There you are.' Wat nudged Cwen. 'They'll be out of the workshop. Gone. We can get on with the weaving.'

'Yes, but..,' Cwen began.

'I thought this was what you wanted?' Wat whispered to her.

'I didn't think that it would be so, well, you know. That they'd be gone just like that. I thought it would be more of a, erm..,'

'What?' Wat asked with a mischievous smile.

'Nothing,' Cwen clamped her mouth shut and looked quite grim.

'Good luck, lads,' Wat thumped them both on the arm. 'It's a grand place, London, but mind how you go. Watch out for the Normans.'

'We will.'

'And the Saxons.'

'Right.'

'And if you see More with a ferry, don't get in.'

'We won't,' they chimed.

'Oh,' Wat added. 'And if you come across anyone who wants a good quality tapestry, you know where to send them.'

They decided that the short walk to the Crypel Gate would be the best way out of London as it was the fastest.

Hermitage had the uncomfortable thought that the Normans were watching him and would put on a murder just for him.

He didn't know how Ranulph de Sauveloy would react to having his execution cancelled, and even though Wat and Cwen told him that that was someone else's problem now, he still worried about it.

The journey back to Derby felt quite lonely, even though Bart and Siward had not been with them on the way down.

They wouldn't be waiting when they got back, nor would they come home again.

And Bart had been quite useful on occasion. He did have some good ideas and was an extra pair of hands when it came to an investigation.

Still, as he told himself at the end of every murder, with any luck, he wouldn't have another one.

Howard of Warwick

But then, he never had much luck either.

Finis

Brother Hermitage will return in:

Murder 'Midst Merriment

And you can read the exciting opening below.

Murder 'Midst Merriment

Prologus:

It was the noise that did for old Jeb.

He was used to the dark, the dark didn't worry him. After all, his particular trade needed the dark. The darker the better. A good strong moon brightening the scene could make a mockery of his night's work.

Of course, he was the only one who called it a trade. Others had a lot of names for it, and trade wasn't one of them. Still, at least he keeps himself to himself, the others would comment as they closed their doors and windows.

And he was used to the noises of the dark as well. The night creatures about their business were no concern of his. The cough of a sheep, the bark of a fox, the sudden flurry close by as an owl took its prey.

But this was unnatural.

His mind hopped through all the possibilities, starting with the most sensible.

Devils. There was demon work abroad and he was about to be caught up in it. Was that a laugh he heard off in the distance? Decent folk wouldn't be out in the woods laughing. It had to be devils.

They were probably laughing because they were going to take him at any moment for their devilish purposes. The priest in town had talked about devilish purposes, and while Jeb didn't have any ideas what they might be, and the priest hadn't gone into details, he didn't want them happening to him in a dark wood.

But if it was devils, wouldn't they have been on him by now?

What else? Could this be his time? Was this the way it went? Angels had come to take him; to waft his soul from his body and take it to paradise. That would be a cause for laughter.

He recalled why he was out in the woods in the dark and thought angels taking him to paradise was probably unlikely.

He quickly dismissed the idea of people being out here making this noise. It was not the natural sound of people in the dark of the woods, and he should know. This was entirely raucous and its makers clearly cared not who heard them. People out in the woods at night did their best not to make any noise at all. That way lay trouble.

The local authorities might not care what you were up to, but the Normans took a far less reasonable approach. They seemed to think that the woods were theirs to do with as they wished and they unfairly assumed that anyone they caught was up to no good. There was a good chance that anyone they caught really was up to no good, but it was still unfair simply to assume that.

If this was Normans, it would be the first time Jeb had heard any of them laugh.

All other options eliminated, it had to be devils. The question was, what sort, and would he be able to avoid their attentions?

Then, the most serious and entirely reasonable of all the reasons for the noise occurred to him. He took one breath and held it as his blood froze. The Wild Hunt.

Herne the Hunter was abroad this night with his pack of ghostly hounds. Obviously, he was abroad every night, but had chosen the woods around Derby just when Jeb wanted to use them. Cruel fate!

Was there any point even trying to hide? The dread hounds would have his scent already. The huntsman was probably holding them back at this very moment, just to savour the instant of his death.

Everyone knew that Herne commanded the night, but no one thought they'd be caught in his bit of it. It was like a bolt of light in a storm; there was no point worrying about it because it always hit someone else.

Recovering some of his senses, Jeb dropped onto his front and crawled through the leafy floor until he reached a large oak. He prayed that the noise of his passage would be drowned out by the demonic cackles.

It was hard to tell exactly where the hunter's ghastly laughter was coming from, but he thought he got the tree between him and it.

Not that the trees themselves weren't in league with Herne, of course. They would bend to his will if called, and there was nothing to be done when the trees were against you.

Jeb considered his options, which were few and largely hopeless.

Stay where he was and hope that he wasn't noticed.

That was simply ridiculous. This was Herne the Hunter, for heaven's sake. Even ancient Aldfrith, who claimed to have once been Derby's foremost hunter would be able to find Jeb hiding behind a tree. Aldfrith was more ancient than hunter these days and his hound's sense of smell must have died years ago, if it could stand to sit at Aldfrith's feet.

Herne had the powers of a God, and spotting people who hid behind trees would be the work of a moment.

And that was forgetting his hounds, all wide-eyed and loathy. Jeb knew the tales as well as anyone.

Herne's pack didn't even need to catch his scent, being as how they could smell a man's soul. And Jeb knew that his soul would be particularly pungent.

Run away?

Same problem. The moment he broke cover and headed back for the town, the ghastly pack would be on him. He could see the red eyes of the dogs in his mind, urged on by the red eyes of Herne's hunters. For some reason, it was the red eyes he feared more than anything. Seeing things with red eyes was more than he could bear.

Frozen by the conclusion that doing anything at all would lead to his hideous death, Jeb's eyes danced left and right looking for some miracle of escape.

Perhaps he should chance a glance around the tree to see exactly what he was facing. Dare he tell himself that this was not the hunter at all, and there was some reasonable and entirely earthly explanation?

Could it be simple travellers, lost on the road, or not knowing how close Derby was? They had made camp in the woods and were even now enjoying their company, perhaps with ale and food.

Jeb sniffed the air and couldn't detect anything earthly, but perhaps they were too far away.

There was one final dread possibility that he hadn't seriously considered; the Normans themselves.

Who else would feel at liberty to cause this much disturbance in their precious woods? True, he had never seen a Norman in anything other than a bad mood, but that could be because he was Saxon, and they didn't like Saxons.

Now they were on their own, they were behaving like

normal people. Well, normal for Normans.

Convincing himself that there was no mystical origin to this disturbance, mainly because all the mystical options led to his horrible death, he decided that he would chance a look around the tree.

If it was the huntsman and his hounds, then perhaps it was best to get it over with. If it wasn't, he might still have the chance to get away.

Keeping as close to the ground as a very thin snake, he slithered his way around the base of the tree and looked off into the depths of the wood.

His view was partly blocked by the broadening trunk, but he did detect a flicker of light, dancing between the branches some way off. It didn't look ghostly from here, so he risked a sigh of relief.

He raised himself onto his knees, still clasping the tree for protection, and tried to make out what was going on, and who was doing it.

It was definitely a fire, but then fire could be made by man and spirit alike. Shadows cast by the light flickered across the dark ground and the looming trees, and even if they were entirely natural, their aspect shook Jeb's wits.

'What are you doing?' he hissed to himself as he emerged from the tree and moved very slowly closer.

Whoever or whatever this was, he needed to be further away, not nearer. Curiosity was all well and good, and the subsequent gossip and tales might be worth something, but not at the expense of his soul.

Still, he reasoned, if he could report to the town that there were Normans in the woods, it might put him in good stead. He hadn't been in good stead for many a year.

Dropping to his hands and knees, he edged through the

trees until he could see that this gathering had settled in a small clearing. The fire blazed in the middle and didn't look or sound very ghostly.

He could make out shapes sat around the fire, all of them with their backs to him. This made sense as the wind, although light, was blowing the smoke away from those who basked in the warmth.

At least there were no loathy hounds.

Sounds of conversation reached his ears but the words could not be made out, so he could not tell if these were Saxons or Normans.

It appeared to be a small band, from what he could see. Only three shapes were illuminated by the fire, but there could be more out of sight.

This was as close as he was prepared to get. If he could hear their murmured conversation, they would hear his progress through the dried leaves of the forest floor. He would have to be satisfied with what scant information he now had.

Content that he was at least going to escape this encounter with his life, Jeb started to slowly inch his way back. He kept a close eye on the fire, in case anyone might move and see him.

Just as he thought he was at a safe distance, the central figure by the fire leant forward, almost as if bowing to the flames.

He froze in an instant and even stopped breathing, hoping he would appear to be some natural feature of the forest.

All of the most deep-seated fears that he had managed to put away, roared back through his mind and body as the figure by the fire stood and revealed its dark shape to a background of licking fire.

The height of this form was beyond reason. Surely, no mortal man could stand so tall. The head almost seemed to be at the level of the trees, it's shadow mixing with those of the branches.

When it turned to one side, Jeb simply threw his hands over his head and buried his wailing face in the woodland floor. Let the fates do with him what they would, he was beyond hope now. He had brought himself to this place and now there was no escape.

It was as plain as dark against light, and Jeb could not deny his eyes. The human form by the fire might be giant, but there was something blood-chilling about the shape of the head; it was probably the antlers.

Murder 'Midst Merriment,
coming soon to a book near you.

Made in the USA
Monee, IL
30 May 2024

59118260R00184